The Triad Conspiracy

By David Gatesbury

Strategic Book Publishing and Rights Co.

Strategic Book Publishing and Rights Co.
12620 FM 1960, Suite A4-507
Houston, TX 77065
www.sbpra.com

ISBN: 978-1-62516-792-7

Book Design: Suzanne Kelly

To Marianne

CONTENTS

INTRODUCTION

When looking back on history we see how the League of Nations (1920-1945) failed. This organization's principal purpose was to maintain world peace. Its primary goal was to prevent wars and international disputes through negotiation and arbitration. The League did not have a military force and relied on the Great Powers to enforce resolutions. It had successes and failures, but was ultimately powerless at preventing aggression by the Axis Powers. Germany, Japan, and Italy withdrew from the League to pursue their dictators' aspirations.

In 1938, prior to the Second World War, the free world gave into Adolf Hitler's rants by handing over the Sudetenland districts of Czechoslovakia to Nazi Germany as a way to bargain for "Peace in our time." Czechoslovakia had no voice in this compromise, and on 16 March 1939 that entire nation fell to German occupation. The world stood by and said little when Japan overran Chinese provinces without provocation. Today, the poses and postures of Benito Mussolini rate a comical figure, but not so when he invaded and annexed Ethiopia in 1938, or in 1940 when he signed the Tripartite Pact with Germany and Japan.

The United Nations is structured much the same as the League of Nations and has many of the same problems. As long as loudmouthed dictators spout untruths and distortions while making threats against other nations before the U.N. General Assembly, world peace is threatened.

There is strength in unity, and an example of this came when Iraq invaded Kuwait. Saddam Hussein learned what happens when one nation stands defiant against world leaders speaking with one voice. Yet it wasn't the U.N. that acted, but a group of nations forming a coalition that kicked the Iraqis out and freed Kuwait. These forces considered ousting Hussein from power at that time, but Arab nations participating in the military action threatened to break up the coalition. However, if Kuwait hadn't been an oil-rich country, and Iraq had not stood to gain control of a large portion of the world's oil supply, the coalition may not have acted so swiftly. In the wake of Saddam Hussein's capture at a later date, Iraqi government officials openly voiced their displeasure with the United Nations' failure to help their people during decades of oppression by the deposed leader.

In January 2003, U.N. members voted Libya, one of the worst sponsors of terrorism, the chairman of their Human Rights Commission, despite opposition from the United States and human rights groups. It is a well known fact that Libyan leader Col. Muammar Qaddafi was behind the downing of Pan AM Flight 103 in 1988, which took the lives of 189 Americans. What were these people thinking? Muammar Qaddafi fell from power in August 2011, but unfortunately, the West has little influence over incoming transitional governments replacing such regimes.

The U.N. also failed to bring an end to the Bosnian-Serbian war, as the NATO Alliance stepped in to bring an end to that conflict. For the U.N. to play a stronger role in maintaining world peace there must be changes introduced, for there is corruption in this organization, and funding has disappeared. Chapter VII of the United Nations Charter addresses how to deal with aggression and ruthless dictators. Yet this written agreement for maintaining peace has done little to prevent aggression and oppression, and world leaders need to clearly define the organization's role or continue facing failures.

When one nation bullies another, should there be military action before a multitude suffers? Should action be taken against totalitarian states run by dictators who slaughter their people and commit atrocities to remain in power? At the completion of this book, war-ravaged Syria is in a two-year civil war with over 93,000 lives lost, and yet, the United Nations is powerless to do anything about it. As the death toll rises, various sources report confirmation of chemical weapons used by Syria's government in this conflict. How many Syrians must die before the U.N. acts against Bashar Hafez al-Assad?

When a U.N.-Arab League envoy arrived in Damascus, Syria under the leadership of Kofi Annan on a mission to halt violence there, he declared that further militarization would make matters worse. This was not what a people outraged by the brutal murder of fellow citizens wanted to hear. Assad's regime has used military force to crush all rebellious opposition, and as a head of state exerting control with an iron fist, he will only step down under the threat and pressure of military force. While Assad denies responsibility for what's taking place in his country, insisting he is not accountable, a diplomatic solution is unlikely and more are sure to die. U.N. members must commit to taking a stand against corrupt leaders like Assad, or the U.N. is destined to fail, just as the League of Nations did.

One of the most serious problems is that members of the Security Council have a dubious record. Russia is Syria's closest ally, and while Syria snubs the world while killing thousands of its citizens, Russia stands by Bashar Hafez al-Assad. Vladimir Putin, a former KGB official and currently the Russian President, has made it clear that he does not want foreign intervention with regards to Syrian affairs.

Russia gives the impression it wants improved relations with the West. However, ties with the U.S. have faltered under Putin's leadership. According to an international press agency, in Brussels on 30 April 2009, NATO ordered the expulsion of two Russians over the Estonian Spy Affair. A diplomat reported the expulsion of two Russian agents in connection with the case of Herman Simm, an Estonian jailed for twelve years for treason. Simm was convicted of handing over more than 2,000 pages of information to Russia's SVR Foreign Intelligence Service. The two expelled Russian diplomats were not believed to be directly involved in this spy incident, but one of the expelled Russians was the son of Vladimir Chizkov, Moscow's ambassador to the European Union.

On 28 June 2010, the FBI arrested ten people dubbed "illegals" for allegedly spying for Russia while living covertly in the U.S. These agents were tough spies for the FBI to catch. The Bureau made the arrests in the Northeast, charging them with failure to register as foreign agents, a crime less serious than espionage, which carries up to five years in prison. Courtroom documents alleged that these defendants lived in the U.S. posing as Canadians and American citizens. Two ring members were husband and wife, raising concerns that Moscow had recruited and planted others. Prosecutors charged the suspects with following Russian Intelligence orders to become "Americanized" enough to infiltrate policy-making circles to acquire a wide range of information on U.S. weapons. The court cited numerous communications intercepted by the FBI, but there was no clue about what sort of information the agents provided to their Russian handlers.

Court papers indicate that Anna Chapman, who the media quickly branded a *femme fatale*, was about to go to Moscow, and viewing her as a flight risk, the FBI moved in. The then-twenty-eight-year-old Chapman, a sultry beauty with striking red hair, became a high-profiled tabloid darling. Said to be a savvy Russian agent, she made a weekly Wednesday intelligence report to Moscow while working undercover in Manhattan real estate. Her arrest, along with those of the other operatives, broke up the largest foreign intelligence network discovered on American soil since the Cold War.

At the courtroom hearing, prosecutors described Chapman as a "practiced deceiver." Assistant U.S. Attorney Michael Farbiarz called the evidence "truly overwhelming." He noted Chapman in particular, saying she was a sophisticated agent of Russia with extraordinary training.

Russian officials initially denounced the arrests as "Cold War-era espionage stories" with elements in the U.S. government attempting to offset the relationship between Moscow and Washington.

Our relationship with Red China's communist government has improved over the years, as they love trading with us, but they hardly view us as a friend. At or near the time of the Soviet Union's collapse, eastern European nations found freedom from the Soviet's handpicked dictators, leading to the unification of West and East Germany. The Russians are no longer governed by a hard-line communist regime and those eastern European nations that were considered Soviet satellites are now independently self-governed. These changes in Europe did nothing to change the situation in Southeast Asia, though, and those nations under Communist China's sphere of influence at that time are still under Chinese influence today. What the U.S. represents is much the opposite of communism, and since communists govern China, they view us as their enemy. People who've lived through the Cold War era should understand this, but there are many who think the wave of change in Europe opened the door for change elsewhere, and that China is our friend and ally.

Communist China has propped up the North Korean government since the Korean War, and they still support North Korea by supplying them with practically everything. The main reason for this is that if North Korea fell and merged with South Korea to become a democratic republic, as happened with Germany, it may serve to undermine China's government.

Many regard North Korea as nothing more than one big concentration camp, and it is pathetic how its citizens are starving. The physical stature of its people is shrinking from malnutrition, as South Korean citizens have grown in height. When it was reported that North Korean authorities were arresting citizens for not crying hard enough after the death of their longtime leader Kim Jong-Il, I could have laughed, but the fate of those people isn't a bit funny.

I believe China props up this wretched nation's puppet government to taunt the West, using North Korea's nuclear ambitions to harass neighboring nations. The idea is that Communist China needn't provide the North Koreans with everything so long as they lend them nuclear weapons and missile technology as a way to gain leverage to acquire food and other provisions from other countries. The West will do what it can to slow down the spread of nuclear weapons by giving much needed aid to North Korea, and as a result relieve China of the burden. Where is this backward and diminutive country going to get missile and nuclear technology, unless China gives it to them? For the present, China is in control, pulling the strings, and they stand to lose nothing with this charade.

It shouldn't take a long leap of understanding to grasp why, whenever there are meetings with Western countries, the North Koreans insist that Chinese officials sit on their side of the table. While China supplies this regime with everything entering that country, they have a great deal of influence about what happens there. In addition, if China was a sincere member of the U.N. Security Council and seeking peace, all they'd have to do is threaten to cut off North Korea's supplies to initiate change and quiet them down.

On 11 April 2012, the North Koreans tested a missile under the claim that it was launching a satellite. I find it ridiculous that a nation that cannot feed its people is building missiles. Another strange thing that I don't find a bit surprising is that the launch site was at Tonchang-ri, about thirty-five miles from the border with China. Had any other nation set up a launch pad that close along China's border, Chinese officials would've regarded such a move as a threat, but it's not a problem when they're dictating how things are run in North Korea. Had India or Pakistan made a similar test launch thirty-five miles from their border with China, this most assuredly would have placed those nuclear nations on the brink of a full-scale war.

No doubt, the United Nations is destined to one day fail, for there is little unity in this organization so long as Russia and China represent the U.N. Security Council. If world leaders cannot find common ground for blocking the ambitions of dictators, we're sure to repeat history and once again find the world engulfed in turmoil. If the way the U.N. approaches these problems is not erroneously distorted, perhaps it is human nature that is flawed, which is certainly a possibility.

Lastly, while sanctions against Iran have taken their toll on its economy, they have done little to slow its pursuit of nuclear weapons. The leaders of Iran are fanatical extremists, determined to arm themselves with nuclear capability, and they will continue this endeavor no matter how much their people suffer. The world is changing, and if they succeed, it is sure to become a far more dangerous place.

CHAPTER 1

An Unexpected Turn of Events

The morning sun reflected off a two-story Victorian-style home with cobalt blue siding and white shutters located at 3411 Arlington in Staten Island, New York. A black ornamental iron fence bordered the sidewalk with short, well-trimmed hedges running on each side of the walk leading to the front porch. A tall pin oak with sprawling branches provided shade for the yard. The house was coming to life as Louise Hagen, a kindhearted, thin, silver-haired widow who handled most of the house chores for the Morelands over the past two years, was in the kitchen making breakfast. A live-in maid of sorts, she almost always wore an apron with a design of yellow flowers when cooking, keeping mitten potholders in roomy, waist-high front pockets.

Linda Moreland was getting ready for work, and she'd set out a striped, short-sleeved pullover shirt and tan pants for her only child, a five-year-old boy named Allan, to wear to preschool. Allan had been home from the hospital only a few days after undergoing treatment for a liver disorder that impaired his growth, robbed him of energy, and left his hair sparse and stubby.

Shaking him gently to wake him up, she kissed the child on the cheek as he began to stir, and she stroked the short, bristly hair, saying, "C'mon, lazybones, time to get ready for school."

"OK, lazybones," he responded with boyish enthusiasm, sitting up in the bed to wave goodbye to her with a bright smile on his face.

Linda came down a flight of stairs to an L-shaped entry hall, gazing into a large mirror that gave a view of the oversized doorway to the living room that contained French provincial furniture. She left a black attaché case on the floor and placed her purse on the shelf below the mirror that supported an assortment of ceramic birds. The most prominent pieces were a cardinal with a bold crown, holding its head tilted to look at the viewer, a nesting robin feeding its babies held center, and posed on the right was a colorful, proud parrot.

Glimpsing her appearance after having put much time into getting herself ready for her position as a fashion designer at a Manhattan-based firm, this vibrant and alluring slender blonde had once been a model. Dressing stylishly and businesslike for the day, she wore a white ruffled blouse with a soft peach bow and slim-fitting black skirt. She approached her job with vigor, and had a flare for arranging and color-coordinating the gowns she worked with, giving a touch that often enhanced a creation. Her vivacious personality and aspiring self-confidence had helped her gain a key position with Mona Shelton, a leading designer.

Mrs. Shelton, an affluent woman who took pleasure in the pageantry and fanfare of fashions, was particular about the way she wanted her exhibitions run. There had come a time when Mona had her hands full entertaining prospective buyers, and Linda had stepped up to consult clients by exhibiting a few alternative alterations that stirred their interests. Linda showed an eye for accentuating the looks of extravagant gowns that helped close sales. She had an appealing knack for communicating with people that caught Mona's attention, and a bond had been forged. Linda had later presented a portfolio of sketches and photos of herself wearing her own homespun business outfits that had impressed the fashion mogul. Mona had gone on to introduce a new line under the designer name "Adrianna," and had arranged for Linda to manage it for her. While Mona paraded outrageously excessive gowns, Linda presented a lucrative line of conservative but fashionable dresswear for the career-minded workingwoman.

Hearing the tapping of a car horn, Linda knew the taxi she'd called for was waiting. She grabbed her purse and the attaché case before going down the hall to wish Louise a good day and rushing out. The breakfast Louise had made for her would remain untouched, but that was the routine, and Louise would see to it that Allan was ready in time to catch his ride to school.

Settling in the backseat of the cab, contemplating the activities she'd planned for a 3 p.m. fashion show at the Waldorf Astoria in midtown Manhattan, Linda had a lot on her mind. The taxi dropped Linda off at the dress shop where she pointed out updates the girls making alterations would need to know, and noted changes in the presentation to open the modeling exhibition. She had a luncheon engagement at noon to meet Mona Shelton at Tony's, an Italian restaurant two blocks from the Waldorf Astoria. Especially known for its pasta dishes, the place had rich décor and a warm, welcoming atmosphere. Photographs of famous Italians in the entertainment field spanned the walls, and she'd occasionally recognize an actor or athlete dining there, as it was a favorite meeting place for iconic figures making the rounds in the New York area.

From the restaurant's entrance, Linda spotted Mona's frosted hair at a table for two by a window. Sophisticatedly well-dressed and with slightly overdone makeup, Mona projected a wealthy image, and she had a beaming grin upon seeing Linda coming her way.

"I took the liberty of ordering you a strawberry daiquiri," said Mona. "I hope that's alright. Or would you prefer a Bloody Mary?"

"No, that's fine," replied Linda, placing her purse on the table and leaning the attaché case against the wall before sitting down.

"Just look at you," remarked Mona. "You look ravishing."

"Oh, Mona, I don't see how that's possible with how hectic this day's been with organizing this show."

"How's Allan?"

"He's very conscious about his hair because kids at school are giving him a hard time, but it's starting to grow out."

The waiter brought their drinks and took their orders, and Linda then opened the case she'd brought to show Mona photos of the dresswear she'd be promoting that afternoon. When the waiter arrived with their meals, conversation halted, and Linda whisked away the photos to make room for the dishes.

Two men sitting at the bar finishing their drinks had their backs to the restaurant's main floor. One took notice of Linda through the mirror on the back of the bar and studied her facial features. Baby-faced, blond, and stocky was Hermann Gensler, who wore a gray suit and steel-rimmed eyeglasses. His dark-haired companion, John Mehlnick, sat to his left. Mehlnick was a large man of Romanian descent with five o'clock shadow, and the only person in the place wearing sunglasses; he had the looks of a Mafia figure. The left sleeve of his dark blue pinstriped suit jacket loosely rolled up to his elbow gave clear indication he had no left arm.

Gensler stood from his barstool to pull the wrinkles out of his sport coat, using his reflection in the bar's mirror as though straightening his tie while taking a long look at Linda. He inconspicuously nudged his partner with his elbow to get his attention, and Mehlnick turned to him, placing his right elbow on the edge of the bar.

"What is it?" asked Mehlnick, his eyes on his drinking glass.

Gensler nodded to the mirror. "Take a look at the blonde sitting by the window."

One-armed Mehlnick shifted his position to look in the mirror, clenching his glass to raise it to his lips and consume a mouthful of bourbon and crushed ice, uttering, "Very sexy."

"Take another look," said Gensler, "and this time, instead of scoping out the legs, see if you notice anything familiar about her face."

Instead of using the mirror, Mehlnick nonchalantly turned his swivel bar seat around to focus on Linda, and lifting his glass to his lips, his hand froze. After recognizing her, he placed his drink on the bar before raising his sunglasses to make sure of what he was seeing.

Gensler spoke beneath his breath. "Don't stare, you idiot."

Mehlnick turned to face the bar and lifted his sunglasses again to look at her in the mirror. Gripping his drinking glass firmly to pull it in front of him, he spoke quietly, saying, "Except for the woman seated with her, she may be here alone."

"It appears that way, but agents could be shadowing her. Get the car and wait for me outside."

Mehlnick read in his partner's expression that he was serious about formulating a daring plan, and keeping his drinking glass close to his lips, he said, "You're not seriously thinking about trying something in broad daylight?"

"Shut up and do as I say. Get the car and watch for me out front."

Mehlnick got up and downed the remains of his drink, his eyes scanning the room. "What if the heat gets turned up?"

Gensler responded insistently, "I'm not going to make a move unless I'm sure we have a good opportunity to act."

Mehlnick went outside, and while casually walking past the restaurant's glass front, he eyed the two women through the windowpane.

Mona looked at her watch. "You'd better get going, Linda. I'll take care of the bill."

"I'll see you later at the show," said Linda. Eager to make certain preparations for the fashion event were ready on time, she picked up her purse and the attaché case before hurriedly leaving the restaurant.

When stepping outside on the walk, Linda didn't notice the man in the gray suit following close behind. Nor was she aware of the gray four-door Mercedes-Benz idling at the curb half a block away. As she started up the busy street toward the Waldorf Astoria, the automobile lurched forward and quickly caught up to the man tailing her on foot who gave the driver a hand signal.

Linda had a thousand things on her mind when the Mercedes sped up to the upcoming corner to cut in front of her at the crosswalk. The driver jammed on the brakes, causing the front end of the car to sink before leveling off. Standing near the car's back door, she avoided stepping off the curb, tilting her head to glimpse the driver of the car wearing sunglasses. The one-armed driver placed the gearshift in park, stretched to lean between the bucket seats to pull the handle on the rear passenger door with his right hand, and threw it open. He looked over the rim of his drooping sunglasses at her. "Excuse me. Could you give me directions to the Chrysler Building?"

Linda hadn't replied, and as a forceful hand caught her by the neck bringing her downward, a hard shove drove her forward into the automobile's backseat. The person pushing landed on her backside, and his weight prompted her to raise her legs. At the same time the automobile accelerated, weaving while picking up speed with the door swinging shut.

Overcome with panic, and struggling fiercely to get out from beneath him as they swayed with the car's movement, she twisted and strained to push free of his hold, screaming, "Let me go!" Fighting desperately, she released her purse and the attaché case to claw at his face, tearing off his eyeglasses. He stayed on her, trying to hold her down and control her fast-moving hands to protect his face.

Fear escalated, and unable to shake loose her abductor, she whimpered at the terror of knowing she was losing her fight for freedom. She kept up the struggle to push him off and kept clawing at him until her fingernails dug into the left side of his face, peeling flesh away.

He struck at her brutally with his clenched fist, his knuckles clipping her brow, but the next punch slammed into her cheekbone, knocking her out cold. She fell limp, and he shoved her body behind him to the back of the seat so he could scoot forward and take an upright position.

"The bitch damn-near took my eye out," came through his gritted teeth, and straightening up, he reached over the back of the front seat, rapping the rearview mirror with his knuckles until he could view his reflection. Examining the scratches she'd given him, he then reached for a handkerchief from his coat pocket. Dabbing the bloody cuts in the side of his face with the handkerchief, he shouted, "Slow down before you get us pulled over for something as stupid as speeding!"

"OK, just keep that wildcat off me," Mehlnick snapped back, and stopping at a red light, he rummaged through the glove compartment to present a plastic tie strap to Gensler. "Here, bind her wrists with this before she comes to."

After securing her wrists, Gensler looked inside the attaché case to view its contents. Seeing photos of sashaying models, he commented, "I thought I'd find government documents in this briefcase, but all that's here are photos of females." Gensler spread the pictures out on the front seat for Mehlnick to see. "What do you make of this?"

Mehlnick took his eye off the road to give the pictures a quick glance. "I don't know, but let's get her back to base and let the others sort it out."

They drove to an abandoned six-story apartment building, and when Linda came to, she first noticed a stench in the air coming from a nearby industrial plant. Trying to move, she discovered straps pinning her down to a hospital bed, and she squinted as she felt a puffy tenderness under her left eye. Taking on a worrisome expression as she recalled the punch she received in the car, she wondered about the intentions of these men who preyed upon her. She attempted to jerk her shoulders free again, but the straps wouldn't budge.

Her mind racing with fear, a helpless feeling of vulnerability swept over her as she surveyed her surroundings. A ragged shade hung crooked in the room's only window, flaking flowered wallpaper covered the walls, and the ceiling near the outside wall had discolored as a result of a leak in the roof. The room was nearly empty except for the narrow bed she lay on and a broad desk paired with a lamp that had a flexible, spiraling neck aimed upwards in the company of a wooden chair. The desk drawers were facing her, and she saw her purse and the attaché case she'd carried lying on the desktop with photos spread of the models she'd shown to Mona earlier.

She thought they must've targeted her for a purpose, and believed it had something to do with Mona, since she had been in her company just before the abduction. Seen with a wealthy socialite, she considered they'd kidnapped her for monetary gain, but if that was so, then they should've gone after Mona. Concluding something else must've drawn them to her, and speculating on what that something else was, drove her to near panic, but the way they had her tightly strapped down made it almost impossible to get free.

Taking a deep breath, she got a whiff of smoke from a smoldering cigarette left in an ashtray on the desk, and then heard the distinct ringing of her cell phone from inside her purse. Having no idea where she was, she saw the phone as her only contact with the outside world and immediately drove her shoulders against the straps to loosen them, but the fasteners wouldn't budge. She realized the importance of reaching the phone: the authorities could find her location by picking up the signal it transmitted, utilizing the triangulation of cell phone towers. She tugged desperately against the straps holding her down once again to gain her freedom, but her efforts were getting her nowhere.

After a few seconds, the phone stopped ringing, and she heard voices outside the room. The echo of a door closing and footsteps coming nearer gave way to the thought she had little chance of escape. The room's door opened, and a thin, dark-haired woman with high cheekbones made her entrance, giving Linda a long, calculating look as she closed the door behind her.

"Ah, I'm glad to see you've come to." Her husky voice carried a German accent that mimicked Marlene Dietrich, and Linda gave no reply.

The woman's cold demeanor did nothing to make Linda feel comfortable, and her smile was little more than a sinister grin that created dimples in her lean face. The woman went to Linda's purse to find the cell phone. She removed its batteries and commented, "You and I have some important issues to discuss, and I'd prefer no interruptions."

Leaning against the edge of the desk, she picked up the lit cigarette, and after taking a deep drag crushed the cigarette out in the ashtray. She then spoke with a reassuring tone as smoke expelled with her spoken words. "My name is Adele, and I don't want your stay here to be any longer than necessary."

Linda finally said, "What do you people want? Why are you holding me here?"

"I'm glad you asked, as conversation is so much better when there are two participating. We require information on the Triad MX-11 project."

"Triad—MX-11. I don't understand. What is that?"

"Fraulein Werner, as long as you tell us what we need to know, you have nothing to fear. Give us the information we need and you can simply walk right out that door."

"But my name isn't Werner, and if you look in my pocketbook you'll find proof of who I am."

An ugly, intimidating smirk grew on the woman's face. "You're not seriously expecting us to accept the identification you're carrying."

"You're making a mistake," Linda insisted excitedly, as her concerns heightened for the outcome of the encounter. "You've got to believe me. My name is Linda Moreland."

"Linda Moreland?"

"Yes!"

"And you've never heard of the Triad MX-11—the Triad Satellite?"

"I don't know what it is you're talking about."

The woman shook her head, giving Linda a pitiless look of disdain. "You're only going to make it hard on yourself playing this silly game."

Opening the wide top desk drawer, the woman revealed surgical instruments displayed on a white sheet, and Linda's eyes enlarged with a look of terror.

"I have the afternoon free and we have ways of making you talk."

Linda began screaming, "Help me! Somebody help me!"

"If it makes you feel any better to shout, go ahead and scream your lungs out. No one can hear you."

"Someone, please help!"

"Have it your own way," she said, acting sure of herself as she removed a folded white cloth from the drawer.

"Listen to me," Linda pleaded, "you're making a mistake. I'm not the person you think I am."

Looking at Linda disappointedly, she jammed the cloth in her mouth and then took a wide roll of gray duct tape from the drawer as though getting ready to place a strip over her mouth. Pausing, she removed the cloth and said, "I'll give you one last chance to talk."

Linda swallowed to clear her throat, and spoke calmly but insistently. "My name isn't Werner, and I don't know how to convince you otherwise, but I'm not the person you think me to be."

The woman responded with a straight face, quickly jamming the cloth inside Linda's mouth before ripping free a piece of duct tape and strapping it across her mouth. From deep in the desk drawer, she removed a pair of rubber gloves and put them on, and picked up a small bottle containing a pale green liquid to remove its cap.

"I was hoping to avoid using the serum because the process takes hours, but we're prepared to do whatever's necessary."

Linda watched wide-eyed as the woman moistened a cotton swab with alcohol and wiped her forearm at the bend in the elbow where she detected a blood vein. Taking hold of a syringe and biting down on the needle's cap to pull it off and expose the needle's stem, she ran it through the rubber skin covering the bottle's top. Careful about the minute dosage drawn, she withdrew the needle from the bottle while commenting with the cap still held at one side of her mouth, "You may have witnessed a similar solution used to extract information from others. Now you'll discover firsthand the affects of psychoactive medication in a potent form of sodium amobarbital."

Tensing up, Linda's eyes widened when focusing on the syringe held by the woman's index and middle fingers with the needle upended, tapping it with a fingernail to get a bubble to the surface. She squeezed the end of the syringe with her thumb, and the pressure applied caused a short stream of the liquid to squirt.

"Now hold still," the woman said, and as the needle came into contact with Linda's arm, her eyes bulged. She cringed as the needle punctured her skin and the injection began. The woman checked Linda's pulse before leaning her backside against the desk, casually lighting another cigarette and exhaling a trail of smoke. "You should be feeling something soon."

The woman's voice suddenly deadened as a strange feeling rushed over Linda, and she tried fighting the drug to keep her senses, but it was useless. The drug's effects intensified while a dizzying sensation overtook her and blurred her vision. A blot of red appeared on the ceiling that expanded until it was running down the walls. Squinting and blinking, she shook her head while rigidly squirming. The red faded, but the walls began to swell in waves, and for a moment she saw the woman as a silhouette figure.

Overcome by hot and cold flashes until nauseated, Linda now saw the woman as a distorted figure checking her eyes with a penlight. The drug's influence accelerated as illusions took on new forms of imagery, envisioning the projected light as a blazing sun. Checkerboards of various sizes appeared in her field of vision, shifting as they rotated clockwise, turning with ever increasing speed, and replaced with more of the same in succession. Caught up in this sequence, her mind couldn't keep up with the drug's mind-bending effects, and she fought to keep conscious as long as she could, but soon she lost all touch with reality.

CHAPTER 2

The Interrogation

Sometime later, Linda's mind was still in disarray, but just beginning to get a hold on consciousness. The desk lamp's bright light showered her face with heat emanating from the light bulb. Finding its brilliance unbearable, she kept her eyes closed, seeing nothing more than a golden haze through her eyelids. The drug had instilled in her an overpowering propensity to yield, compelling her to react to the urgent need for answers. There were questions from a male's calm voice, and at other times, clamoring shouts from another male that resounded in the inner recesses of her mind. When the words fired at her came in spurts of impatient frustration, she sensed intimidation, but could do nothing but put up with the badgering. Two voices were coming across with an engaging, commanding tone, but having seen only one set of eyes with great detail staring back at her, she could not resist the demand that she look deep into them.

Drained from the ceaseless questioning, her body still held down rigidly by the straps, these relentless people held her prisoner in a controlled environment where they kept pressure applied to force her to divulge information. The calm voice had first introduced questions dealing with her identity, and when she had difficulty answering, the voice put forth simple reasoning to unlock answers she struggled to provide. Leading questions went into an area she was unfamiliar with, connected with the intricate design of a high-powered laser, light refraction, energy sources, and computer systems, all beyond her range of intellect. When she had no answer she'd stall or mumble and ramble on, and that's when the shouting occurred, ordering her to clarify or expand on her answer. She lastly gave clear and concise answers on questions touching on her personal life and her son Allan.

Sensing the presence of others lurking about the room, she knew gripping fear as she tried listening to the trade of indiscernible words. She then heard the distinct voice of the woman calling herself Adele, saying, "I saw her eyes blink soon after giving her the injection to counteract the serum. She'll be coming around soon, and we should give her at least one hour of rest before instructing her. Otherwise, how can we expect her to retain what we tell her?"

A man spoke with a tenor voice and an impatient attitude. "The central question is whether using a barbiturate derivative to extract information has made her compliant."

Another man – the calm voice she'd heard – replied in a foreign accent, "There are limitations to what we can accomplish with the little time we have, but I believe what we're attempting here is the most sensible solution. We've tapped into the subject's subconscious and probed her thought processes to enable us to see quite keenly her strengths and weaknesses. Trapped and longing for escape has made her more susceptible and submissive to certain persuasive commands. In my observation, I've found her strongest character makeup to be of maternal instinct, making her a good candidate for doing as we've asked with reasonable predictably.

"This woman has convictions engrained in her personality, and what I've done is implement the power of suggestion to raise her faith, trust, and confidence as a way to bolster and reinforce her own natural tendencies. If you've listened to the phrases I've used, you know my intent is to surpass the very ideals that already appeal to this individual's psyche. I've affirmed their prevalence for overcoming any barriers that may cause interference for the pretext of achieving our goal. The strong will and natural obligation of a protective, devoted mother will guide her to do what is necessary to deliver what she sees as fulfillment and closure to her problems. Should a conflict enter in,

13

her threshold for commitment will rise to cancel that preamble, and she'll suppress these thoughts while focusing on the task at hand."

The tenor voice again amplified from the individual standing close by. "Enough talk. Over the next forty-eight hours we'll know if our efforts have been futile. Provided other measures we've taken fall into place accordingly, I don't think what we're asking of her is outrageously difficult. However, Adele's right. She'll need rest before she's given further instructions and is released, as she'll barely be able to walk in an hour's time."

Someone switched off the lamp and in the still darkness, the ringing voices that had tirelessly pounded her ears now granted her ravaged mind peace, allowing Linda to doze off.

She woke up later bewildered and withdrawn, feeling as though she'd awakened from a nightmare. Everything at first looked foggy, and she did all she could to hold on to the fading present with conscious awareness proving elusive. Her mental faculties working without order or any true purpose, she couldn't concentrate long enough to comprehend all she'd been through. Picking up the sickening stench of an industrial chemical in the air, she saw dim sunlight peeking through the top of the window shade, a sign it may be nearing dusk.

Attempting to move in the dim surroundings, the straps confining her rustling movement, she caught the attention of Adele who sat in the wooden chair by the desk reading a book by the desk lamp. She closed the book with one hand and placed it on the desk, then scooted her chair out to give her enough space to stand. Adjusting the lamp's flexible neck by turning it upward so its light would reflect off the ceiling, she came around to open the window shade. She stood at Linda's side to assess her condition.

Adele examined her drowsy eyes, released levers to unlock the bed's wheels, and moved it to one side with a jerking motion that made Linda queasy.

Sensing the woman undoing the straps, Linda hung on to consciousness, blinking to correct her blurred vision, but the lingering effects of the drug left her judgment cloudy. Still confused about why they'd abducted her and what this mixed-up mystery was all about, she kept hoping they'd release her. Her head snapped sideways as her eyes enlarged to catch sight of a hairy, two-foot long caterpillar crawling up the wall, but then the vision evaporated.

"See something? There may be some residue of the drug coursing through your veins, but it will wear off soon and there will be no long-term effects. Now try sitting up. I'll be here to lend support if you start to fall."

Linda sat up, feeling weak and light-headed. The woman aided her to move off the bed and take an unstable stance on her own.

"Careful, you're still a little groggy from the straps restricting your circulation, but once you've walked around a little that will pass."

Linda gave no acknowledgement, and Adele guided her about the room before leading her to the chair at the desk, where she sat down. Gradually returning to some level of normalcy, she felt uncertain about what was coming next.

Adele sat on the corner of the desk gazing at her, sounding trusting and reassuring when saying, "There's no need to worry. All of your personal belongs are here on the desk, and you'll be leaving shortly."

The woman's words were encouraging, and after glimpsing her purse and the attaché case lying on the desk, she stood and proceeded to straighten out her clothing in preparation to leave. The lamp used during her interrogation attracted her attention, and she looked at it, thinking about all she'd been through.

Seeing no shoes for her to wear, Linda was soft-spoken when she asked, "Where are my shoes?"

"You lost one of them sometime earlier when you were picked up, but I have a comfortable pair of walking shoes for you to wear." Adele presented her with a plain pair of black slip-on shoes with low heels. "They may be a little large for you, but I'm sure they'll do."

As Linda put the shoes on, Adele spoke coldly and with a stern tone. "You have nothing to be afraid of, Mrs. Moreland.

Yes, we know you're who you say you are. When you wouldn't answer our questions and elaborate, we knew something was amiss."

Brief relief came in knowing that these people had realized their mistake. Linda hoped her bizarre abduction and interrogation was over, but suspected they weren't quite finished with her.

"Look at this, Mrs. Moreland." In the woman's hands she saw a striped shirt similar to the one she'd placed out for Allan to wear to school earlier in the morning. Linda's eyes locked on the shirt as she confirmed in her mind that the shirt belonged to Allan. Adele bluntly asked, "Do you know who this garment belongs to?"

Linda's lackadaisical state caused her to reach out to touch the shirt with concern for her son. She wondered how this person came into possession of the garment, and said, "Allan."

"It belongs to your son, doesn't it?" she snatched the shirt from Linda to get her attention. "Your son's life depends on you understanding what I'm going to tell you, so it's important you listen carefully."

Tears sprouted from Linda's eyes, and she wiped them as she listened.

The woman opened a manila file on the desk to reveal typewritten papers and a color photograph of Linda, but she immediately knew the image wasn't hers. The female in the photo shared a remarkable likeness to her, but she made the distinction best by how this person wore her hair: shorter, straighter, and perhaps a shade lighter than her own.

"When we picked you up we thought you were this woman. You can see there's a strong resemblance, but we were mistaken and we're sure others can make the same mistake. Her name is Evelyn Werner, and by acting in her place, you'll bring freedom to your son. In other words, for one short evening we need you to be this woman and gain access to information we need. You're to take this file with you, as there are steps outlined for you to take, telling you exactly where you are to go and what we expect you to bring back to us. You're to perform this task tomorrow night, so use what little time you have to give these papers a thorough going over. Success depends on how well you perform acting as Evelyn Werner, and failure means never seeing your son again. It's that simple."

She stuffed the file in Linda's handbag, adding, "Remember this, Mrs. Moreland. Should we learn you've gone to the police or FBI, we'll have no qualms about doing away with your son."

Having said all she intended, the woman helped Linda out of the chair, her legs momentarily unsteady, and ushered her to the door. They walked into a spacious stairwell landing that had up and down accessibility. The slightest sound echoed off the floor's octagon mosaic tiles.

Thinking the building to be a multifamily dwelling, she mustered the strength to walk down the stairs. She moved awkwardly, her hand clinging to the handrail, as Adele carried her purse and briefcase. They cut through a vacant lower level apartment to exit the building into an alleyway. It was night already and a light above the door protected by an oval screen attracted a swarm of flying insects.

The woman pointed to the street running crossways at the end of the alley. "At the end of the alley, go right to reach the first street corner, then go left, and keep walking until you've reached the following corner. We instructed a cabby to pick up a woman standing at that intersection, and it should be coming soon so don't dawdle. If you want to see Allan again, be extremely careful tomorrow night. You'll find our next meeting place in the file." She then turned and went back inside the building, bolting the door behind her.

Dazed by all they'd put her through, Linda felt demoralized, as though these individuals had violated her. Weak, fatigued, and uncertain of what had happened, she started wearily toward the street as she'd been told to do. The events seemed more dreamlike than real, for these were people who had no sense of conscience or pity. Feeling a sudden urgency, she needed to know if these people had in fact kidnapped her child, and her steps quickened.

The quiet walk in the cool night air helped stimulate her senses, stepping up her pace even more, but she was confused about which way to go at the end of the alley. After turning right to move in the direction of streetlamps, she turned left at the following street corner to move along hurriedly and catch up with the cab which she hoped to see soon.

At the next intersection, she waited at the corner, unaware of two men watching her from a gray Mercedes parked down the block. She didn't see a soul in sight. Smog trapped the stench of a chemical plant in the night air, and the drug's lingering effects fueled the delusion someone was stalking her in this blighted neighborhood. Staring across the street at barren brownstone row houses that had broken out bay windows and stark black doorways made her paranoid and fearful of this gloomy district.

A short distance down the street she saw a large neon sign hanging vertically over the walk. Its glowing reddish-orange letters spelled out the word "MISSION." A minute later, she flagged down an approaching taxicab, and climbing into the vehicle, she heard the driver, an old-timer, ask, "Where to, ma'am?"

"Staten Island—3411 Arlington," she replied. With all that had transpired, her only thought was to get home to see Allan waiting for her. The idea of him not being there sickened her, but this tormenting episode was so perplexing that she had trouble grasping exactly what they'd put her through. Not knowing what to think, she kept recalling flashbacks of an intensive interrogation under that blinding light. The gentle motion of the car ride nauseated her. She closed her eyes and leaned back in the car seat. Time slipped away as she drifted off.

CHAPTER 3

More Questions and Answers

"It was 3411, wasn't it, miss?" said the cabdriver as he searched for addresses on houses. There were but a few doors to go before reaching her home.

"Yes," Linda blurted out, "3411 Arlington." Her eyes opened wide to recognize familiar houses, as she perked up with surprise that she was already home.

Seeing the charge registered on the meter, she quickly gathered money from her purse to pay the driver, and slamming the car door behind her, she rushed to the door of her home. Stepping inside the foyer and leaving the attaché case leaning against a wall, she saw Louise sitting in a chair in the living room while a uniformed policeman sat on the sofa.

The sight of an officer in the living room quickened her heartbeat, and miserably frazzled, she rolled her eyes to keep welling tears from spilling over. Turning to the wall mirror to see a haggard appearance that fast needed changing, she placed her purse on the shelf beneath the mirror to grab a brush and makeup kit.

"Linda," Louise called out, entering the hallway to see Linda whipping back her hair with a few quick brush strokes.

"I'll be right there, Louise." Seeing glossy, glazed eyes and a bruised left eye, she made a rapid, fumbling attempt to cover the bluish-purple skin with makeup.

Louise began chattering. "I've been worried sick, Linda. Where have you been and why haven't you called? Allan is missing. One minute he was in the backyard playing, and then he was gone!"

Linda now knew they had Allan, but remained calm. She understood the importance of keeping her composure. Wondering how best to cope with the situation, she turned to Louise and conjured the only story she could think of, saying, "There's nothing to worry about, Louise. Allan's father picked him up."

"Mr. Moreland picked up Allan this afternoon?"

"Yes, he was supposed to call before he came by."

"He didn't say a word, and I've been so worried. You should've called to let me know he was coming for him. You have no idea how serious this situation has become, because the police had asked me if I believed Mr. Moreland had taken him and I told them I didn't believe so."

Fighting anxieties, Linda pulled herself together. "I'm sorry I didn't have time to call, but it's been such a crazy day."

"It's gotten crazy here too. I've had a policeman here for hours, and I don't see how you were so busy that you couldn't have phoned. I've tried reaching you all day, leaving you half a dozen messages, and when they told me you weren't at the fashion show, I didn't know what to think. Mona Shelton phoned the house numerous times wanting to speak to you and I didn't know what to say to her but to suggest that she try your cell phone."

Linda took a deep breath. "The reason I couldn't get to a phone or answer calls was because I was managing the show and entertaining clients."

Louise was throwing a fit. "You'd better come in here now and explain to this officer why I wasn't told about Allan's father coming for him."

Running her fingers through her hair to pull strands over the bruised eye she'd tried to cover with makeup, she entered the living room to face the police officer.

"Ms. Moreland?" said the tall officer, less than thirty years of age, coming to his feet.

"Yes, I'm she." Trying to appear relaxed, Linda smiled.

"I'm Officer Nash, and I'm here because Mrs. Hagen reported both you and your son as missing."

"It's all a terrible mistake." Linda added cordially, "Please, won't you sit down, and I'll try to clear this up as quickly as possible."

Louise interrupted Linda with a curious look. "Isn't Mr. Moreland in San Diego?"

Standing in the middle of the room, Linda ignored Louise, asking the officer, "Have you had coffee?"

"Had plenty, thanks," he replied, returning to his place on the sofa and opening a notepad.

"I'll have a cup please, Louise," Linda said to give her time alone with the officer, sitting down in the armchair and folding her hands to hide her nervousness. "I'm really sorry about all this trouble, but Allan went to live with his father in San Diego. All of this could've been avoided if my husband had called before picking him up."

"Your husband's an officer in the Navy and stationed in San Diego?"

Linda lowered her voice. "Yes, he's been stationed there over a year now. However, Officer Nash, I'm not trying to pass the blame for this unfortunate misunderstanding, but I discussed this with Louise the night before last. She's been a little absent-minded lately, and part of it is that doctors have diagnosed her in the early stages of Alzheimer's disease."

Louise came from the kitchen to give Linda a cup of coffee, wearing a look of disgust after overhearing her last comment, and returned to the kitchen. The coffee tasted bitter to Linda, and she immediately thought the drug injected into her had temporarily affected her taste buds.

"Mrs. Moreland, ordinarily we wouldn't have designated you as a missing person, but Mrs. Hagen was insistent something had happened to you, and when we couldn't locate you at the fashion show we presumed the worst. We sent a car to the Waldorf Astoria at 4:30 and those officers reported you weren't there. As a result of that, my supervisors are going to demand that I have answers detailing your movements up till eight o'clock, so I need you to tell me where you were for my report."

21

"I don't think it was so much that I wasn't there, but that I was difficult to locate, and surely anyone who went down there can verify that we were busy working a fashion show."

"Yes, but they had you summoned over the hotel's intercom system, so I'm going to need more to explain why you were thought to be absent from the hotel."

"I was in and out of wardrobe making dresswear alterations. When you're in the dressing room you can't hear what's going on up front, and people were paging me over that speaker system throughout the day. Frankly, after a while you become oblivious to those calls. It's simply impossible to take care of everything and everybody, and that's why I told the girls not to interrupt me when I was in the dressing room. I'm sure, had they known it was official business, they would've located me, but at the same time, they may have considered I'd responded to those calls in some way."

"OK, you managed this fashion show this afternoon, but that still doesn't explain your whereabouts this evening. Our investigation has your fashion show scheduled to run from three to five, and it's now after eight, but the last person I have reported as seeing you is your employer, who had lunch with you. Let's get past the fashion show and concentrate on your movements between five and eight. Assuming you left the show at five or five-thirty, where were you from then up till eight o'clock this evening?"

Under stress to find a way to cut the conversation short, she continued manufacturing a story. "I met a gentleman friend after the event, and we had dinner together at the hotel."

"Surely it didn't take you two and a half hours to have dinner?"

"Well, this friend had a room at the hotel and we spent some time in his room." She paused to sip coffee. The officer kept his eyes on her while waiting to hear more. "I suppose if I have to offer more details I can, but I'd rather not give you his name since he's married."

The officer raised a brow. "I don't think that will be necessary."

She faked a smile. "The big mistake I made was turning off my cell phone at the beginning of the show and afterwards forgetting to turn it back on."

The officer made notes filling out his report, and then asked, "Are you sure you previously discussed your husband picking up the child with Mrs. Hagen?"

"Positively. I distinctly remember explaining to her that I'd decided to let Allan live with his father, and that he'd come by this afternoon to pick him up. He was supposed to call first, but he apparently didn't."

"Then you didn't say good-bye to your son?"

"No, I told him goodbye last night so he wouldn't get emotional, thinking it may be easier on him for me not to be present when his father came. You know how kids can be."

"What's puzzling is that no one picked up any of the child's belongings."

Linda found one lie leading to another, leaving her to worry that talking too much could show she was rattled. She calmly replied, "I'd left a small luggage bag inside the kitchen door. My husband must've come around to the back, met up with Allan, and reached inside the door to grab the bag without saying a word before leaving. That's my husband for you, and he'd confessed to worrying that I'd change my mind about allowing him to take Allan to California. If he'd just called as I'd asked him to it may have jogged Louise's memory, and we could've avoided taking up your time."

Feeling squeamish, the caffeine in her coffee made her jittery as she watched the officer jotting down information.

"Alright, Mrs. Moreland, I think I've got enough information to complete my report."

She sat her cup on the end table and conducted herself as naturally as possible when leading him to the door. Speaking apologetically, she said, "I'm sorry about all the trouble this has caused. I should've called Louise myself and made certain she understood, but I didn't expect this would happen."

"That may have saved us all some headaches."

"Goodbye, and again, I'm sorry," she said, closing the door behind him.

Overcome by exhaustion, Linda leaned against the wall, unable to get Allan out of her mind. Thoughts of him in the hands of those heartless, callous people made her sick. As much as she wanted to ask the police for help, she dared not risk gambling with her son's life. The kidnappers' brutal methods had convinced her they were deadly serious. There was no doubt in her mind that they would stop at nothing to accomplish their goals, and crossing them by informing the police of the situation would cause them to kill her son.

Uncertain about what to do, and agonizing over thoughts of what they might do to Allan if she failed them, she was on the verge of tears. Her mind racing, she clasped her hands over her nose and mouth and stepped back into the living room, collapsing on the sofa, her face sinking into the seat cushion as tears gushed forth.

"Linda, has he gone?" Louise called out from the kitchen, and hearing no response, she came to the living room to find Linda weeping. She knelt down beside her. Pulling her close to look in her eyes, she'd sensed all along that something was terribly wrong, and asked, "What is it? Linda, what's happened?"

Sobbing, Linda said, "They've got Allan," and broke down in tears all over again.

"Who's got him?"

"These people. They want me to get something for them."

"You're not making any sense, Linda. I'd better get Officer Nash back here."

Linda caught the sleeve of Louise's blouse, and with urgency in her eyes and voice, she said, "No, you mustn't. They told me they'd kill him if I went to the authorities, and they meant it."

"But you have to go to the police, Linda."

Linda shook her head. "As soon as they've learned I've spoken to the police they'll kill Allan."

"What are you going to do then?"

"I'll have to get them what they want."

"Linda, if you won't go to the police, I will."

With a desperate, determined look in her eyes, she gripped Louise's arm, pulling her close, and insisted, "You're not calling them!" Linda's hold relaxed as she calmed herself. "Allan's my child. He's all I've got in this world, and that's a decision you have to let me make. If something happens to him, I'll be the one who's left to suffer, so please promise me you won't interfere."

"Alright then. If you feel that strongly about it, I promise not to get in the way, but if these are the kind of people you think they are, they can't be trusted."

Linda couldn't hold back the onrush of tears. "Don't you understand? As long as they have Allan, I'm at their mercy, and I've got to do as they've asked." Staring into space, she put her hand to her cheek, smearing the tears running down her face. She whimpered, "Louise, what if I don't get him back?"

They sat down on the sofa together, and Louise turned tearful as she embraced Linda while rocking her in her arms.

"Oh, Linda, you must give some thought to going to the police. There may not be a lot of time to do something about this, and later you'll blame yourself for not calling them."

Their tears subsided, but Linda was coming down from the drug the kidnappers had administered to her, leaving her mind descending into chaos as her world was unraveling. She felt as though she'd fallen into the bleakest, blackest pit, and in this wretched state she lost consciousness and fell asleep in Louise's arms.

Having never seen Linda so emotional before, the way she'd collapsed in her arms told Louise she was exhausted. Certain she wasn't going to get any more information from her, she left her stretched out on the sofa and covered her with a blanket. Having given her word she wouldn't contact the police, she decided to talk to Linda about Allan sensibly in the morning.

Linda wrestled with an inner conflict in her sleep, partly generated by the drug, and reliving haunting visions of what she'd gone through left her mind in turmoil. The horror of not knowing who the people who'd stolen her child were gave her intense anxiety, and in her mind she fell into deluded dreams. Finding herself imprisoned and tormented by Allan's cries for her, she couldn't find him no matter how hard she tried. Huge, penetrating eyes came out of the darkness chasing after her; the pupils were brown, and the whites of the eyes clear with dark circles surrounding them. Pressure heightened to find Allan as she ran from the domineering eyes, and when she found an exit, she saw the way blocked by her abductors—two tall, faceless companions standing before the woman Adele, who stood grinning. Throughout the night, she ran inside herself with grim hopelessness leading to the same torturous results…

CHAPTER 4

Preparations

Linda woke up early the next morning with her first thought for Allan, and the nightmarish reality of not knowing where he was gave way to fear for his safety. Unable to cope with his abduction, mental anguish festered in her mind until her heart actually ached for her child. The strangers holding him weren't deviants in the usual sense, but people that took children for any reason couldn't be normal by any stretch of the imagination. It made her sick to her stomach that she couldn't do anything to get him back, and with nowhere to turn for help, all she did was sit and stare while thinking about him.

Louise came to place a tray of food on the coffee table, and from one of the pockets of her apron removed utensils wrapped in a napkin to put with it. "I thought you may be hungry when you woke."

Linda's thoughts brought tears to her eyes, and even without having eaten for such a long time, she was still without an appetite. The only way she could function was to cling to the belief they hadn't harmed Allan, but more importantly, she knew his future depended on what she did from here on. Trying to focus on what she needed to do to get him back, she settled down and began looking about for her purse, as she recalled a file placed inside it detailed the kidnappers' demands.

"Have you seen my purse, Louise?"

Louise remembered seeing her purse on the shelf below the mirror in the entry hall and went to bring it to her. Wanting to be of some help to Linda, after handing the handbag to her, she sat down in an armchair prepared to offer her assistance.

Linda opened the handbag wide, but outside of Louise's line of vision, to remove the manila folder. She began sorting out typewritten papers, glimpsing the 8x10 photograph of Evelyn Werner. She saw what first appeared to be a wallet-sized photo, which was a photo ID connected with the Department of Defense.

She began nibbling on fruit Louise had sliced and prepared for her while delving into the papers and studying the typewritten instructions, giving less and less attention to the food as she did so. The ID card was referred to as a clearance badge; a small clip connected to it made it easy to attach the badge to a pocket or the collar of clothing. Similar to the size and shape of a credit card, a photo of Evelyn Werner was centered on it, and beneath it were bright blue markings and a red emblem indicating top level clearance. The reverse side gave instructions in case of loss, directing the finder to drop the card into any mailbox which would forward the article to FBI Headquarters in Washington, D.C.

Louise kept still in her chair as she watched Linda's eyes scan the papers, but then asked, "What do they want you to do?"

"I don't think we should discuss it, Louise."

"Linda, I know I promised, but I was hoping you'd see things differently by morning. As emotional as you were last night, I couldn't get anything out of you, but you'll only get yourself in deeper trying to bargain with kidnappers."

Linda placed her hands on her head. "Louise, please don't do this. I've got far too much to think about, and Allan's best chances for survival depend on my doing as they ask. You have no idea what they're like. There's little they won't do to get what they want. They abducted me from a busy street corner at noon in Manhattan. The instant the police are involved, they're sure to find out, and then they're liable to kill Allan, so I'm going to ask you again not to interfere. I'm asking you for Allan's sake and as a friend—don't make this any more complicated than it already is."

Gathering up the papers and putting them back in the file, Linda left the room carrying her purse, starting for the stairs to shower and put on a change of clothes.

Louise rose out of her chair and came to the hallway, saying, "Linda, wait."

Stopping midway up the staircase, Linda turned and said, "How I can make it any clearer, Louise? I don't want you getting involved. Please do as I ask, and stay out of this."

Louise's expression looked serious as she replied, "I was going to ask if there was anything I can do to help."

Linda's shoulders slumped. "Yes, you can make an appointment for me at the beauty parlor."

Louise looked confused as she watched Linda go up the stairs.

Soon afterward, Linda heard Louise calling upstairs for her. "Linda, they said they can take you in two hours, but they inquired what services are needed."

Linda shouted down, "Just a shampoo and a cut."

Stuffing the file beneath her pillow as she prepared to shower, she saw her troubles doubling by considering the kidnappers' request. What they wanted her to do was not only illegal but downright criminal. It seemed outlandish to think she could pass for this other woman she resembled, but unable to think of anything but Allan, she had no choice in the matter—she knew she must appease these people. Stepping inside the shower, isolation behind its doors rekindled nightmarish memories from the interrogation, intensifying her misery. The helplessness she knew at the time stirred emotions, and while crying, the shower's spray of hot water washed away her tears.

She clasped her hands over her eyes when visualizing the lamp's blinding light, hearing questions projected with authority from a dark figure looming over her.

How long has the MX-11 been in operation? What is the energy source powering this laser weapon? What is the range of the Triad Satellite?

The questions kept coming, sharply spoken words pounding her mind with amplified pitch and annoying repetition.

You engaged in work involving the MX-11 project. You helped develop the laser for the Triad MX-11, and you must open up and answer my questions!

The influence of the drug they'd injected into her compelled her to answer, but as much as she wanted to comply, she didn't know how to, and her mumbling left her interrogator agitated. Her hands moved, cupping over her nose and mouth as she became engrossed with the degrading recollection of what occurred in that dark room. She turned, remaining still as hot water showered her back, seeing shadowy figures moving in and out of her line of sight.

She envisioned a set of cold, penetrating eyes, encompassed by dark circles and paired with black eyebrows, staring into her own. She wrapped her arms around herself. It was as though these eyes had the ability to see into the depths of her mind and read her thoughts. Their constant stare left her unable to breathe, and to escape them she quickly lathered up and rinsed off before stepping out of the enclosure to dry off.

She put on her robe and went back to study the papers and consider their plan, wondering if she could enter an aeronautical defense plant in Washington, D.C., and lead people to believe she was Evelyn Werner. She'd have to go beyond a maximum security area, locate a safe, and seize a NATO file on what the kidnappers referred to as the MX-11. On top of everything else, they wanted her to do it tonight…

Her instructions were to find a file with NATO on the cover, accompanied by the North Atlantic Treaty Organization's official star-shaped emblem. She was to look at the first page inside the file to make certain it read "MX-11, CODENAME: TRIAD, LAB TECHNOLOGY—ENGINEERING DESIGN."

Linda went down the hall to the family's computer room where she looked up NATO in an encyclopedia, and there was the emblem, a sort of geometric design in the shape of a star. Looking at it, she knew that what she was thinking about doing meant treason and going against everything she believed in, but overriding her reasoning was the convincing threat they'd kill Allan if they didn't get the file.

She returned to her bedroom in a mental tug-of-war. As much as she was determined to do anything to get her son back, her conscience kept eating at her. She knew what she planned was wrong, but she also knew her child's life relied on success-fully acquiring this file. Unable to imagine life without him, she saw no other way out. Her commitment to her son outweighed any common sense angle, as she couldn't go on living knowing her failure had resulted in his death.

Linda put on a pale blue blouse and black slacks, and she placed the file in the folded layers of a quilt in the middle bot-tom drawer of her bedroom dresser. Yet she kept wondering what the MX-11 was and if turning this document over to these people would constitute the crime of the century?

Compelled by something she didn't understand, she felt mixed emotions, like the reluctant shoplifter who knows he's going to get caught but can't say no to the prospect of stealing. Linda knew that if the authorities caught her it would mean years of imprisonment, but a commitment to her son hung over her, bringing on a pressing urgency to succeed. Unable to sup-press thoughts that her country's defense may somehow hang in the balance, she took comfort in the idea that she wouldn't have done anything wrong until she'd actually penetrated the govern-ment facility. However, once she entered that building with the intention of obtaining secret information, she'd be past the point of no return and criminally liable.

Thinking these unsettling thoughts caused her to develop a pounding headache, and she pushed them aside, making use of the time she had to make preparations for her trip to Washing-ton. She went to the hairdressers to have her hair styled boyishly plain with little curl to help her look like Evelyn Werner. After stopping by the bank to get airfare, at quarter to three in the afternoon she returned home. Louise wore a surprised expres-sion upon seeing how Linda had her hair shortened.

Momentarily looking at each other, Linda finally com-mented, "It'll grow back." She then went upstairs, thinking, *My hair will have plenty of time to grow back when I'm doing life in prison for espionage and the theft of top secret material.*

Linda brought the file out to look at the 8x10 photograph of Evelyn Werner, gazed at her own reflection in the dresser mirror. A weird feeling came over her as she saw she had an incredible likeness to the woman, leaving her surprised she could look so much like a complete stranger. To learn she had a look-alike was oddly annoying: there was a slight variance in hairstyle, as Linda's hair was still longer and had slightly more wave and curl in comparison to the woman in the photo.

Reexamining the face in the photo inspired her to speak out loud. "No wonder they mistook me for her. She could pass for my double."

A rap came at the door and Louise entered, catching a glimpse of the photo before Linda flipped it over. They exchanged a stare.

"Linda, I think I'd feel better about all this if I knew what these people wanted from you. I'm only asking about it out of concern for you and Allan."

"I understand, but I can't discuss it with you because if something goes wrong and things get more complicated, I don't want you implicated in any way. What you don't know can't hurt you, and I don't want you to be in anyway responsible."

"Responsible for what? The way you're acting is telling me you're going to do something dangerous, and I can't help feeling you're making a serious mistake by not going to the police."

Linda, knowing she needed Louise's cooperation, spoke calmly. "If the kidnappers should find out the authorities are involved I'm likely to lose contact with them. In that event, it may be months or even years before I learn my son's fate, and if any harm should come to Allan because you brought the police into this, I'll never forgive you. Now I know you're thinking about calling the police, and it's only fair that you think about the consequences because once you make that phone call it's out of my hands."

"Look at the risks you're taking, Linda. After they get what they want, what's stopping them from doing away with the both of you?"

"That's a gamble I've got to take, and right now I don't see how I have any other choice. I'm proceeding with faith that once they've gotten what they're after it'll be over. If I thought the police would improve Allan's chances I'd go to them, but I'm convinced that once they know the police are involved they'll kill him, and where's that going to leave me?"

"You can't blame yourself."

"It's not a matter of who's to blame but what it's going to take to achieve Allan's safe release. I don't want any harm coming to him. If I can accomplish what they want done tonight, I should be able to bring him home tomorrow, and after it's over with and he's safe, I'll go to the authorities."

Louise stood there looking at Linda, wanting to somehow convince her to go to the police, but knew she was getting nowhere. "You're going out tonight?"

Linda nodded. "Should I succeed at what I'm setting out to do, at ten o'clock tomorrow morning I'm expected to deliver them what they want, and then they'll give me Allan. Now think about Allan's position—your calling the police could result in his death, and how will you feel then?"

With that, Louise left the room.

Linda believed she'd done a good job of reasoning with Louise, but she still couldn't be sure whether she'd phone the police, and this worried her. Unable to stand another day of not knowing her child's fate, she watched the clock, trying to keep a clear head and focus on what she needed to do. Arranging to catch a six o'clock flight to Washington, D.C., with a nine o'clock return flight, she used the little time she had left before her departure to memorize information in the typewritten papers. Feeling cornered like never before, and afraid of forgetting something, she jotted down particular details on a piece of notepaper.

Approaching the hour to go to the airport, she was turning into a nervous wreck, but determined to go through with it, she phoned for a taxi. Concerned Louise might look for the file, she decided not to return it to the dresser, but hid it beneath a rug runner in the hallway, leaving it tucked away at the hall's far end near the linen closet. She thought there'd be little foot traffic there with less chance of Louise finding it. Not long afterward, the cab arrived and Linda threw on a tan blazer before coming down the stairs.

Louise stood looking out the door's glass, and when she turned she saw how dispirited Linda appeared.

"Louise, please try to understand that this is something I've got to do."

"What time should I expect you home, so I'll know when it is a police matter?"

"I should be home before midnight, and if I think I'll be any later than that, I'll call."

"Do you need money?"

"No, I stopped by the bank earlier."

The cabdriver tapped his horn twice. They hugged, and Linda went out the door.

The taxi took her to Newark International Airport in New Jersey, where she boarded a jet airliner. In flight, she felt jittery as anxiety gripped her. *It's a frame of mind*, she told herself. *Keep calm*. Linda continued reassuring herself, but imagined she'd fall to pieces before the night was over.

Unable to stand much more of this unnerving misery, she felt uneasy about accomplishing this heist to bring her son home. It would either be over tonight if she got caught, or tomorrow she'd complete the trade at ten o'clock in the morning, expecting to gain Allan's freedom when she delivered the file to a cemetery in Brooklyn. She went on to analyze the kidnappers' motives for wanting to get their hands on this document, feeling they'd pushed her to act fast to acquire this file so as not to run the risk of her going to the authorities. The information it contained obviously meant a great deal to them, and she believed they were likely working for a foreign government.

Only just realizing her son was without the pills he needed to treat his liver condition was just one more thing to contend with. However, she knew that if she got him back tomorrow as planned then it shouldn't be a problem. She tried concentrating on the challenge she had ahead of her in Washington, D.C.

CHAPTER 5

Washington and the
Point of No Return

The plane touched down at Washington National Airport near dusk. Minutes later, Linda waved a taxi down and directed its driver to take her to the Aeronautical Defense Agency Headquarters.

The driver, who was familiar with the area, knew where she wanted to go as the facility employed thousands of people. When the taxi pulled up in front of the government installation, Linda saw a well-lit entrance to a parking area. At the gate's entry was a small glass building housing two uniformed guards. She got out on the far side of the street, noticing a large sign on top of the guard shack with black lettering and reflecting lights that read:

Aeronautical Defense Agency Headquarters
Department of Defense
—WARNING—
U.S. GOVERNMENT PROPERTY
RESTRICTED AREA
PARKING FOR FEDERAL EMPLOYEES ONLY

Linda stood outside the taxi while paying the driver, and saw in the distance a modern building of brick and glass blocks.

Pinning the plastic badge to the collar of her shirt, she said, "I expect to be about forty minutes to an hour. Any chance of meeting me back here around then?"

"Well," began the chunky driver, looking at his watch, "I'm about due for a break, so I'll go get a cup of coffee and be back here in less than an hour."

"I'd appreciate that," she said, presenting him with a twenty dollar tip. "You won't let me down?"

"I'll definitely be back before 8:25 p.m., miss."

As the taxi pulled away, Linda checked her watch to see it was 7:25 p.m. Crossing the street, she sighted the guards, who noticed her. One seemed hardly interested, while the other kept an eye on her. As she came closer into view, he seemed to recognize her with the badge she wore and gave her a short hand wave.

Passing through the main gate and maintaining a steady pace on the long walk to the building, where a wide staircase led up to a set of glass doors, she believed she was making the worst mistake of her life. With the last rays of daylight came encroaching darkness, and she felt tense hearing her heels clatter against the concrete, while a cool breeze ruffled her hair. Anxiety grew as she neared the headquarters entrance, and it occurred to her that security guards may be monitoring her movements through surveillance cameras. Her conscience stirring, she felt as though she wore a shroud of guilt for her intent. She knew that by passing through the doors she'd be making a serious infringement on the law of the land. Still, these thoughts were in vain, as her legs went on carrying her in the direction of the doors, and a persistent motherly instinct became an unrelenting driving force controlling her actions.

Allan's survival depended on her succeeding, so she saw this as something she must do. She also worried about impersonating Evelyn Werner, someone who probably held an important position here and came to this location on a regular basis.

It's not too late. You haven't done anything wrong, she thought while glimpsing the set of doors ahead of her.

Determination overcoming common sense, she spoke out loud, as if to give herself a word of encouragement. "Dear God, don't let me fail."

Her legs carried her up the steps like an automated figure, and she pushed open the door on her right to enter the building. Her instructions told her to be prepared to show a guard behind a desk on her right the ID badge, and she paused, turning her shirt collar to make the badge easily viewable. Behind a long counter, a middle-aged black guard reading a newspaper glanced to recognize the badge before waving her on before turning his eyes back to the sports section.

Moving along, she walked down a corridor trying to locate an elevator, and slowed down when taking notice of a sign on her right that read:

WARNING
ALL PERSONNEL ARE SUBJECT TO SEARCH WHILE
ON THIS INSTALLATION

Just beyond the sign was the elevator, and grateful to find it empty, she pressed 5. She withdrew the paper from her purse that she'd made notes on from the typed instructions, and suddenly aware a hidden camera probably had her in view, she tucked the paper inside the right hip pocket of her blazer.

After reaching the fifth floor, she stepped into a hallway branching off in three directions and turned left as instructed, passing by another wall sign that read:

WARNING
CONTROLLED AREA
AUTHORIZED PERSONNEL ONLY

Soon, she came to another checkpoint where a security guard inspected her purse at a counter, and while checking its contents the guard made the friendly comment, "Working late tonight, huh?"

Linda just smiled, and when the guard finished, she tucked her purse under her arm and followed the hall until she came upon a glass door with a slotted, electronically-controlled device connected to the frame. She'd learned from her instructions that she'd come across such a door, but hesitated on what to do.

There's no turning back now. In thinking this, she was prepared to accept all consequences for her actions. Remembering to remove the ID card from her collar, she inserted the bottom side of the card until the red emblem and bright blue markings for levels of clearance were no longer visible.

The door slid sideways for her to enter, and after she passed through, the door closed automatically. She paused to re-clip the badge to her collar. Up ahead she saw another security door, and when approaching it she saw that this one did not have a slot for her to insert the badge. This door had a compact pedestal attached to a wall, and as much as she thought it could be a security device, she wasn't certain. What puzzled her was that her instructions hadn't made mention of it, and she placed her hand on the door in hopes that it would open automatically, but nothing happened.

Now what? she thought, and seeing no way to get through this door, as much as she didn't want to ask the guard for help, she saw no other way of going beyond this point without assistance. Going back to the guard would attract attention, but at the same time, waiting too long to ask for help would certainly serve to make this predicament worse and arouse even more suspicion.

Taking a deep breath, she reversed direction, using the badge again to make passage through the first door, and came to approach the guard who'd searched her purse minutes before.

She tried appearing dumbfounded when approaching him, as if to show no understanding for why she couldn't pass into the next security zone, saying, "Excuse me, but I can't get by that security door."

"Didn't your badge work, or was it the second door?"

"The second door is the one I couldn't get through."

Walking back to the first door together, Linda used her badge to gain passage to the next security door, and when they came to it, the guard said, "Go ahead and place your hand on the scanning plate."

Just now fully realizing the pedestal attached to the wall was a scanning plate, she understood that this device could read handprints, and knew it wouldn't recognize hers. However, she had no choice but to place her hand flat against the glass plate, and dancing light waves read her hand's skin impressions, but it did not open the door. Even though there was no warning alarm, she knew security personnel must be monitoring this access door and had received an alert signal to draw their attention.

The guard responded by saying, "Step back and I'll see if I can get it to work."

He placed his hand on the plate and light waves scanned it, and this time the door opened. "They've spent millions on technology to provide security, and there's still an occasional glitch in the system."

Linda heard a voice coming through a radio attached to the guard's belt as a security technician asked what the problem was. Detaching the radio to respond, the guard replied, "I have Evelyn Werner with me. The pedestal couldn't read her hand print, so I'll check her thoroughly here before allowing her to move on from this point."

The guard squared-off with her while scrutinizing her facial features and unclipped her badge from her collar to examine the photo and make a comparison. Returning the badge to her, he said, "Alright, Miss Werner, you may pass, and I'll put this in my report, but don't be surprised if this happens again, as it usually does after it's occurred once. To prevent future delays I'd suggest stopping by the security office on the first floor. They'll run a tracer on your hand print again to correct the problem on this end."

Linda entered through the door and continued on her way to find the office she was in search of, thinking they'd told her to come here after six because that's when the building would have less foot traffic. A stunning portrait of George Washington hung from a wall at the hallway's end, and the reality that she was betraying her country came to her, but she shut this idea out of her mind.

Following the hallway, she passed the ladies' restroom and soon came to an oversized metal door on her right marked with bold red lettering:

**MX SYSTEM
TOP SECRET**

A digital panel on the wall electronically operated the door. Having memorized the access code, she didn't have to check the notepaper. The numbers lit up on the panel as she pressed them in sequence, the door slid sideways into the wall, and she stepped forward into a dark room. The door closed behind her and the glow of moonlight through glass block windows on the far end of the room helped her to see an outline of chairs, desks, and tables. Seeking a light switch, she saw a glowing one inch square button on the wall, and uncertain about the button's function, she took a chance on pressing it. The button activated the door she'd just entered through to open it again, and it soon went back to a closed position to leave her wondering what to do next.

Her eyes quickly adjusted to focus on another nearby switch, and when flipping it rows of florescent lights in the ceiling blinked before flooding the room with light. Immediately drawing her eyes were stars and stripes—Old Glory hung like a lone sentinel in a corner, and there were four desks evenly spaced within the room. Something she didn't expect to see were navy blue curtains covering the walls on her left and right. Her instructions had told her to go beyond the curtains and locate a safe containing the file.

Going to the curtains on the right side of the room, she drew them open by pulling on a cord. They parted from the center to reveal a global map covering the entire wall. Done in fine detail, the map had an array of flags and color-coded pins scattered across the continents. She closed the curtains immediately and went to the curtains on the opposite side of the room. Drawing them apart exposed a black and chrome safe centered in the middle of the wall, and on each side of the safe were shelves holding volumes of books and files. She went to the safe's shiny circular dial, notched and stamped in fine numerals of tens up to 100, and she unfolded her notepaper to make sure she had the combination correct. As instructed, she spun the dial counterclockwise three times to clear it. Crossing zero again, she carefully pegged the numeral 47, reversed the dial to stop on the numeral 34, and then she reversed the dial again to 79 before lastly turning the dial back to 23. Thinking that should do it, she gripped the handle firmly to give the door a big yank, but it didn't budge.

Carefully and precisely repeating each step again, she pulled the safe door's handle hard, but was unsuccessful at opening it.

"No, God, no—I don't believe this." At a loss of patience, she took a deep breath and exhaled. "Either I'm doing something wrong or there must be a slip-up in the combination."

After giving the combination a third try, she shook her head, figuring the combination must be wrong and gave up, asking herself, *Now what do I do?*

Feeling pressed for time, she turned to face the alignment of desks in the room. It occurred to her that some absentminded person may have jotted down the safe's combination at their desk to make it readily available, and she went to the nearest one. She first checked the phone's bottom, the bottom of a lamp, and then started rifling through drawers, checking the back of the drawer's facings to see if someone had attached the written combination to it.

Careful to leave things as she'd found them, she proceeded to the next desk. A wall clock indicated it was already a few minutes after eight o'clock, leaving her concerned about catching her cab ride. Hearing the electronic door to the office start to open, she sat down to open a hard-backed manual for computer components, pretending to read as someone stepped into the room.

Linda kept her eyes on the book as she resisted looking at this person, but sensing the individual staring at her, she finally looked up. A tall, red-haired man with a pinkish complexion, in his late forties and dressed casually, nodded with a smile as if to say hello.

"I didn't know you were still working in this sector. I hope by now you've had time to tour the many attractions here in Washington?"

"No, but I hope to one day soon."

"Washington, D.C., is one of the most beautiful cities in the world, and to make your stay here a memorable one you need to walk through the National Mall, take in the monuments, and explore the Smithsonian Institute."

Linda felt pressed to say something, and commented, "I've seen them from a distance."

Seeing the curtains drawn, he went to the safe to work the combination, and although it was impossible for her to read the numerals he turned the dial to, when he pulled the lever, it opened. Shuffling through files until finding the one he was searching for, he tucked it under his arm, and placed his hand on the safe's door as though getting ready to close it.

Linda nervously uttered, "Would you be kind enough to leave the safe open please? I'll be finished in a few minutes and I have something I need to return to it."

"Sure." Taking his hand from the safe's door to leave it open, he started toward her with a pleasant smile. "Something must have you stumped to be working here so late, but with your stubborn persistence you're certain to figure it out."

Uncomfortable with the attention she was getting from this person, she managed to break a smile and her eyes shifted from eye contact with him to the book she held in front of her.

"I'm seeing a different look about you. Perhaps you've changed your hairstyle?"

She looked up at him. "I used a blow dryer earlier this evening after showering, and it may have given it some fluff."

"You look nice, and as long as you're going to be in Washington for awhile, I hope to be seeing you again soon."

He then left the room, and with him gone, Linda quickly moved to the safe to go through a stack of manila folders, most of which were marked Department of Defense. Some had the symbol of a bald eagle posed with wings spread open and its head turned to one side, talons clenching flags of NATO and the

United States. These were files of the utmost importance. Her instructions specified that she find a file titled NATO and that had the organization's emblem on the cover. Sighting a file lying separately on a shelf, she saw **NATO** in bold capital letters at the top of the file, and recognized the star-shaped emblem.

Opening the file cover, she read:

MX-11
CODENAME: TRIAD
LAB TECHNOLOGY—ENGINEERING DESIGN

Kept separate from other files, she believed the TRIAD file must have great importance, but for now she could only think about how she was going to get the document out of the building undetected. Instructed to exchange the file cover with one of the others, she did so, presuming the trade was to put off others from learning the file was missing. She left the original file cover containing different information lying on the shelf where she'd found it, and placed the Triad papers inside a file that had a symbol of an eagle on its cover.

She closed the safe door, and seeing the wall clock read 8:20, she wondered if the taxi was going to be waiting for her when she left the facility. Thinking she may still have time if she hurried, she thought, *If I lose my ride to the airport, what am I going to do?*

Knowing the guard would search her purse, Linda now had to devise a way to get the file out of the building without him seeing it. Thinking she had to somehow hide it in her clothing, but not wanting someone to enter the room and surprise her when she was most vulnerable to exposure, she remembered the ladies' room down the hall. Removing a roll of transparent tape from a desk drawer, she put it in her purse and tucked the file inside her blazer, and then left the room as she'd found it.

Looking up and down the corridor without seeing anyone, she backtracked to the ladies' room where she took one of the stalls. Placing her purse with the roll of tape and the file on the tank lid, she removed her blazer and blouse and hung them on a protruding hook attached to the stall door. She positioned the file beneath her bra, flat and firm against her stomach, with the file cover fold down so nothing could fall out, and then strapped the file to her by wrapping the tape around her three times. Believing she had the file secured, she slipped into her blouse, and checking the time on her wristwatch, she saw she'd been inside the building for nearly an hour. Time was running out to meet the taxi and, doubtful the driver would wait for her, she now expected she'd have to take a later flight back to New York.

Throwing her blazer on, she left the roll of tape hanging on the hook and hurriedly left the restroom to go down the corridor to get to the elevator. The door controlled by the pedestal scanning device opened automatically from this side when activated by a motion detector. When approaching the next security door at a fast pace she felt her collar for the ID badge she'd need to open it with, and gasped when discovering the badge missing.

Knowing security wouldn't allow her to walk the halls of the facility without the ID badge, she doubled back in search of it. Irked by the threat of getting caught stealing this document, she began perspiring as her eyes scanned the floor of the hallway. Returning to the ladies' room, she found relief seeing the badge lying on the stall floor and snatched it up.

She leaned against the stall wall while taking a deep breath of air. *What am I going to do if that cabdriver isn't out there waiting for me, and how will I get to the airport if he isn't there? I didn't even see a filling station anywhere nearby.*

Regaining her composure, she left the ladies' room and this time made it through both security doors without a snag. Connecting the badge to the collar of her blazer, she went down the hall and stopped at the checkpoint, where the same guard that searched her purse earlier did so again.

Taking the elevator to the ground floor, she walked past the main desk, where the guard waved her on to exit into the cool night air, and she looked up into a clear twilight sky. Walking from the building to the entry gate, she was breathing easier, but she knew it wasn't over yet. It wouldn't be over until she arrived back home safely in Staten Island with the file in her possession.

Nearing the brightly-lit entrance gate, a federal patrol car with emergency roof lights rolled up to the guard shack. It seemed strange for this car to show up just as she was leaving the facility. Passing through the gates of this installation was the final stage of the task, but she thought the guards may be waiting for her to actually exit the property before making an arrest to strengthen their case for theft. Lacking confidence and shivering all over, she watched as a guard came out to meet the patrol car and have a word with its driver.

"Don't get paranoid," she said under her breath. "Keep calm."

The guard standing next to the car watched her go by, saying, "Good night."

Linda gave a casual wave, but her worries intensified when she noticed the taxi wasn't waiting for her. It was after 8:30. She'd halfway expected the cab not to be here, but the federal patrol car now posed an unforeseen element as she wondered if it caught the guard's attention that she didn't have transportation.

They must think it odd to see someone leaving this installation this late at night on foot, she thought, with her emotions see-sawing. Unable to shake the suspicion that these guards were watching her, she moved at a fast walking pace to get away from the installation as quickly as possible.

Crossing the street to get to the sidewalk on the opposite side from the government employee parking area, she continued distancing herself from the headquarters' gate. Headlights from a car coming up behind her cast her shadow out before her in elongated fashion, and she stopped when she heard the vehicle pull up behind her. She turned and squinted to look into its blinding headlights, studying the elevated crown on the car's roof line—*the federal car!*

When the silhouetted figure of a man stepped out of the car, she feared that guards were going to arrest her, and her first instinct was to run, but she knew it was useless.

"Miss, do you still need a ride?"

It took only a second for her to realize it wasn't the patrol car after all, but the cabby who'd returned for her.

"I came around once and waited for five minutes for you before thinking you'd already caught a ride." He opened the door for her, adding, "I'm glad I came back."

"So am I," she replied with a sigh of relief.

Having missed the 9 p.m. return flight, Linda had to wait two hours for the next one, and she used her cell phone to call Louise, letting her know she'd be arriving home later than expected. Louise once again voiced her concerns, but Linda calmed her by reassuring her that everything was fine, leaving her with the impression that she expected to gain Allan's freedom the next morning.

On the return flight, Linda had mixed emotions about what she'd done. She knew that handing over the file to those individuals was terribly wrong. From her seat on the plane, she kept mulling over events from the time of her abduction, as thus far she'd been unable to rationalize or see the full scope of her problems.

Succeeding in this theft put things in a different light. She began to think about what her country stood for, and the great sacrifices people had made to make America what it is today. *It's not too late to prove the loyalty you have for your country.* However, the file represented hope to her and now that she had it, there was no turning back.

You'd make a fine patriot, she thought of herself, still sorting things out while considering trading the file for her child's freedom.

She wanted to do right by going to the police, but the thought of the kidnappers killing her son was something she couldn't bear. She couldn't deny Allan this chance for life, not without making an attempt at saving him. The idea of the authorities discovering her son's dead body was not the kind of closure she was willing to gamble for. She'd received clear warning of what would happen to Allan if she went to the authorities, and the experiences she'd had through her abductors told her these were the kinds of people whose threats she couldn't take lightly. Believing she could best safeguard her child's fate by making the tradeoff, it was only the love for her child that kept her going. However, her conscience wouldn't give her rest—the item she carried was possibly of great importance to national security.

CHAPTER 6

Making the Exchange

On the taxi ride home from the airport, a mental tug-of-war resumed to give Linda unsettling thoughts about the outcome of tomorrow's exchange. She knew she may be fooling herself by believing she could trust these people, but she'd begun seeing those dark, penetrating eyes in her mind, a vision that commanded her to comply. The eyes gave warning that the threat against her son's life was real, and by doing so, exerted influence over her. The imposing, watchful image of the brown pupils gave a sensation of oppression, as if reminding her of these callous people's lack of conscience, for she did not want to risk losing her son. She dare not defy people who would lose no sleep over murdering a small boy, and by eliminating him, they'd also be discarding a potential witness. The tight grip they had over her made her see she must give them the file for the release of her child. As she leaned back in the car seat, the pressures of a pounding headache made her want to give her mind a rest.

It was after 1 a.m. when Linda arrived home, and the lamp and television were on in the living room. Louise, who was usually in bed and asleep by 9 p.m., was slumped in the armchair, but her eyes opened the moment Linda entered the house.

"I didn't think you'd be up," Linda said, going to a nearby table to use the remote for switching off the television.

Slowly rising out of the chair, Louise straightened up. "I didn't want to go to bed until you were home. You're still not going to tell me what they asked you to do?"

48

Linda looked down while pacing the floor. "I'd rather not say, but I've stolen for them, and after Allan's safe I'll worry about the consequences."

"Don't you think under the circumstances the police would be willing to cooperate with you and take steps so as not to endanger Allan?"

Linda rubbed her eyes, beginning to feel irritable. She understood Louise meant well, but she couldn't stand any more pressure with the headache she had from thinking about everything. She remained calm. "Maybe, but I'm not going to gamble with Allan's life. I'm meeting the kidnappers in the morning and bringing them what they asked for."

"Have you eaten anything?"

"I grabbed a sandwich earlier at the airport, and right now all I want is to get some sleep." Linda moved into the foyer to prepare to climb the stairs to the second floor, but paused long enough to say, "I want to thank you for the support you've given me."

"I don't know if I've done right by allowing you to do this on your own, but it will help if they release Allan into your hands tomorrow."

Starting up the stairs together, Louise said, "Mona Shelton called and asked that you phone her at your first opportunity."

Linda nodded, and at the top of the stairs, they said good night to each other. Louise went into her bedroom.

Linda took off her blouse, removed the tape holding the file to her body, and placed the Triad file beneath the rug in the hall with the original file that contained her instructions. Drawn to Allan's room, she sat on the edge of his bed to lift a stuffed panda bear he favored. Lying back to rest her head on his pillow, she held the panda close and dozed off. Awaking a short time later, she went to the bathroom to take two aspirin, and set her alarm for 7 a.m. Tossing and turning for what seemed like hours, she found herself beneath the blinding lamp undergoing interrogation, and then came those dreaded eyes entrenched in her mind. The contrast of the dark brown pupils and whites of the eyes, and dark circles surrounding them, looked at her with such depth, as though they could see inside her mind. The vision soon turned into a reoccurring nightmare, much like what she'd experienced the night before. She heard her son calling for her while Adele and her two faceless companions waited around every turn, and those haunting, unrelenting eyes chased after her throughout the night...

These visions gave Linda little rest, and awaking just before the alarm was set to go off, she dressed to get ready to leave the house to meet the kidnappers. She had no way to confirm her son was alive, but kept telling herself that, for the short period of time they'd held Allan, it didn't make any sense for them to harm him. Not wanting to be late or give the kidnappers an excuse not to release her child, she fetched the files from the hallway, combining the MX-11 file with the original file they'd given her. However, when picking up the MX-11 file, she glimpsed the symbol of an eagle on its cover, and then opened it to see exactly what she was trading away for her son's release.

The first page read:

STRATEGIC DEFENSE HIGH-ENERGY CHEMICAL LASER TECHNOLOGY

In the privacy of her bedroom, she sat on the bed giving the document quick study, and flipped a page to come across blueprints for a strange celestial craft with a futuristic design. The main body had the form of an upright capsule, and projecting from each side were two large oblong sails or solar panels. Three arms protruded down from its top, and at their ends were what she thought resembled ray guns.

The next several pages were detailed diagrams and literature covering specific components of the Triad satellite. A few pages illustrated the laser's power source and its conversion into energy and emission. Some of the designs covered the system's link to solar energy, describing in technical wording a newly-developed glass in the solar shield partly comprised of crystallized diamond fragments for magnifying light refraction many times over. Furthermore, there were pages on heat-sensitive, infrared sensors for early warning and target tracking, and even more on guidance control and navigational system components.

Skimming through the pages, she thought, *I'm sorry I looked at it now*, but she had, and she couldn't just close the file and forget it. She recalled how during the Reagan White House years the term "Star Wars" came to describe satellites capable of shooting down missiles launched to target our country. Even though technology of the time fell short of making defensive satellites with this capability, she wondered if science had made the leap to building such defensive weapons. There was no question that computer technology was progressing at an awesome rate, but if the country had developed such a satellite defense system, it was keeping it hushed from the world.

Fast becoming aware of the importance of this information, as it held the highest secrecy with regards to national security, she knew it could be quite harmful if this file fell into the wrong hands. The blueprint designs she handled were sure to hold great value in the eyes of the enemies of democracy, and to allow such knowledge to leak out had powerful implications. Continuing to glance over documents in the file, the decision whether to complete the trade now weighed heavily on her.

Her mind went from one extreme to the other, comparing her son's welfare to the crime she was committing, but the vision of those eyes was tipping the scale. Those penetrating eyes staring her down, as if burning a hole in her brain, claimed her concentration, and she began experiencing an intense headache that wouldn't allow her to think straight. She closed the file, placing it beside her, and the intense, pounding pressure caused her to lie back on the bed in the fetal position.

Amid this inhibiting spell, the storm raging in her mind became unbearable, and her eyelids closed. At that moment, deep-rooted devotion and a constant longing for her child gave her peace of mind. She now understood that if Allan was to have any chance for survival, it was up to his mother to fight for his life. Cleaving to the idea that she had but one chance to get Allan back, she saw the way clear for removing turmoil and confusion. It now seemed logical to finish this task to get Allan returned to her, and she found relief preparing to meet with the kidnappers.

Her instructions had her meeting with the kidnappers at Mount Sinai Cemetery in Brooklyn at 10 a.m., and she phoned a taxicab company to arrange for a car to pick her up. Not liking the secluded location of their meeting place, but unable to do anything about it, she knew she had plenty of time to get there before the appointed time. Continuing to suppress her guilt, overriding any questionable thoughts was the hopeful eagerness she had to gain her son's freedom. She could hardly wait to hold her child in her arms.

Just as Linda was putting on her blazer, a knock came on her bedroom door. Louise stuck her head in to say, "Your taxi is outside, and Mona's on the phone."

"I can't contend with Mona right now." Stuffing the files in her purse, Linda started down the stairs with Louise keeping pace behind her. "Would you tell her that I've already left the house, and that you'll have me call her when I've returned home?"

"Won't you at least tell me where you're going? What if I don't hear from you? What am I to tell the police?"

Linda reached the front door. Opening it, she said, "I'm going to the Mount Sinai Cemetery in Brooklyn, and I'll either call you or return by twelve noon."

"Linda, wait." Louise reached in one of the deep pockets of her apron to present to her a cylindrical cartridge. "I want you to take this."

Seeing it to be a gray miniature spray can that had a fine printed label, she asked, "What is it?"

"Pepper spray I sent away for some time ago."

"I'm going voluntarily, I don't think…"

"You take it," Louise insisted, putting it in the hip pocket of Linda's blazer, "and don't be afraid to use it." They embraced, and Louise said, "Do be careful and bring that boy home safely."

Instructing the cabby to take her to Mount Sinai Cemetery in Brooklyn, Linda sat tense in the car. No more was there shame or guilt over what she'd done, only the hope of recovering her son. Driven across the Verrazano-Narrows Bridge into the heart of Brooklyn, the taxi turned onto a busy boulevard, and soon they rode parallel with a cemetery. A four-foot-high stone wall with a spiked iron rail on its top bordered the cemetery, and she knew she wasn't far from Prospect Park, just west of it. Linda had a strange inkling this location resembled the neighborhood where the kidnappers had taken her, as some of the area looked run-down with slum-like row houses and large abandoned brick buildings.

The taxi went through the cemetery entrance and fifty yards inside, a huge stone mausoleum with marble pillars and wide steps stood like an ominous fortress. Linda took notice of its tall oversized doors, and when passing it, at the far end of the building she saw steps leading down to a maintenance door.

Coming to a fork, the cabby asked, "Which way, miss?"

"Keep to the right please, and follow the road till it ends at a circle."

Louise's words echoed in the back of her mind *You can't trust these people.*

Still totally dedicated to getting Allan back, Linda now couldn't suppress the cold reality that, once the driver dropped her off, she'd be at these people's mercy. Nearing the end of her ride, she became fearful for her own life, remembering their brutal methods, and dreaded facing them alone. Soon she'd have to for Allan's sake. Stresses in her mind grew steadily with apprehension, and in her wondering the raw realization of losing her son clamped down on her mind. Unable to imagine life without him, for her future peace of mind she knew she must comply with the kidnapper's demands.

There's no reason they shouldn't give him to me, as once I've given them what they want they've achieved their goal, she thought, as though trying to reassure herself that she was doing right.

When the taxi reached the circle at the end of the road the driver pulled over to the side, and Linda showed her nervousness when stepping outside the cab to pay the driver.

"Want me to wait?"

"That won't be necessary, but thanks anyway."

His eyes squinted. "Are you sure?"

"I'll be fine. I'm visiting my parents' grave, and my husband will be along shortly to pick me up."

Watching the taxi drive around the circle to disappear down the road, Linda then gave attention to her surroundings. Stark monuments, stained and discolored from age, encompassed the area, and in this quiet stillness she walked about in the bright sunshine, passing a stone bench on a concrete slab outside the circle drive. If not for the circumstances, she could've found peace in this tranquil setting among the tall, mature trees providing shade for the grounds about her. A breeze cut through the treetops, whipping branches back and forth. In the distance, she heard faint street sounds, but she couldn't see the road beyond the sloping cemetery grounds.

Expecting them to come soon, she impatiently stood at the curb, and knowing her son's life relied on the trade working, she checked her watch to see the time was 9:55. Looking down the snaking road, she saw no one, and once again scanned the barren tombstones spaced randomly outside the lane. Standing beneath the shade of a sprawling tree, she thought how this was the first time she'd been to a cemetery since her mother's death a few years ago. Finding her mother a few hours after she'd passed away, she'd tried to put the experience behind her and remember her as the kind person she was.

At 10:13, a black Cadillac limousine came down the lane, rolling at fifteen miles per hour, and upon reaching the circle, it pulled over to the curb and stopped. A woman dressed in black emerged from the automobile's backseat, a veil draped over her face from the wide rim of the floppy black hat she wore. In her left hand was her handbag, and in her right, a bouquet of assorted flowers. She left word with the driver before walking in a slumped-over manner to stand before a gravesite. After spending a few minutes there, she placed the flowers at the base of a heartbroken angel with long drooping wings posed over the grave. She then returned to the limousine, and as soon as she got in the car, the vehicle came to turn around at the circle and left the way it had come.

Watching the car disappear down the lane, Linda then went to sit on the stone bench. Growing impatient, she looked at her watch to see the time was 10:23, causing her to ask herself, *Where are they?*

Minutes later, a breeze rustled the treetops, a cloud created a shadow that slowly rolled across the landscape, and while uncertainty festered in her mind, she clung to the thought they would come. The sun broke through the clouds. Determined to stick it out, she avoided checking her watch, but questions lingered as to how much longer they would make her wait.

At 10:46, another black limousine appeared down the lane, and she thought it may be the same one. It looked identical to the first, and was coming at the same slow pace. She stood observing the car's approach to the circle. The limousine progressed to make its turn at the circle, and it surprised her when it stopped before her and the rear passenger door opened. Getting out of the car was the woman wearing the wide-rimmed, floppy hat. Leaving the car door open, she approached Linda at a brisk walk, her purse hanging by a strap from her arm.

"Do you have the file?"

Recognizing Adele's distinct accent, Linda's eyes barely penetrated the veil to see her features. "Yes, I have it. Where's Allan?"

"Your boy's fine," she replied, sticking out her hand with her palm up, her fingers twitching. "The file first."

Linda felt reluctant to give her the file, but opened her purse and handed it over with the original file and the clearance badge.

Without a word, the woman thumbed through pages, and then commented, "This isn't what we want."

"I brought you the file you asked for. Where's my son?"

Adele placed the file under her arm. "In the safe, do you remember seeing a stainless steel case holding a computer disc?"

Linda's face turned to anger. "No, I didn't, and that's not what you asked for."

"A stainless steel case the size of a common CD case," and she demonstrated the size, making a squared off interpretation with her index fingers and thumbs to illustrate its circumference.

Linda moved toward her, "I told you, NO!"

Backing off, the woman pulled from her purse a .22 caliber semi-automatic pistol. "Get back!"

"We had a deal: the file for my son."

"If you want your son back, you'll get us a stainless steel compact disc case with the word TRIAD engraved on the lid." She handed over to Linda the clearance ID badge she'd need to enter the defense installation again.

Linda's eyes began to tear up. "How can I trust you? You didn't even bring him."

"I can assure you he's safe and close by. Just deliver us the disc and he's yours."

"I don't think I can do it. There's a hand scanner for reading skin impressions you didn't tell me about, and you didn't give me the correct safe combination. I'm telling you it's impossible for me to go back without drawing suspicion."

The woman signaled for the driver to pull nearer. "Have it your way, but if you want to see your son again you'll have to get us the disc." She then spoke reassuringly. "It's not like we're asking you to do something you're incapable of, not after you've acquired the file. Once we have the disc, I promise your son will be returned to you and we won't trouble you again."

Adele kept the pistol pointed at Linda as she backed up to the limousine to stand beside the car door. "Bring the disc to Our Savior Roman Catholic Church at 11 a.m. tomorrow. That's just a few blocks from here. Go to the west confessional. While we examine the disc you and your child will be reunited, and once we know the disc is genuine, you'll both be given your freedom."

She sat down in the car seat, and before closing the door, added, "All we want is the disc, Mrs. Moreland. We intend to fulfill our end of the bargain, but we simply need information contained on that disc. Your son is depending on you, so don't make the mistake of going to the authorities. You're sure to regret it if you do."

Linda's eyes expressed the anguish she felt as she watched the woman pull the car door closed, and the limousine drove away. Infuriated, but at the same time ready to cry, she made a mental note of the car's license plate number. When she placed the badge inside her purse, she grabbed an ink pen and jotted down the number.

Seething over how they'd manipulated her, all she could do to let out frustration was to strike her fist against her thigh, and she became more exasperated as she walked back to the cemetery entrance. Seeing how everything stood in the kidnappers' favor, she no longer had faith in them delivering Allan to her. The idea of going back to Washington looked useless, for it was too simple and easy for them to pull the same move. Thinking about her son, she again remembered he was without his prescription pills, and as much as this concerned her, there was nothing she could do about it.

Thoughts of Allan brought on choked-up sniffling until she broke down in tears, and she thought, *Louise was right. They can't be trusted. Why couldn't I have seen this?*

By failing at getting Allan back, she now saw how she had to go to the authorities, and noted her ability to arrive at this decision without experiencing the confusion and constraint she had before. Inasmuch as she didn't fully understand what power these people had held over her, she'd begun to grasp how they'd dominated her mindset to constrict her range and scope of thinking. She came to the realization that since the time of that diabolical interrogation, her mind had been limited in its ability to challenge ideas that clashed with her obligation to obtain the file. So long as she had concentrated on retrieving her son safely, there was no consternation to initiate those paralyzing headaches that inhibited her mind and left her unable to function.

Although she couldn't be sure of what had happened, she found a change within herself, and felt an uplifting sensation, as though there was no longer anything restricting her line of thought. It was as though the intense frustration she'd just experienced allowed her to break free of the hold they had over her, and yet she knew it wasn't that simple. She'd fulfilled her commitment by presenting the file to these people, and either by doing so, or by their failure to deliver her son as promised, it broke a link. An urging element pushing her to obey the kidnappers' requests no longer existed, as if it had been cancelled and unlocked. Diverging ideas enabled her to suddenly see what she couldn't before.

Using a powerful drug to tap into her subconscious and reveal her deepest, innermost thoughts, and by reading her mind, they learned how much Allan meant to her. Knowing she'd go to great lengths to protect Allan, they had used the bond between mother and child to their benefit, as leverage to force her to acquire the file. It may have been the influence of this drug that left her vulnerable to a form of mind control or power of persuasion. Their demands taking precedence over her thoughts and actions, she had been resigned to being a willing participant in the theft of the file for her son's sake. They'd convinced her that accomplishing this theft would lead to a favorable outcome, which it had failed to do, and this may have been what broke the psychological hold they had over her. The concept was mind-boggling, and the most absorbing aspect to all of this was that deep down inside, she wasn't completely aware of what all this entailed.

She'd known from the outset that the right thing to do was to seek help from the authorities, yet had felt compelled to attempt getting her son back by doing what the kidnappers had demanded of her. Now feeling liberated, recalling short segments of that interrogation brought enlightenment and the insight to see how she had had no choice in acquiring this file, as if something in her subconscious mandated that she go through with their plan. She knew that governments, including the United States, had experimented with all sorts of different methods to control people's minds, and it was frightening to think these people had manipulated her in such a way. Even with this cloak lifted for her to see how this came to be, she could still envision those forever-stalking eyes, and it was this set of cold, penetrating eyes that enabled her to conclude they'd actually hypnotized her.

Despondent about what the future would bring for her, Linda knew her only hope lay with going to the FBI. She'd have to confess her role in the theft of top secret material to help expose and identify the kidnappers. Looking back at how she'd breached that defense installation in Washington, D.C., she knew this act wouldn't be likely to win her favoritism with government officials, and she didn't expect much sympathy from them.

Her walk took her to the mausoleum, and as she scanned the aging structure, it looked as if it hadn't been opened in ages. Her eyes strayed from the building's architecture to notice a narrow walk leading from the curb to steps near the building's corner, where a maintenance door had a window reinforced with wire mesh. She soon came to the cemetery's entrance and looked both ways before crossing the boulevard. Her aim was to get to a phone directory to look up the address of the FBI, and give them an account of what happened. She started for a filling station two blocks away.

Finding the station boarded up, graffiti everywhere, and an outside telephone vandalized, the cord cut, she used her cell phone to call Louise. She let her know the outcome of the meeting, and told her she was going to the FBI to seek their assistance. Louise looked up the office address for the FBI in lower Manhattan and gave it to her, and then Linda phoned for a taxicab. She didn't have long to wait, and when giving the driver the Manhattan address for the FBI, she asked him to be careful no one followed them. Worried, while making an analysis of the people holding her child, she wondered what they might do to Allan if they learned she'd gone to the authorities.

CHAPTER 7

Looking to Get Help

A rriving at the government building, Linda met a tall African-American FBI agent named Andrew Godfrey, who after hearing a portion of her story, led her to Special Agent Kenneth Barnes's office. The door to his office was open and Godfrey presided over introductions, saying, "Mrs. Moreland, this is Inspector Barnes. He'll be handling your case."

Godfrey closed the door and Barnes, an astute-looking middle-aged man with graying dark hair, dressed in a gray pinstriped suit, reached across his desk to shake her hand. "Won't you please sit down, Mrs. Moreland, and tell us all about your problem."

The three seated themselves and the two FBI men listened as Linda gave a detailed account of all she'd gone through. She started with how these people had abducted her from a Manhattan street corner, the interrogation, the theft of a classified document, and updated them to the present.

Upon her finishing, Barnes said, "The identity card and instructions they gave you, where are they now?"

"I gave them back their instructions with the defense file I'd taken, but I still have the ID badge, and I also have some handwritten notes I'd made to aid me last night when in Washington." Linda presented to Barnes the clearance badge and the notes she'd made that contained the safe combination which hadn't worked when she tried opening the safe. "I brought the badge with me to the cemetery because I thought they might ask for it, and I didn't want to give them an excuse not to release my son to me."

Barnes glanced over the badge and the notes, and then turned to Godfrey. "Notify the Defense Department immediately, and I'll keep these articles here until they decide how they want it handled."

"Alright," replied Godfrey.

"You say you got the license number off that limousine?"

"Yes, I wrote it down on that paper I gave to you."

Barnes copied the number on a piece of stationery and gave it to Godfrey. "I doubt if we'll have much luck with the number, but run it down anyway and let me know what you come up with." He then looked at Linda. "Do you have a photograph of your son we can keep?"

Linda removed a picture of Allan from her pocketbook, and Godfrey took it and left the room.

Barnes placed a pen and notepad on the edge of the desktop. "While everything's fresh in your mind, I want you to write down your story, and any information you think may be helpful to us. Sometimes the smallest detail proves important in taking us in the right direction. For instance, we need descriptions of those individuals holding your son. We'll need everything you can remember about this apartment house they took you to, and anything else that might prove useful to our investigation."

"I've tried remembering details about that night, but my head was still buzzing from the drug they'd injected me with."

"Perhaps you saw a street sign, or the name of that mission you saw just before you were picked up by that taxi could be significant in leading us to their hideaway."

Linda bowed her head in despair. "It was a yellow cab, but I didn't even get a good look at the driver. I was concerned about getting home to find out if they really had my son."

Barnes escorted Linda to a conference room across the hall where she sat down at a table, and he said, "Just write down all you can remember and do the best you can with it."

Linda looked up at him. "Do you think I'll get my son back safely?"

"I can't predict the future, Mrs. Moreland, but things certainly wouldn't be any worse had you come to us in the beginning. As it is, you've probably leaked highly-sensitive material to these people that may leave our nation vulnerable to an attack." Before stepping out of the room, he added, "I'll be in my office if you need me."

In the hallway, Barnes saw Godfrey approaching and asked, "What was Washington's response?"

"The Defense Department wants to keep the story hushed for security reasons, and insists their own agency take over the investigation. They'll have someone down within the hour and they'll expect to see a full report."

"When this Defense Department official arrives, show him to my office."

After thirty minutes, Godfrey returned to get what Linda had written, and then left the room without saying a word. Overwhelmed by her predicament, Linda couldn't get over how coldly Barnes acted toward her. It was obvious he was angry. She knew exactly what they thought—in their eyes, she was a traitor, but it wasn't their child these people had taken, and at this point she knew she'd be facing prison time for what she'd done. She could see herself at the arraignment on capital charges in a federal court—her life ruined, and as bad as it looked, it was only a matter of time before the media caught the story. Ashamed and yet ready to face whatever life threw at her, she worried mostly for her son's sake and she was hopeful they could recover the file she'd stolen.

The door to the room opened, breaking her weary stare, and a man with dark hair stood in the doorway holding a brown attaché case. Wearing a light tweed sport coat, a brown tie, and tan slacks, his face looked fortyish and had character, holding a serious expression with raised eyebrows. "Mrs. Moreland?"

"Yes." She began to stand.

"Please, don't get up." Closing the door behind him, he sat the attaché case flat on the table. He then presented, from the inside of his sport coat, a card identifying him as a special agent for the Defense Intelligence Agency.

Sitting down across from her, he had possession of the ID badge and notes she'd made. "My name is Jack Matheson, and I've been assigned to your case. I haven't had much time to get acquainted with what we're up against, but from what I understand, the people who have your son are expecting you to return to the Aeronautical Defense Agency Headquarters in Washington tonight. There, you are to obtain a computer disc in a stainless steel casing. Is that correct?"

"Yes, that's correct."

"And tomorrow at 11 a.m. you are to bring the disc with you to a church in Brooklyn?"

"Yes, Our Savior Church."

"Understand that if I'm short with you it's because we're pressed for time, and incidentally, the license number off that limousine came from a stolen car, giving us no leads. Are you sure you can't help us more with this apartment building they interrogated you in? You made mention there was a strong chemical odor in the air. That's the kind of details we need."

Matheson took out a pen and used it as a pointer to go over what she'd written. "In these notes, you mention seeing a mission, but nothing more. You saw a sign which read vertically 'MISSION' in neon lights, but you didn't see any other name on the building... We're trying to track down the driver of the cab who picked you up that night, but there was no call made to the Yellow Cab Company to pick up a stranded woman as they led you to believe. I'm assuming someone may have approached the cabdriver with a couple of bucks and told him where to find you, and with that he soon arrived to pick you up."

"I've tried remembering, but they had me so doped up I couldn't think straight. They kept a light concentrated on my face, and memories of those hours are fragmented by the drug they'd given me."

Reading further, he stated, "You didn't provide much description of your abductors, except the woman."

"I struggled with one man in the backseat of a car for a few seconds when they first abducted me, but he almost immediately knocked me out cold. I only caught a glimpse of his face, but I believe he had blond hair, and I remember scratching his face. The driver of the car wore sunglasses, had dark hair and dark features as though he may have been Italian or of Middle Eastern descent." Linda paused before saying, "If I may say something, Mr. Matheson, what's stopping the FBI from capturing these people at the church tomorrow and negotiating their freedom for my son and the file?"

Matheson used the top of the pen to scratch the side of his head. "The people who've orchestrated your son's kidnapping are probably going to send someone to the church who they consider expendable. The woman and the driver that met you at the cemetery this morning were merely following orders, and may be no more than pawns in this. Their arrest may hinder any chance of getting your son back, for they may not be interested in negotiations of any kind. My guess is that they're watching the church and anything out of the ordinary happening there is sure to attract their attention, so it's not going to be that simple. I might add that you've gone to great lengths to get your son back, Mrs. Moreland, and as a result, you're going to have to face some serious criminal charges."

Down and rejected, Linda's head hung low. "I've admitted to my mistakes and I'm sorry for what I've done, but that boy is all I've got in this world."

"You deliberately engaged in the theft of high-level, classified material, and somewhere along the line it must have crossed your mind that these people can't be trusted. Yet you went ahead with their scheme. You knew exactly what you were doing, and you can't even be sure if your son's alive now, can you?"

"I don't know if he's still alive, and that frightens me, but at the time, I had no confidence in the police getting him back for me."

"We share your concern about your son, but if you'd come forth immediately our government would be considerably more sympathetic about your problems. You've done something to threaten our national security, and as a result of that, you've made few friends. Depending on how this plays out, you may very well end up spending the rest of your life behind bars.

"However, because of the possibility of future events involving these people, and the threat they pose to our nation's security, my department has authorized me to recruit you to help us capture these people. You want your son, we want these people, and with your assistance, we may be able to apprehend them while bringing closure to this mess before it leaks out to the media. As crazy as it may sound, the State Department wants them bad enough that they're considering giving clearance for you to return to Washington to obtain the disc and complete the deal."

Her eyes widened. "You want me to give them the disc?"

"Basically, we want to use you as bait to catch all of them. That's not going to be easy, but by cooperating, you'll be helping your son and vastly improving your own position."

"I'll do anything you ask."

"I have to caution you that what you'll be doing is extremely dangerous, and backing out later is not an option. If you work with me and assist in the capture these people, I can only promise that if you go to a trial at a later date, I'll be there to testify on your behalf. I have to warn you that if the media exposes this to the public, there's a strong possibility that all deals are off, and that means I may be unable to do anything to help your situation. It's a cold proposition, but that's the best I can offer you, and if you're killed in the service of your country, it's not likely anyone will ever know."

"Well, I'm willing to do all I can to help."

"That's good. From the moment this fell in our laps we've banked on your cooperation, and while my department will do everything possible to get your son back, I can't guarantee anything. I'd like to point out that because of the secrecy involved we'll be working with little help from others in my agency, and for your own protection no other government agency has ties with this operation."

"What makes you think I can fool the kidnappers?"

"I don't know that you can, but you've proven you have nerve. Not just anyone could've accomplished the theft of that document." He returned to her the badge and the handwritten notes she'd made to aid her in acquiring the file. "One more question: do you think the opposition could've followed you here?"

"I'm almost positive I wasn't. I was careful to look because they'd warned me about going to the police, and I'd asked the cabdriver to look out for anyone following us."

"Let's hope they didn't, for it's my duty to inform you that these people may kill you the moment they become suspicious of our involvement. They have all the earmarks of a crafty collection of characters who may already know you've sought help, and there's little they won't do to get their hands on this disc you're going after tonight. Even if they pick up on the fact that you've gone to the authorities, they may not kill you immediately because of the disc's importance, but you are under the threat of extermination. I know this may not sound like good advice coming from me, but if you meet with your son and get an opportunity to escape, I strongly recommend that you go for it and run for your life."

Matheson leaned back in his chair. "We are interested in knowing how you obtained that file from Washington last night. Even though you'd assumed the identity of Evelyn Werner, it's hard to believe you were able to slide through all those security measures."

"Would you mind telling me who Evelyn Werner is?"

"She's a German physicist who helped develop chemical lasers equipped on the Triad Satellite, a defensive space-based weapon with advanced airborne lasers. About three months ago, you may remember the launching of a satellite our government described as a new weather satellite, which was in actuality the launch of Triad. Anyway, the afternoon they abducted you in New York, Evelyn Werner presented an updated report on our success with the MX-11 or Triad Satellite project to NATO advisers just before the United Nations General Assembly convened. Her visit to New York helps explain how this mistaken identity came about, and why they targeted you as a prospective mark. I have to admit, Mrs. Moreland, you bear an uncanny resemblance to Evelyn Werner—you're a dead ringer for her. Can you offer any reason for this likeness?"

"No, I can't."

"In my opinion, you're far too much of a look-alike for it to be a mere coincidence. Perhaps as we probe with our investigation something will turn up."

After jotting down Linda's telephone number, he then examined her cell phone, and afterwards handed her his card. "You can reach me at this number anytime, day or night." Matheson then looked at his watch. "We need to get you home as quickly as possible, and I want you to follow last night's timetable, so you have a few hours before you have to catch that plane this evening. I suggest you go straight home and try to get some rest, as I suspect they may be tracking your movements."

"Do you think they've killed my son?"

Trying to be supportive by leaving her with hope, he said, "What would they gain by harming a defenseless child? As I see it, your boy is a very valuable bargaining chip, and until we know otherwise, there's every reason to believe he is safe. You'll do best by remembering you're the only link to his survival, and the way you stand up to these people may have the most bearing on whether he makes it through this."

Linda then explained, "Something I didn't mention before is that the woman who gave me the injection used the word amobarbital to describe the drug used. They were trying to extract information from this Evelyn Werner, but when I couldn't answer their questions, they knew something was wrong. I keep seeing a pair of penetrating eyes belonging to an individual whom I believe to be of Indian or Pakistani descent, and who spoke with an accent. It may sound far-fetched, but I think they may have hypnotized me. However, since delivering them the file, I no longer feel constrained.. Does that make any sense?"

"Sodium amobarbital has both sedative and hypnotic properties which deprive a person of the faculty of reason to break down their inhibitions. After administering the drug to make you submissive, they soon learned you weren't Evelyn Werner. Then, understanding the need for your cooperation, they resorted to using a hypnotic suggestion to gain your committal for the theft of that file and to strengthen your will to get the job done."

"You sound like an expert on the subject."

"You may not realize it, but your subconscious has probably fought whatever means of persuasion they used all along. I'm glad you brought this to my attention because the group I suspect is behind this is prone to using such techniques."

Matheson ushered Linda to the hallway and signaled for Godfrey to come for her. "You understand, of course, you'll have to get the disc the same way you seized that document last night. In case you're watched by one of the guards who may be working for the other side, it's essential that you succeed in the theft of the disc without being detected and without our help."

"But what if I'm caught?"

"If that happens, they may have ways of finding out through any number of different sources, and then they'll know of our involvement, so don't get caught."

"Yeah, but like I've already told you, there's that scanner, and I still don't have the correct safe combination."

"Just follow through with the same time schedule you used last night and I assure you everything will work out fine."

"This doesn't get any easier, does it?"

Matheson spoke reassuringly. "No, it doesn't, but I'll catch up to you later this evening and explain more details."

Godfrey came to Linda's side. "Mrs. Moreland, I'm going to take you to where there's a taxi waiting to take you home."

Matheson added, "We've arranged to purchase your plane tickets to and from Washington tonight using the same airline you'd used, and you'll be able to pick them up under your name at the counter near the departure gate."

Matheson watched Linda leave, feeling certain about the kinds of people he'd be dealing with. He recalled a run-in he'd had with a notorious criminal organization trafficking in the sale of arms and intelligence secrets led by an elusive figure named Emeric Kleistner. Wanted by the CIA, Interpol, and the FBI, Kleistner and his henchmen as of late were working to extract intelligence secrets from government-employed contractors providing technical support for the Department of Defense in the United States. Two years ago, Defense Intelligence caught on to a fouled-up conspiracy arranged by Kleistner to attempt to kidnap a nuclear physicist and his family. The idea was to use the scientist's family members as leverage to engage his expertise in devising a rudimentary trigger component to arm nuclear devices, as reportedly commissioned by the Iranian government.

Kleistner's plan had failed when Matheson and a colleague tracked him to his hideout in Queens, New York. He and others in his organization had barricaded themselves in a building in a commercial district where they held the scientist and his family hostage. After a six-hour standoff, authorities deployed a counterterrorism SWAT team to storm the premises and a shootout ensued. The scientist and some of his family members ended up critically wounded, but they had all survived. Kleistner and his people had a prearranged escape route whereby they'd previously tunneled into an unoccupied building located next door. When shooting broke out, they exited through that neighboring building and gunned down Matheson's partner in a hail of bullets. Matheson had taken a bullet in his left side above the beltline. Kleistner and others he was in league with escaped in a patrol car left running, and sped off into the night.

Matheson wore a scar beneath his ribcage from the ordeal, and forever wanting to avenge his partner's death, he expected this to be one of his most challenging assignments. He knew he'd have his hands full trying to bring Kleistner to justice while at the same time looking out for the safety and wellbeing of Linda Moreland and her son.

CHAPTER 8

Returning to the Scene of the Crime

Linda's thoughts and worries had run awry in seeking a solution for her son's return, but going to the authorities for help provided her little comfort. Before today, she'd never even heard of the Defense Intelligence Agency. Uncertain how much help Jack Matheson was going to be, she'd have to return to Washington again tonight, and he had made it clear that secrecy was of great importance for securing Allan's safety. When arriving home, she told Louise everything—what she'd done to acquire the file, the Defense Department's response, and went further by divulging what the government expected of her. Louise saw how nervous Linda was about returning to the capital to obtain the disc, and assured her she'd done the right thing by going to the government.

That afternoon, as it neared time to catch the plane to Washington, she saw the difficulties she had ahead of her as she glanced over her notes of the kidnappers' instructions. Reorienting herself with her movements from the night before, she familiarized herself with the layout of the government building as best she could recall in her mind. Looking at the badge that was in part key to her entering a restricted area, she studied Evelyn Werner's image while hoping she could rely on Matheson's help for acquiring the disc.

Later, the horn of a taxi signaled Linda that her ride had arrived. She gave and received a hug from Louise at the door. Wearing the same blazer she'd worn the night before, she had her purse tucked under her arm when climbing into the vehicle. She instructed the cabdriver to take her to Newark International Airport in New Jersey.

During the cab ride, she had growing concerns about the task ahead of her. She remembered how she'd tried emphasizing the complications she'd had at that government installation to Matheson. The hand scanner and the fact that she didn't have the correct safe combination posed huge problems. She expected to hear from Matheson soon. If she couldn't get past that scanner, it would be impossible to pull this off. Even if the guard allowed her to venture beyond that point, how was she supposed to get inside the safe without the correct combination?

She thought Matheson might greet her at Newark Airport because he mentioned he'd catch up to her and he knew the flight she'd be taking, but she didn't see him there. She resisted the urge to call the phone number he'd given to her out of concern the kidnappers may be watching her, and she didn't want to draw suspicion. Matheson had stressed that she keep the same timetable, so she got on the plane hoping to meet him at the Washington airport.

After the plane touched down in the capital, she briefly looked for Matheson at the airport terminal. With no sign of him, she caught a taxi in front of the terminal. Soon arriving at the government base, she saw the parking area beyond the fence at the defense installation nearly empty, and the same two guards were in the glass-enclosed building.

Standing outside the taxicab paying the driver, she tipped him twenty dollars. "I'd like for you to return in one hour, and if I'm not here, would you mind waiting a few minutes for me?"

"Sure, miss." Then the taxicab was driven away.

Walking toward the gate while pinning the badge to her collar, Linda passed beneath a streetlight near the main entry gate. One of the guards she recognized from her visit the night before waved her on. Following the same path she'd taken the night before, she approached the headquarters building, and checking her wristwatch, she saw she was within minutes of keeping last night's timetable. Tonight the wind was calm, and the clatter of her heels against the concrete served as a reminder to buy a pair of soft-soled shoes on her next purchase of footwear.

Pushing open the door to enter the building, she turned her collar to display the ID badge, and the same guard she had seen the night before gave a nod. Progressing well enough to reach the elevator, she pushed the button, and two men came to stand behind her to wait for the elevator. When the elevator doors opened, the men allowed her to enter first, and she stepped back to give them space, saying, "Would you press five, please?"

The two men got off at the fourth floor, and when the elevator reached the fifth floor, she stepped forward to take the corridor on her left. She soon came to the desk where she waited while the guard searched her purse, the same guard who had examined its contents before. Pondering how she could go no farther last night without his aiding her in getting past the scanner, she wanted to avoid seeking his assistance tonight if possible. With nothing said about that incident, and having passed this brief inspection, she tucked her purse under her arm and followed the corridor to the first electronically-controlled glass door.

Removing the badge from her collar, she inserted it into the mechanism's slot. The door opened, and up ahead she saw the security door with the scanner. Feeling intimidated by this security device, she now held concern that placing her hand on the scanner might activate warning alarms to throw the place into a panic. Sensing someone coming through the first door behind her, she turned around and saw Jack Matheson.

She drew a deep breath. "I was wondering when you would show up."

"Assuming everything went smoothly up till this point, this was the first place I expected you to encounter a problem, and you're right on time." He placed his hand over the scanner, which gave them passage to move on, and they walked the corridor quietly together. Soon passing the portrait of George Washington, they came to arrive at the door marked:

MX SYSTEM
TOP SECRET

Matheson allowed her to access the code to open the door, and she did so without checking the notepaper she carried with her, but this time the door didn't open. Turning to Matheson with a confused expression, she expected him to provide assistance.

"As soon as the agency learned there was a security breach they changed the code for this door. That's standard procedure." He entered the new code and the door opened. Matheson stepped inside the room to switch on the lights while saying, "You weren't nervous, were you? After all, you managed without my help last night."

He drew the curtains open to expose the safe. "When checking the guard's nightly report we learned how you got past the scanner. However, we weren't sure how you'd gotten inside the safe. The kidnappers gave you what was previously the correct safe combination, but after security was broken sometime ago, the combination was changed, and the code to open the door for this room changed at the same time. Since that time, the individual that provided you with the ID badge acquired the new code for the security door, but hadn't as yet gained access to the new safe combination, leaving us curious about how you opened it."

Matheson worked the safe's dial in correlation with the combination. "So how did you get the safe open?"

"A middle-aged man with red hair came in who acted as if he knew me, or like everybody else, I suppose he mistook me for Evelyn Werner, and he opened the safe. I was sitting here at this desk when I told him I had something to return to the safe. I asked him to leave the safe door open, which he did."

"I see. You'd made no mention of that before, and we wanted to know how you accomplished getting the file without the new safe combination."

"When turning the file over to those people I told them they'd given me the wrong safe combination, and made mention that they'd neglected to warn me about the scanner, but they never asked how I pulled it off."

Matheson turned to her. "I may as well tell you now that the people holding your son are well aware that we changed the combination, so they're sure to suspect that you've gone to the authorities." He pulled the handle and safe's door opened. "I understand your ex-husband is a naval officer. Is he aware that his son was kidnapped?"

"No, he doesn't know anything about what's happened, and I'd prefer that he not know, at least not for the time being."

He reached inside the safe to bring out the disc. It was as Adele had described, a stainless steel casing the size of a standard compact disc case with the word TRIAD engraved on the lid. Matheson handed it over to her. Linda caressed the printing with her fingertips.

Matheson secured the safe and closed the curtains. "You're probably thinking there's a disc containing vital information inside that case, but it's merely a blank computer disc. The only way someone would know it's blank is if they inserted it into a computer. However, we're working to produce an edited version of the original to place in your possession. Although we made a few modifications in the alternate disc, it will still contain highly-sensitive, classified material. Much of the encrypted information is in code, so they'll find deciphering it difficult. We're not making it easy for them.

"I'll turn the disc over to you only when it becomes necessary, and we've decided it's best for you not to take it with you to the church tomorrow. It's too easy for them to take the disc and dispose of you, so at the meeting you'll insist on seeing your son to make sure he's alive. They should accept your motive, as it's natural for you to want to know your son is safe, and it will help buy us time to step up our investigation while fully assessing the situation."

He pulled out the desk chair for her to sit down, saying, "Why don't you take a seat for a few minutes while we talk... You look tired."

"I feel exhausted. I haven't been able to eat or sleep regularly since this nightmare began, and thinking I'm to go to that church tomorrow without bringing the disc with me isn't going to be helpful. They're probably hyper-paranoid as it is, and they're surely not going to be happy about that situation."

He sat on the corner of the desk, facing her. "Seeking an end to the Second World War, our leaders looked to scientists to develop *the bomb*. Now we live in an age of concern for a nuclear confrontation, and although we and the Russians have made efforts to reduce our arsenals, the number of countries with nuclear capability continues to grow.

"As early as the 1950s, our nation has tried building an effective missile defense program to shield us from intercontinental ballistic missiles, and we've had some success. In recent times, the United States, with the cooperation of its NATO allies, has been able to harness a form of energy with the capacity to power a high-energy laser as part of a space-based defense shield. This research and development resulted in a technologically-advanced satellite as part of NATO's strategic defense. Originally called the MX-11, the Triad Satellite carries three sophisticated lasers capable of delivering simultaneous strikes. Tracking a range radius of up to 3,000 miles on the Earth's surface, the Triad is equipped with heat sensors, enabling it to detect and destroy a missile at its initial launch or boost phase. A few of these satellites could virtually eliminate the threat of a large-scale nuclear attack, and over the next two years, we've scheduled the launch of two more to go into space.

"The file you gave to those people contains blueprints and records covering the Triad Satellite's design and its functions, which may have given these people what they're after. However, the disc covers the laser weapon in depth, with extensive research and valuable filmed laboratory experiments, as well as several important tests. Tests of particular significance record beams emitted from the Triad Satellite from outer space and their entry into the earth's atmosphere. These demonstrations were narrated by your look-alike, Miss Evelyn Werner. The first shows the sinking of a World War II destroyer in the South Pacific. The second shows a beam striking a ground-based missile launched, carrying a dummy warhead, and exploding in flight. Triad exceeded expectations by intercepting a Polaris missile launched from a submerged Navy submarine, taking it out less than two minutes after leaving the water.

"A few years ago, intelligence sources began picking up information leading us to believe we have a leak in the CIA, as highly-classified material from this very office began disappearing. For a time, we believed there may be a Russian agent operating in the ranks of the CIA, and we thought the importance of gaining information about Triad made it essential for the Russians to activate him. His role would have been to attain what information he could on this satellite's capabilities.

"We recently discovered a leak in information connected with an electronics expert and computer engineer named Charles Harding. Harding assisted in the design of the Triad Satellite, and he had sometime in the past sold information to an outside party, quite possibly the same people who are now holding your son. Before we could apprehend him to learn exactly what he compromised, he took his own life.

"Harding's suicide may have marked the end of our investigation, but strong evidence of a double agent working in this building comes from the ID badge carrying Evelyn Werner's identification the kidnappers supplied to you. Only someone with special clearance could've duplicated this badge, giving us solid proof of a double agent, and we think he was probably present for the time of your interrogation. This person produced that clearance badge within hours of your abduction and provided instructions enabling you to gain access to that classified document last night. Harding knew the interior layout of the building, and would've known the access code for this office and the prior safe combination, but it wasn't Harding, as he's been dead for over a week. The door code and the safe combination changed when he killed himself, and like I've already said, these people were able to furnish you with the new code for the door, but had not yet procured the new safe combination."

"But if it's that important, and this individual had access to that information, why didn't this double agent take the disc himself?"

"CIA officials have clearance to enter this office, but as important as the Triad Satellite is, I'm sure Moscow wishes this agent to maintain his unique status, and will only risk blowing his cover when it's absolutely necessary. Washington believes it may be worthwhile gambling, or perhaps even sacrificing, the disc to identify this mole threatening our national security, as he's the prime force behind this leak. Our main objective is to lure him into the open, using the disc as bait. When favorable circumstances for obtaining the disc present themselves, we're counting on this person to come forward. Should we be fortunate enough to catch him but lose possession of the disc, we figure we're ahead in the long run. However, should we blow this chance and still lose the disc we'll be losing big—real big.

"Since practically no one is above suspicion, we don't know what information this operative has access to, but regardless, we would most definitely prefer they didn't get their hands on this disc. This may be our only opportunity to expose who this individual is, and regardless if he and the kidnappers he's working with are aware of our involvement, they'll have to make an effort to acquire the disc. It's far too valuable for them not to."

"So you're not so much trying to catch the kidnappers of my son as you are aiming to entrap the individual who's behind the Defense Department's breach in security?"

"Like I said in the beginning, we'd like to capture the whole bunch of them, but that's not going to be easy. Holding this agent in reserve, the Russians have commissioned a shadowy network of spies led by a man of ruthless cunning named Emeric Kleistner to get the information they're after."

From the inside pocket of his jacket Matheson produced a photograph. "Here, take a look at his photo so you'll recognize him if you see him. There are few photos of Kleistner in existence, and this one taken in his youth shows him in military uniform, when he was an East German official. Considered highly intelligent, he had a driving ambition to move up quickly in the ranks of the secret police, gaining a brutal reputation while operating with cold-blooded efficiency. Soviet-dominated Warsaw Pact nations adhered to a philosophy of controlling the people by the use of fear, and he had no qualms about committing murder to gain favor with his superiors to advance his position. At the age of twenty-five, Kleistner landed a position third-in-line in East Germany's high command, closely overseeing the heavy-handed Stalinization tactics of that regime.

"His career was on the rise when the USSR's hold over Eastern Europe began showing cracks. Poland and East Germany broke free from the Soviet sphere of influence in 1989, and soon afterwards, the Soviet Union collapsed. Disillusioned by this wave of geo-political change, Kleistner's wish was to carry on the social science of authoritarianism in a *closed society*. When East Germany merged with West Germany, he took refuge in Yugoslavia's melting pot of ethnic factions. A nation in economic and political turmoil, caught up in a war of barbarism, he aided Serbia's Communist party leader Slobodan Milosevic in a wave of systematic genocide. Always keeping in close contact with the Russians, nearing the end of that conflict he moved on with a collection of neurotic, sadistic thugs to evade charges for war crimes.

"Their movements run with a map of global unrest, first stopping at Beirut, Lebanon, where he used his Russian contacts to move outdated Soviet armory in arms deals with radical terrorists. After a short stint in Damascus, Syria, he took up residence in the Republic of Yemen, where he sold arms to Somali rebels. For a short time laying low in Iraq, he turned up next in Pakistan where he arranged arms sales to renegade tribal lords. Pakistani authorities were able to intervene before he completed a deal for high-tech weaponry with a high profile terrorist organization, possibly Al-Qaeda or Hezbollah.

"Kleistner became a prolific dealer in the arms trade business, and well-trained and experienced in the craft of espionage, he recruited dangerous people to do his dirty work, paying them well. However, the CIA and Interpol were tracking him so he had to remain on the move to avoid arrest and prosecution. When capturing an agent working undercover in Bangkok, Thailand, they murdered him and removed the victim's head and hands before disposing of his body, making identification difficult. His detailed knowledge and elaborate planning has stifled law enforcement authorities while allowing him to remain secretively aloof and, for a time living in Canada, he did work for various foreign powers. There's a big demand for Western technology, and not just with the Russians and Red China, but even countries who are supposed to be our allies vie for technological support. Oil-rich Third World countries controlled by radical extremists are the worst, as they're willing to pay a big price for military hardware, and his organization has the ability to market such materials."

Matheson reflected before having another thought. "When you said you believed you were hypnotized, it stuck in my mind, as intelligence sources have recently focused on locating an individual by the name of Sadhan Rishankar. A provocative and obscure figure, he reportedly allied with Kleistner and his compatriots when they were in Pakistan. A doctor of philosophy and a mystical spiritualist, he's wanted by the nation of India under the charge of extorting a large sum of money from a government official through the use of hypnotism. The warrants for him allege that while treating a high-ranking official in India's Treasury Department for Parkinson's disease, he coerced him into giving him over $2 million. He may very well be the man you described as having hypnotized you.

"Our relations with the Russians may have relaxed somewhat, but they are still considered a threat with their nuclear strike capability. Even though they've adopted a democratic system of government, we must remain vigilant for the possibility of a hostile party coming to power. Vladimir Putin is a former KGB official who has a strong hold over Russia, and he often gives mixed signals about where he's taking the country. We've developed the Triad Satellite for defensive purposes, but the Russians undoubtedly have sighted its offensive capabilities and feel threatened by it. We believe they've launched a massive effort to collect every piece of data they can to pinpoint the satellite's vulnerability, and we're convinced they've engaged Kleistner's assistance. Nowadays operating in cloak-and-dagger fashion, he and his people have targeted contractors doing work for our government's Defense Department for the purpose of extracting classified information."

Matheson stood. "Tomorrow will be a crucial day, as much depends on how they react to your not having the disc when you show up at that church. I don't think you'll have any problem sounding convincing when demanding to see your son, but it's to your advantage to make them play it that way so we can be sure he's still alive. When you leave the church, they may put a tail on you, so I'd advise going straight home before calling to inform me how the meeting went."

He checked his wristwatch to make sure Linda had time to make her scheduled flight. "You've got a plane to catch, and since it wouldn't be wise for the two of us to leave the building together, I'll wait around here for another hour before leaving."

He ushered Linda to the door, but before pushing the button, he turned to her and said, "You know we're counting on you to get out of this building and back to Staten Island without our help."

Linda looked at the stainless steel casing she held in her hand. "Why didn't the kidnappers have me get this last night when I was here?"

"I think the file gives them what they're after, but the disc was returned to the safe yesterday, which gives us more reason to suspect there's a double agent at work here. The disc was in New York as part of that briefing Evelyn Werner gave to NATO advisers, so whoever's supplying these people with information has carefully tracked the disc's location. Learning the disc would be returned to the safe on short notice, they must've decided to send you back again tonight to obtain it."

"You're matching me up with dangerous people. Am I going have any protection at the church tomorrow?"

Matheson shook his head. "Not at the church. They'll be watching you there like a hawk and someone showing up who remotely resembles a government agent could cause you to get your throat slashed. My guess is that they'll be angry when finding out you came without bringing the disc, so be careful tomorrow, Mrs. Moreland."

Linda moved into the hallway alone, placing the disc in the hip pocket of her blazer for concealment, and buttoned her blazer to stop the coat from flopping open when she walked.

She successfully made it past the fifth floor checkpoint and took the elevator down to the main floor, feeling as if she were in limbo until getting past the guard in the lobby and reaching the outside. On her walk to the main gate, she felt more at ease, experiencing relief upon seeing the taxi waiting across the road.

During the taxi ride to the airport, she thought the disc might trigger the metal detector at the airport, so she put it in her purse. There was still the chance the disc would draw attention, but she thought airport security viewing it on the X-ray screen could mistake it for a make-up kit or a compact disc player.

At the airport, Linda got through the terminal checkpoint without complications and soon was in flight, but things Matheson had told her stuck in her mind. During the hours they'd abducted and interrogated her until the time they released her, these people hadn't had a lot of time to produce the Evelyn Werner ID badge. This meant it hadn't taken the kidnappers long to determine she was telling them the truth about who she was. When probing her mind they'd concluded she'd do all she could to protect her child, convincing themselves she was a worthy candidate for posing as Werner. However, what seemed most important was that she'd be dealing with deadly, dangerous people who made their living by killing and through bloodshed for their own personal gain.

Knowing how merciless these kidnappers were, Allan was constantly on her mind. She wondered how his health was without his medication. She also worried how the meeting with the kidnappers would go tomorrow at the church when they'd learn she wasn't delivering them the disc. Of course, they wouldn't be pleased when learning she had shown up without it, but insisting on seeing her son made good sense, for she did so much want to see Allan to know he was OK. However, soon the time would come when she would have to turn the disc over to them. She held concerns for what was going to happen to both her and her son from that moment on.

When arriving home that night, Louise whipped up a tuna fish dish as a quick meal for her, and Linda felt better after getting something in her stomach.

"I'm to meet with the kidnappers tomorrow, and Jack Matheson, the agent in charge, insists I not take the disc with me."

"That was the main demand of the kidnappers, so what does that mean?" Louise asked with a look of concern.

"Before delivering the disc, the government wants me to insist on seeing Allan to make certain he's alive. One of the kidnappers, a woman, told me that I'd be able to see Allan at the church, but I don't think Matheson believes they'll have him there, and I don't trust them either."

"You went to the authorities for help. Aren't they doing anything about this?"

"It's like I told you, they're acting in secrecy, and they need time."

"But what if these people are not willing to wait?"

"Matheson's relying on their need for the disc to make them compromise and allow me to see Allan before a trade is made." Worn and tired, Linda stood up. "I've got little choice but to do as he says."

Without another word, Linda went upstairs to her room, and at first not knowing what to do with the disc, she decided to hide it in the bottom of a shoebox in her closet. Thinking about all Matheson had told her about these people made her uneasy, and just before going to bed, she knelt at her bedside and made a fervent prayer for help to bring her son home. She'd gone to great lengths to acquire the file and endured wearisome turmoil to get the Triad disc to trade for her son, and now she had tomorrow's meeting at the church. Her distressed mind wouldn't let her uncoil, but much needed sleep eventually prevailed.

CHAPTER 9

Dealing with Shrewd People

Mounting problems allowed Linda little sleep, and awaking tired and withdrawn, she prepared to go to this church to meet with her son's kidnappers. Matheson had described them as the kind of people who'd stop at nothing to get what they were after. Weighing heavily on her mind was that not delivering the disc was certain to make for a confrontation.

Nearing the time to go to the church, the telephone on the secretary desk in the living room rang, and Linda saw on the receiver's ID window that it was Mona calling. Not wanting to answer it, but knowing she'd only phone again later to put Louise in a difficult situation, she picked up the receiver. "Hello."

"Linda, it's Mona," the virile voice of a woman responded. "Do you think you'll be coming to work today?"

"Mona, I've been meaning to call you, but I've got some serious problems hanging over me."

"It's Allan, isn't it? I knew when you weren't there for the start of the fashion show that he must've taken a bad turn."

Linda heard the taxi's horn outside when replying, "As a matter of fact, it is about Allan, and it happened so suddenly that I haven't been able to keep my head straight."

"I'd told you the minute something of that nature occurs to simply drop everything and go, but I wish you'd at least taken an opportunity to phone me to let me know his condition. I knew you had troubles, and I've tried phoning you, but that house-maid of yours is afraid to tell me anything about what's going on. Anyway, I took your place making the presentation and then managed the entire fashion affair."

"I'm sorry for not calling you, but it's just that I've been in a tight corner looking after him and worrying about his wellbeing."

"Yes, dear, I can understand you've had a lot on your mind, and as far as I'm concerned, you've earned the time off, but you need to at least give me the consideration of a phone call."

Linda heard the taxi's horn again. "I know, and I apologize for not phoning."

"We can manage without you for a few days, but can you tell me how he's doing?"

"I think he's going to pull through this OK. Thanks for your concern, Mona, and I'll call you in a day or two."

Linda hung up the phone, rushed out to catch her taxi, and getting in the vehicle, she said, "Our Savior Catholic Church in Brooklyn."

The cabdriver said, "That's on Eighth Avenue near Prospect Park, right?"

Linda wasn't sure, but remembering seeing a street sign for Eighth Street or Eighth Avenue, she replied, "I believe that's correct."

On her taxi ride to Brooklyn, she kept wondering what the kidnappers' reaction was going to be once they learned she hadn't brought the disc. Remembering what Matheson told her about these cold-blooded people, she couldn't suppress the thought that this ploy was going to endanger both her and her son. However, she thought it made sense to demand seeing her son before handing over the disc, and the fact that they placed considerable value on the disc was the one thing giving her the leverage to buy Matheson time.

Adele had instructed her to go to the west confessional, and even though Linda wasn't a Catholic, she'd once attended a wedding ceremony at a Catholic church with a friend when she was young. The friend, who was a Catholic, pointed out the confessionals in that church and explained how within their confines parishioners confessed their sins to a priest as a way to repent and ask for God's forgiveness.

Deep into Brooklyn, she saw the gothic pinnacle of Our Savior Church in the distance, a symbol that raised hope of seeing her son, and the steeple clock read 10:50. Before long, the taxi's tires grazed the curb as it came to a halt in front of the immense church. After paying her cab fare, she stepped out of the vehicle. Sidewalks on both sides of the street were clear of people, and she walked toward the tall church doors to enter through the one on the right. As she passed through the vestibule, the door closed behind her with a loud thud that echoed throughout the building. She went through a set of open doors to enter the heart of a grand old church. There were rows of empty wood benches, but up front she saw a woman in black wearing a hat with a veil seated near the center aisle.

Linda walked down the center aisle toward the altar to approach the female sitting in the third pew, and dreaded confronting the shrewd person she knew by the name Adele. When in this woman's company she felt cornered and frustrated, having to restrain herself and cover up the contempt she had for this female who was in control of her son's fate.

As Linda neared, the female stood, and when their eyes met, she saw a woman in her sixties or seventies that wore a frown. She immediately knew the lady wasn't one of them. Without a word spoken, the woman passed by Linda, taking the center aisle to exit the church, and now she stood alone in the church, gazing about its spacious interior. She saw two A-frame constructed oak confessionals with intricate trim work centrally located on the left and right side of the church adjacent to broad marble pillars. There were three doors to each confessional, and the center one bore a cross, as a man of the cloth normally occupied this space, going from one side to the other to hear parishioners privately tell their sins.

Adele told her to go to the west confessional, and she went to the one on the left side when facing the altar. Entering the confessional and closing the door tight to shut out almost all light, she knelt on an elevated pad facing a screen, and without certainty if someone was listening, she asked softly, "Is anyone there?"

"Are you Linda Moreland?" replied a man's sinister voice that sent shivers up her spine and made her squirm. Unable to place a face with the voice, she tried to see beyond the screen, but only saw a shadowy figure. She replied in a soft-spoken voice, "Yes, I'm she."

"Did you bring the disc?"

"No, I didn't, but I have possession of it."

Silence loomed, and then his commanding voice snapped at her, "Did you misunderstand your instructions?"

"I was told my son would be returned to me when I gave up the file, but he wasn't. I was promised I'd be able to see him today when I came to this church, and before giving up the disc it's only fair that I be allowed to see him."

No response came, and seeing the outline of a distorted shadow moving about, she added, "I need to know no harm's come to him before turning over the disc to you." Linda saw the figure behind the screen shifting again, and when no reply came, she used an assertive tone. "You can kill me, I don't care, but if I don't see him, you'll never get your hands on that disc."

"Alright," the voice came back with a trace of anger. "Had you brought the disc I'd have taken you to your child and after the disc was authenticated the two of you would've been released. As a result of your failure to follow instructions, we'll have to make other arrangements. You'll receive a phone call this afternoon giving the time and place for you to see the boy."

"Why don't you take me to him right now?"

"I want this trade to go off without a hitch, and you've complicated matters by demanding a change in plans. So we're going to accommodate you, but I can't take you to him until I've consulted with others. My colleagues are not as receptive to granting concessions as I am, and your showing up without the disc may rattle them so they'll need some coaxing." Then the voice added, "Do you have a watch?"

"Yes."

"It's important after I've exited the confessional that you wait a full two minutes before leaving. Understand?"

"Yes, I understand."

It was vital to get a look at the man behind the screen for identification purposes, as he could be the so-called double agent sought by Matheson. Within the confined compartment she occupied she heard movement on the other side of the screen, then the opening and closing of the door. Remaining in a kneeling position while turning toward the door, she wanted to crack open the door to have a look, but hesitated, knowing she could endanger her son by making such a move.

Hearing his hurried footsteps, she gripped the door handle firmly to nudge the door open to take a peek, but the angle at which the door opened outward blocked her from seeing him. She stuck her head out far enough to gain an unobstructed view, but he'd already exited by a side door near the altar. There was a short burst of sunlight before the door swung shut behind him, and their carefully arranged setup made it nearly impossible for her to view this person. Had she chosen to enter the opposite door on the confessional, he probably would've made his exit by the other direction, which would've served to block her view in much the same way.

She had another minute to wait, and she thought about how this church's congregation must be a fraction of what it once was. These people must've known it was conveniently vacant this time of day. Waiting a few more seconds before leaving the confessional, she quickly went to the side door, but her adversary had mysteriously disappeared down a hedged footpath leading to the rectory. Closing the door and taking the center aisle to leave by the same way she'd entered the church, a silver-haired priest in a black robe unexpectedly appeared through a door connecting with the altar. He carried in his arms a basket full of flowers, and they exchanged looks before Linda continued down the aisle to exit the church.

"Wait," said the priest, setting down the floral arrangement. Linda stopped to turn to the altar, and the approaching priest faced the altar to genuflect before coming toward her, saying, "Did you come for confession?" Linda had little time to reply before the priest said, "The reason I ask is we hold confessions at 10 a.m. and 4 p.m. on Saturdays."

"Thank you. I'll come back some other time."

The priest then kindly added, "I left some bulletins by the door, and being a new face at our church, you might care to take one."

"I'll do that." On her way out, Linda picked up a bulletin from a table near the door, and seeing the priest still watching her, she then exited the church.

She believed the church, like the cemetery, wasn't far from the building where they'd taken her for interrogation purposes. The character and makeup of nearby buildings reinforced this belief. Moreover, it seemed logical for the cemetery and church to be conveniently close to their hideaway, so they could make quick getaways to reach a place of refuge.

Using her cell phone to call for a taxi, in the time Linda waited in front of the church she listened to recorded phone messages, and there were many of them. Most were from Mona and Louise, trying to locate her from the time of the fashion show when the kidnappers first abducted her. Erasing the messages in their succession, she heard nothing from Matheson, and the taxi soon arrived to pick her up.

After arriving home, she telephoned Matheson. Recognizing his voice when he answered, she said, "It's Linda Moreland. They said they'd let me see Allan. They told me they'd call me this afternoon to set up a meeting place."

"Did they send the same woman to meet you?"

"No, this time they sent a man, and we conversed in the confessional where a screen hid his face. He told me to wait in the confessional while he exited the church, but I still attempted to get a look at him, although the way the confessional doors opened made that impossible. He had the same impatient tone in his voice as one of the men who questioned me when they had me drugged, but that's something I can't be completely sure about."

"You have no true recollection of what any of these men look like, right?"

"If I saw the two men who abducted me, I might be able to recognize them. When under the influence of that drug, they kept a lamp directed at my face, and I only remember the eyes of one of them staring at me from close up, but he may not have been one of those who abducted me."

"You probably did a little more than you should've, and I appreciate that, but I don't want you pushing these people too far. I've tried to avoid it, but I want you to know that I've arranged to have one of our men planted in your home, as there's too much risk involved with you keeping the disc there. His presence will serve as protection for you, and although we're monitoring your phone calls to get voice recordings of these people, he'll tap into your phone service from down in the basement to listen in. He'll be as inconspicuous as possible, but strange noises in the house may bring him upstairs, so try not to be startled when that occurs."

"What time will he be coming, so I can tell Louise to expect him?"

"He and I will come to the rear entrance to your house after nightfall. Be sure to keep the lights down low, and at that time I'll bring you the disc."

"What if I get a phone call to meet the kidnappers before then?"

"That's certainly a possibility. Call me as soon as you hear anything."

Following their conversation, Linda waited for the kidnappers to call, unsure whether they'd contact her by her cell phone or her home phone. At ten till four in the afternoon, her desk phone rang and she answered it. "Hello."

"Mrs. Moreland." A muffled and unfamiliar voice came across the line, sounding as if the speaker was trying to disguise his raspy voice.

"Yes."

She heard nothing but silence, and following a brief disturbance on the line, the sweet sound of a small boy brought her joy as Allan spoke excitedly through the receiver. "Mom, Mommy!"

"Yes, Allan." Her voice cracked as her eyes lit up. "It's me, darling."

"I miss you, Mommy."

"I miss you too." A smile grew on her face as she clenched the receiver with both hands, blinking as tears filled her eyes, and she grabbed a handkerchief to dab them away.

"When are you coming to get me?"

"Soon, I promise, real soon."

Allan's voice suddenly grew distant, and he screamed, "Mommy! I want to talk to Mommy!"

"Allan! Allan!" Her grip on the receiver tightened as she pressed it to her ear.

Now the man's voice returned, sounding maliciously fiendish, "You'll bring the disc to the cemetery at 10 p.m. or the boy dies!"

She heard him hang up, and then she broke down crying.

After regaining her composure, she phoned Matheson, and still sniffling when hearing his voice, she said, "They called and let me talk to Allan, then demanded that I bring the disc to the cemetery at 10 p.m."

"My gamble to gain us more time may have placed you in a dangerous position, but I should've expected something like this. Was it the same man you spoke to at the church?"

"It may have been him, but whoever it was tried disguising his voice. You said they'd be suspicious of the authorities' involvement, and it looks like they are."

"They're no doubt eager to get their hands on the disc, but there's little chance of luring out anyone of any real importance. I expect they'll send the woman with her driver." Matheson paused before adding, "They may come on foot."

"What makes you think that?"

"I've done some checking. That cemetery closes at 5 p.m. every day, and at the time of closing a caretaker runs a chain across the entrance to block cars from entering. They're probably keeping watch on the cemetery, and it's likely they'll come on foot, making my job all the more difficult."

Thinking of the disc's importance, Linda asked, "Am I supposed to bring the disc with me when I go there tonight?"

"You'll have to bring it, but giving you support isn't going to be easy, as after dark they could be prowling about almost anywhere on those cemetery grounds."

"You're not making me feel very confident about the outcome of this meeting. I'm supposed to hand the disc over to them whether they deliver Allan to me or not?"

"I'm not particularly fond of the idea of asking you to go there tonight, but you'll have to bring them the disc, and it won't do any good to resist. They'll simply take it from you forcibly. The State Department authorized you to complete the trade, but there's no way of telling how this is going to play out. They may be earnest about completing the trade but insist on taking you somewhere to examine the disc before releasing your son to you."

The phone grew quiet, and then Matheson added, "I'll see you after dark as we'd discussed, and I'll give the disc to you then."

"OK, but if you're coming after sundown and I'm supposed to be at that cemetery in Brooklyn at ten, that's not going to leave me a lot of time."

"I'm aware of that, but we should arrive with ample time to relay the disc to you before you have to leave the house to go there."

As soon as she was off the phone, Linda informed Louise about a man from the government coming to stay with them, and explained what his function would be. Although she'd grown emotional after first talking to Allan, it gave her pleasure to hear his voice and it reaffirmed her courage and commitment. As afternoon turned into evening, apprehension grew about going to this cemetery so late at night, but she was willing to trade the disc for her son's freedom. In her mind, she was the one taking the chances and it was up to the authorities to catch these people, and yet a part of her hated the idea of cooperating with such ruthless people.

CHAPTER 10

Danger in a
Late Night Rendezvous

The evening forecast projected sunset at 8:19 p.m., predicting cool temperatures with some wind but no rain, and as that time grew near, Linda felt butterflies in her stomach. She and Louise sat at the kitchen table, keeping watch on the stove's clock that illuminated a faint glow, expecting Matheson to show up any minute with another man whom Defense Intelligence wanted stationed in their home. Seeing how time was running out for her to make her ten o'clock rendezvous with the kidnappers, the wait made her nervous. On the table lay the stainless steel casing that, according to Matheson, held a blank computer disc, which she was expecting him to swap for another disc he'd be bringing with him.

At 8:30, she called for a cab to take her to the cemetery in Brooklyn, and at 8:35, they heard tapping on the back door's glass where an alley light dimly produced two silhouetted figures on the window shade. Linda lifted it to recognize Matheson wearing a black turtleneck sweater under a gray herringbone sport coat, in the company of a man who appeared about fifty, wearing a trenchcoat over a dark suit. She opened the door for them. Matheson carried a black dispatch case while his associate lugged a large suitcase. After entering, he moved to one side to make room for the man behind him.

Matheson spoke softly when saying, "I take it you didn't get any more calls?"

"None. I haven't heard anything."

He then made introductions, saying, "I'd like you ladies to meet Walter Koenig. He'll be staying with you until things take a turn for the better, which I hope won't be too far off. This is Mrs. Moreland, and you must be Mrs. Hagen." Koenig shook their hands.

"Pleased to meet you both," Koenig said in a gruff, scratchy voice, which didn't sound at all in tune.

"Walter's got a touch of laryngitis," said Matheson. "I think it's from the changing, cooler weather coming in."

Standing together in the darkened kitchen, Linda wasn't able to view Koenig's features very well, except to see his hair streaked in silver and gray, and he wore black-rimmed glasses. Koenig seemed impatient in wanting to go about his business, and strained his vocal cords when asking, "How do I get to the basement?"

Louise escorted him to a door off the front entry hall. It led to the basement stairs that ran beneath the staircase which gave access to the second floor. She followed him down and in doing so said, "I set up a comfortable cot and chair for you with a pillow and blanket on the chair. If there's anything you need, please don't hesitate to ask."

"I'll be alright," uttered Koenig on his way down the stairs.

"I'll leave this last case for you here on this top step," Matheson told Koenig, but Louise was kind enough to carry the case down for him.

Linda remarked, "Louise is a darling person, and she'll do a terrific job of looking after Mr. Koenig during his stay here. It's going to be a comfort having him around because I've begun worrying about those people breaking into the house to get the disc."

"I'm sure they have their suspicions about your house being under observation, so there's little chance of that happening."

Matheson brought out a cell phone from the inside pocket of his sport coat and asked, "May I see your cell phone for a minute?"

When placing her cell phone next to his, she noticed the phones were the same make and model, and she watched as he made adjustments with both phones, as though checking something.

"They may insist that you go with them to another location to verify the disc's authenticity, and if that happens your phone is equipped with a global positioning transmitter, which may prove useful for tracking your whereabouts."

Linda's eyes told of concerns she had for this late meeting at the cemetery, and she said, "I just called for a cab, and it should arrive soon. I'm assuming you're going to the cemetery too. I mean, I can't very well be expected to be responsible for this disc on my own."

Matheson removed the disc from the hip pocket of his jacket. It was in a clear plastic carrying case. He switched the discs. The stainless steel case now stored a disc containing top secret information. He left the stainless steel case on the kitchen table, sliding the other out of the way.

"I'll be watching your back, but I've got to keep my distance. That means I may have a tough time keeping close watch over you, and they may be coming in numbers to stop someone like me from interfering with their plans. I know it's asking a lot under the circumstances, but it's important that you do what you can to safeguard that disc."

Linda stuffed her cell phone into the inside breast pocket of her blazer and placed the stainless steel casing holding the disc in the right hip pocket of the coat. "I'm not foolish enough to believe this is going to be a simple exchange—the disc for my son – but I hope I'm not asked to leave the cemetery to go somewhere else with them."

Thinking she may be short on money to pay the cabdriver, she said, "I wasn't going to bring a purse with me, but I need to get some cash. I'll only be a minute."

She went to the living room to get her billfold from her purse, stuffing a wad of cash in the left hip pocket of her blazer, and then she heard a car horn signaling the taxicab was outside. When Linda returned to the kitchen, Matheson had vanished. Louise came up the stairs from the basement, and she told her goodbye before leaving the house to catch her taxi.

Giving the driver the destination of Mount Sinai Cemetery in Brooklyn, she believed she had sufficient time to arrive before ten o'clock. Riding in the backseat, looking at the streetlights they passed, she'd gotten a glimpse of the chubby, unshaven driver who looked to be of Italian descent wearing a New York Mets cap while listening to the ballgame. The Mets had just tied the score with the St. Louis Cardinals in the bottom half of the sixth inning. Throughout the duration of the ride, she thought about the risks involved while holding concern for the night's outcome.

The time was 9:25 when the cab pulled over in front of the cemetery, easing next to the curb beneath a streetlamp. The driver said, "We're here."

Linda brought cash out of her blazer to pay the fare, handing the cabby an additional five dollar tip.

He turned and smiled, speaking with a strong New York accent. "Lady, what are you doing at a cemetery at 9:30 at night?"

"Some friends will be along shortly to pick me up."

He chuckled. "Are the friends picking you up vampires? All the landmarks around town and you have to pick a cemetery for a meeting place. You know, I'm not one to give advice, but this isn't the neighborhood for you—there was a guy killed in a drive-by shooting less than a week ago on the next corner. You stick around here long enough and you just might become a permanent resident with your own cemetery plot." Wearing a comical grin, he added, "Hey, I'm tryin' to look out for you here. If you want me to wait around for a couple of minutes until your friends show up, I don't mind."

"It's nice of you to offer, but that won't be necessary," Linda replied, opening the car door to get out.

The driver rolled down his window. "You're no hooker, unless you're a $500 a night hooker, so come on, what gives? Are you making a drug-run for your rich boyfriend?"

Finally making an off-the-cuff remark to end the conversation, she said, "Yeah, I'm looking for vampires selling white powder."

"OK, I'm outta here, but you really ought to ditch the guy." As soon as Linda closed the door the driver sped away.

Linda thought the driver well-meaning, wishing he could come along and keep her company. The thought of taking a lei-surely walk through a cemetery at night didn't sit right with her. A cemetery can project an image of peaceful permanence and tranquility, but after nightfall, it's a downright unnerving place to take a stroll. She stepped over the chain strung across the entrance and started into the hallowed grounds of Mount Sinai Cemetery to reach the circle where Adele had previously met her. The streetlamps' light dimly reflected off the mausoleum, and the monolithic shrine looked eerily foreboding, making her uneasy about the walk she had ahead of her.

Coming to the fork in the road, she went to the right to fol-low the asphalt pavement leading to the circle, and getting away from street lights made for a dark path to tread upon. A full moon broke through shifting clouds to bring light to the cem-etery grounds, giving her an opportunity to see the road ahead with clarity while allowing a sketchy view of aboveground crypts and tombstones. The constant clatter from the heels of her shoes against the pavement made her stop, and thinking about taking them off, she swore to never again wear these shoes when dealing with these people.

Continuing down the paved road, she looked at her wrist-watch and saw she was going to be a few minutes late mak-ing her appointment with the opposition, as it was already ten o'clock. Walking this dark lane to reach the circle was more of a stretch of the legs than anticipated, and stepping up her pace to reach the circle, she found no one waiting for her there.

Quickly growing impatient, she checked her watch again to see the time was 10:15, and she began pacing. Up till now, everything seemed to be running in favor of those holding her son, and they'd been careful about protecting their identities. However, they now had no choice but to come out in the open to get the disc, but who would they send, and would they be escort-ing her son to this location? They had the ability to wage a psy-chological war by making her wait, and the pressure applied by pulling Allan away from the phone as he was screaming for her aroused the contempt and deep-seated hatred she had for them.

If my patience is wearing thin, then theirs must be too, but where are they?

Walking about the circle nervously while keeping watch, she had time to consider the kinds of people they were. By Matheson's own account, they had made killing and kidnapping their life's work. They must've given consideration to doing away with her after getting their hands on the disc, viewing disposing of her a necessity to eliminate her as a witness.

Matheson had made it clear he was working without the assistance of other government agencies and with little help from people within his own department. This was primarily because the Defense Department was seeking to expose a mole or double agent posing a threat to national security, but this individual may have access to a broad scope of information. If a spy who'd infiltrated the CIA had aided these kidnappers to gain possession of the disc, they could've alerted them that she'd gone to the authorities. This meant they may have also learned Matheson was going to show up at the cemetery, and for this reason they may have resorted to a change of plans, leaving her to think they may never come.

Wishing Matheson would show up to relieve her growing fears, she now wondered if something may have happened to him. As much as she didn't want to consider that possibility, she thought by now he should've made his presence known. *So where is he?* The disc she carried contained classified information, which she didn't want responsibility for. At the same time, she couldn't think of why there had been so little progress made in locating the kidnappers' hideout—she'd told them it couldn't be far from the cemetery and the church to narrow down their search area. Success may lie with finding a charity mission in the vicinity of the cemetery and church, as she'd seen a vertical electric sign with neon letters indicating a mission after they'd first interrogated her.

Her mind running frantic with suspicion and fear, she didn't know Matheson well enough to judge his character, although she had faith in him. Still, a person in a trusted position of the government could cut a deal with these kidnappers, turning his head the other way for great deal of money exchanging hands. Not wanting to think such things, she fully understood that for the government to give one agent the job of protecting a disc of such importance, he would surely have to be an individual with an impeccable reputation.

Losing her patience, Linda couldn't resist using her cell phone to call Matheson, and having inserted his phone number into her phone's memory, she read it by a bright header to initiate the call. When there was no answer, this fueled more speculation, and she returned her cell phone to the inside breast pocket of her blazer while surveying the surrounding landscape.

A cool breeze rustled the trees. Hearing something, she turned to see scattered leaves dancing across the pavement, and then looked up at passing clouds, their silvery lining created by the moon. When a shifting cloud blocked the moonlight, a shadow fell across the cemetery grounds, and she grew increasingly uncomfortable with the prolonged wait. Just as it seemed nothing could ease her frustration and anxiety, the wind calmed and everything came to a standstill. It was as though time had stopped. In this stillness, she heard faint street sounds, but when hearing a disturbance from behind her, she twisted her upper body and froze, her eyes scanning the outlying area. Linda sensed someone or something lurking about in the dark, their eyes watching her. But whose were they? Who, if anyone, was out there stalking her? She became alarmed at the threat of a mugger targeting her. Suddenly seeing the possibility of losing the disc to a common thief, she tried convincing herself that she'd waited long enough for the kidnappers, as they must've changed their minds about coming.

The outcome of this night could fall many ways. Feeling the need to assure herself that she was in possession of the disc, she put her hand in the right hip pocket of her blazer and felt for the disc. Feeling the case, she ran her fingertips deeper into the base of the pocket and discovered something unidentifiable—a cartridge-shaped object. Drawing it from her pocket, she found it to be the aerosol container of pepper spray Louise had given her, which she'd completely forgotten about.

The clouds shifted again to give the moon free reign to shine across the land, but the trees produced shadows to hide someone watching her from a distance. Her eyes swept across the cemetery grounds, skimming over still headstones, and checking her watch again, the time was almost 10:50. Thinking they may still come because they valued the disc, and wanting to see this through for Allan's sake, she decided she'd wait until eleven o'clock. Visibility diminished as shifting clouds cut off the moonlight, and while their shadows overtook the land to leave her standing in darkness, she felt vulnerable.

At two minutes to eleven, she once again considered starting back to the cemetery entrance and looked out across the cemetery, listening for street sounds. For a moment, she thought about taking a shortcut by cutting across the cemetery grassland. Even though she wanted to leave in a hurry, she couldn't bring herself to cross that uninviting patch of ground between her and the street—too many hiding places, too much like Central Park.

She couldn't understand why they'd lured her here, then not show up. *Why didn't they come, and what happened to Matheson for him not to make his presence known?*

Feeling as if trouble was creeping up on her, leaving her easy prey, she looked down the long stretch of road she'd have to walk, and then she heard a loud burst of broken glass. It wasn't a sound she liked hearing, and momentarily she thought it could've been an automobile accident, but if it had been a car crash, she hadn't heard screeching tires. Thinking someone may have broken in a car by shattering a window, the idea of staying here was not something she intended to do for much longer.

CHAPTER 11

Moonlight Madness

Hoping to survive this night to see the light of day again, Linda had waited over an hour to meet with the kidnappers, and now she began walking back to the boulevard. Moonlight returned to give a clear view of the pavement's wide path, and noticing the annoying clatter of her shoes, she moved to the grass as a way to quiet her footsteps. Up ahead, the road appeared to narrow between two mature trees, making for a place to expect trouble. She came to one of the trees to embrace its coarse bark while a perpetual wind held steady, looking about and listening while danger lurked in the shadows. Tree branches swayed from another strong gust of wind, and wondering whether someone was waiting for the right moment to pounce on her drew her eyes to scattered headstones.

Linda moved on to meander around a tall bush. Suddenly, the moon cast light on a looming, life-size statue of an angel with a large cross attached to its back. Shadows from the statue's features made it look eerily sinister, and she returned to the asphalt pavement where it seemed safer. She removed her shoes and carried them both tucked under one arm, but her feet began to ache from having stood for so long at the circle and walking on the hard pavement.

Coming within twenty yards of the mausoleum, she saw the fork in the road up ahead. One lane went straight on to another section of the cemetery while the other turned left to pass the mausoleum to lead out to the street. Moving forward, she cautiously approached the ominous structure, and seeing streetlamps at the cemetery entrance, she held concerns about flagging down a taxi this late at night.

Sensing the presence of someone watching her, Linda walked wide-eyed, remaining on the opposite side of the paved road from the mausoleum, and movement near the building's corner startled her. Her eyes fixed on an obscure form coming out of the shadows, a man walking casually who'd just exited the maintenance door at the rear of the mausoleum. She quickly concluded it wasn't Matheson, for he had blond hair, but she didn't run. He wore a gray suit, his steel-rimmed eyeglasses held a gleam, and he stopped at the edge of the pavement to leave the distance of the road's width separating them.

Seeing marks where she'd scratched his face returned the memory of her abduction from a street corner, and the backseat struggle she lost. She still didn't run.

Gensler spoke with not much more than a loud whisper. "Do you have it?"

Wary of danger, while discouraged by the person sent to meet her, she answered, "I have the disc. Where's my son?"

After looking about cautiously, he said, "Follow me, and I'll take you to him."

Watching him start back to the mausoleum, Linda dropped her shoes, slipping her feet into them one at a time, and then she proceeded to follow him at a safe distance.

Leading her to the mausoleum's maintenance door, he descended four stone steps to stand at the door, where he paused to make sure no one was around before pushing the door open. Linda kept her distance, noticing someone had forcibly broken out the door's window and reinforcing wire mesh, leaving a gaping hole in its place. She remembered the sound of glass breaking earlier, which she'd taken for car glass shattering, and she stopped, remaining watchful for what he was up to.

Gensler spoke softly. "Listen, I have a portable laptop computer and it'll only take me a minute to check the disc, but the boy may have to be carried because he's feeling ill."

His comment raised Linda's concern for her son, but she held back from following him, watching as he disappeared through the door and into the black darkness of the mausoleum's basement. A second later, he stuck his head out long enough to say, "I don't have all night. Are you coming for him?"

He went back inside, leaving the door open for her, and as much as she was untrusting of him, she couldn't walk away. If there was any chance that Allan was in there, she didn't want to leave without him, and on her guard, she called out to him. "Allan."

Staring at the open door, she kept her distance from the doorway's threshold by stopping at the edge of the descending stairs, but her eyes still could not penetrate the pitch-black that lay beyond.

"Allan," she called out again, her voice carrying as if she were at the opening to a tomb, and all she needed to do was hear his voice to commit to moving closer. Refusing to descend the stairs without first hearing his voice, she called out to her child with a pleading tone. "Allan, answer me." Standing just a short distance from the doorway, she used a demanding tone while stooping over. "Allan, you answer me."

Gensler shot out of the darkness to grab hold of Linda by her hair and the scruff of the neck, yanking her with a swift jerk to drag her inside the mausoleum, flinging her against a wall.

Pinned so she couldn't move, she quickly realized he was wrapping a rope around her neck, and she tried frantically to get her fingers between her neck and the tightening rope. Fighting to escape, she twisted and turned to catch hold of any part of her attacker's anatomy, but he managed to stay on top of her and out of her reach. Her middle finger clipped his eyeglasses, knocking them to the floor, but the rope pulled firmly to tighten around her neck. In the violent struggle, she lost her balance, falling to her knees. He went down on one knee behind her, jerking the rope back and forth until she resisted no more.

"Enough playing around. Now where's the disc?" he insisted with his teeth clenched.

Linda was in an uncompromising position, and stifled and helplessly frightened, she recognized the malicious tone in his voice as the one she'd heard on the telephone earlier that afternoon.

"Where is it?" His harsh words were spoken loudly in her left ear as he breathed hard.

The squeeze tightened around her neck. She again made an attempt to force the fingers of either hand between the rope and her neck, but it was useless.

"Can't breathe," she wheezed.

The choke hold from the rope loosened and she panted for air, swallowing to clear her throat. "What about my son?"

"Forget the boy and hand over the disc." Then the rope tightened, cutting off her oxygen.

"OK," Linda said in an exhaled breath to surrender, and having no other recourse, she reached into the pocket of her blazer for the disc, her fingers feeling about to get a grip on the disc's casing. In doing so, she rediscovered the pepper spray and popped off the cap while gripping the cartridge. Getting a feel for the direction of the spray nozzle by its fingertip shape, she slipped it out of her pocket.

Hearing him breathing heavily in her ear, she took a deep breath before closing her eyes, and aimed the cartridge at his face. Pressing the nozzle brought its contents out under pressure.

Her eyes picked up a stinging mist as she turned away, gasping for air. The rope tightened intensely as she kept the nozzle compressed. Keeping one hand braced against the wall for stability, she rose to her feet, shoving her attacker and scratching at him. Entangled in a furious struggle, she dropped the spray can to gain a finger's hold inside the rope, but kept on pawing and scratching while clinging to the rope to enable her to breathe.

Gensler, coughing and breathless, turned defensive. She felt the rope loosening, and then came the crunch of his eyeglasses underfoot.

Linda pushed him away to bolt for the door in a stumbling run, her shoulder catching the doorjamb, and she nearly stumbled on the steps only to finally fall on the pavement before the mausoleum. Lying there, coughing and puffing in the night air, she gripped her throat and reached for her ankle that had twisted in the fall. Her ears picked up sound from the maintenance door. Gensler came to the doorway, coughing, panting, wiping his watery eyes, and holding his eyeglasses by the earpiece with his thumb and index finger, the framework bent, both lenses shattered.

Upon seeing her, he dropped the glasses and chased after her.

Linda got up from the pavement and darted into the cemetery grounds. Her heart pumped rapidly as she ran errantly on a weak ankle, past a row of headstones in a patch of moonlight. Inhaling and exhaling breathlessly, she dodged him by turning sharply and running past the still statue of an angel, but his onrushing steps told her he was gaining on her.

Seeing a large shrub coming up on her left, suddenly something caught her wrist to bring her gently to the ground, and she glimpsed Matheson in his black turtleneck sweater ramming her attacker.

As the two men clashed, Linda crawled to where she had a clear view of the blows thrown, and saw one knocked to the ground, his head clipping the base of a headstone. The man on his feet ran away, making it obvious that Matheson was the one left dazed, but he got up rubbing his head, and, without a word, charged after her assailant.

Running full-out for the street, Gensler kept his stride, but he was tiring, and Matheson was gaining ground. When reaching the stone wall surrounding the cemetery, Gensler hoisted himself up by pulling on the spiked wrought iron running along its top. He was going over when Matheson caught hold of his foot, but Gensler kept kicking at him until Matheson held only a shoe. Matheson watched Gensler go over the wall and climbed it to pursue him, momentarily holding a perched position on the wrought iron to view his opponent's next move.

With every passing second, the risk of outside intervention grew, and Gensler wanted to avoid another confrontation with Matheson. Stopping at the curb before a four-lane boulevard, he knew his best line of escape was to cross this avenue as quickly as possible. He rubbed his wet eyes in an effort to correct his blurred vision. They hadn't stopped watering from the pepper spray, and without eyeglasses, his vision was impaired even further, so he was unable to focus to check Matheson's position.

Gensler hobbled on one shoe into traffic, and a driver gave a blast of his horn, but then braked to stop and allow him to cross in front of his car to cut across the street.

Matheson dropped to the sidewalk to follow him into traffic, but passing cars wouldn't allow him to enter the first lane—the drivers honked their horns, and he was losing him.

Pressed to reach the alleyway on the opposite side of the street, Gensler journeyed as far as the yellow line, where he was stuck in the middle of cross traffic. The bright headlights of cars making his vision worse, he wiped his eyes before looking back to see Matheson starting across, and this made him eager to cross the remaining two traffic lanes. He waited anxiously for an approaching delivery box truck—the only obstacle standing between him and freedom. While it passed by him, he turned his head to check Matheson's position once more.

As soon as the truck passed, he stepped over the yellow line, and unable to pay heed to a compact car sweeping in behind the truck, his body contracted before the automobile struck him. The impact knocked him twenty feet before he fell still on his back, his limp body sprawled and straddling the yellow line. An oncoming taxi coming from the opposite direction locked its brakes and skidded over his upper torso.

Matheson waited for traffic to come to a standstill before going to the body lying in the street, seeing blood oozing from the man's nose, mouth, and ears. Before a crowd gathered, he knelt to feel his wrist for a pulse. Gensler was dead, leaving no chance of getting any information out of him. Matheson slipped the dead man's wallet out from inside his sport coat, neatly palming it before stuffing it behind his belt buckle. Unable to find the disc, he realized Linda must still have it.

A woman wearing a fur coat came up behind him. "My husband called for an ambulance. The man jumped out in front of us, and there was nothing we could do."

Matheson stood up and nodded as though in agreement with her.

Awestruck by the lifeless body lying at her feet, she asked, "Is he alive?"

Matheson shook his head no, and as bystanders moved in closer to view the body, a police car pulled up. He backed off to the walk where a tree branch hung over the cemetery wall. The branch's foliage shadowed him from a nearby street lamp, and the sound of sirens signaled that more emergency vehicles were converging on the scene. During the time police were occupied clearing and untangling traffic, an ambulance arrived, and Matheson made his way over the wall without drawing anyone's attention. He looked back over the wall to see paramedics examining the body as policemen questioned people, visually scanning the crowd to see if anyone could pass for an associate of the dead man.

Apparently not expecting this individual to fail, it looked as though they'd sent just the one man to the cemetery.

Linda soon joined Matheson at the wall, and looking through the wrought iron to see what was going on, she asked, "What happened?"

"He was hit by an automobile when crossing the boulevard and it killed him."

Linda's fingertips lightly touched the rope burns on her neck while watching paramedics set the body on a gurney. They covered it before placing it inside an ambulance. Police were still questioning the driver of the first car that struck him, and the cabdriver, to grasp how the fatality occurred so they could complete their report.

Matheson reached inside the neckline of his sweater to produce a penlight to sift through the dead man's wallet, reading out loud the name on the driver's license. "Hermann Gensler. This could be the break we've been looking for. I'll run his name through agency computer files and see what comes up." Tucking the wallet back behind his belt buckle, he turned the flashlight on Linda. "You've got the disc, right?"

"Yes."

Noticing red marks on her neck, he asked, "Are you OK?"

"I think so."

Pulling her by the arm into the glow of the streetlamp, he tilted her head to get a closer look at the marks on her neck. "How did you get these?"

"He and I struggled back at the mausoleum where he tried strangling me with a rope." She shrugged Matheson off while stepping away. "He told me he'd brought Allan to lure me there, and now I need to go back to that building to make sure Allan wasn't left tied up inside it."

They walked to the mausoleum and Linda pointed in the direction of the maintenance door. "Near the far corner of the building is a door."

"Wait here and I'll have a look," said Matheson.

"No, you don't have to. Just let me use your penlight, and I'll see if he's there."

"Why are you acting so indignant? It'll only take me a minute to determine whether he's in there, so wait here."

"I almost got killed tonight, and all you're concerned about is that stupid disc. What if my son's lying in there dead?"

Not wanting to argue, Matheson replied, "Wait here."

He walked away to disappear into the mausoleum's lower level, and she watched and waited for him to return, dreading what he might find.

He finally exited the building and came to her, saying, "He's not there. Come with me. My car isn't far."

Linda followed, keeping pace with Matheson, and it took them ten minutes to reach the west end of the cemetery where he'd parked his Chevrolet Impala. They rode up the street, and crossing the first intersection, they saw flashing lights from police cars at the site where her assailant died minutes before.

Matheson stopped at a drugstore to pick up a jar of medicated salve to treat the rope burns on Linda's neck, and coming back from the store to the car, he found her in tears. The night's frightening excitement had caught up to her, and taking his place behind the steering wheel, he was at a loss for words. He tried to console her, but she moved away.

"I'm not crying for me. If I've learned anything tonight it's that if these people don't get what they want, they're going to kill Allan."

Her crying stopped and she dried her eyes with a handkerchief.

"I wish there was some other way to go about this, but these people are only interested in one thing, and that's getting their hands on the disc. As long as they see an opportunity to obtain the disc, it's unlikely that any harm will come to your child, but once they've learned of my department's involvement, they may break contact with you."

"What if this man's death results in my losing contact with them, then what? We're no closer to getting my son back than when I first came to you. This situation is driving me crazy, and I don't know how much more I can take before I have a breakdown."

There was quiet in the car, and then Matheson began to unscrew the lid to the jar of medicated gel. "Would you like me to put some of this salve on your neck?"

She once again dried her eyes with a handkerchief. "I can do it at home."

He closed the jar and handed it to her. "If they call, how do you intend to handle it?"

"I haven't had time to think about it."

"I'd suggest telling them exactly what happened, leaving me out, of course. He tried strangling you, you got away, and when chasing you across that boulevard a car hit him. Keep it simple. That may or may not be sufficient to keep them bargaining, but it should because they want the disc. Can you add anything?"

"Only that our next meeting will be out in the open. I'm never going back to that cemetery. You keep mentioning how important it is that they not learn of your involvement, but I don't see how they can't know because I didn't have the correct safe combination, and yet I came into possession of the file and now the disc."

Matheson nodded. "It's keeping them guessing, and there's no doubt they're suspicious, but it is of the utmost importance that they remain in the dark about my role in this."

Leaning back against the car door, Matheson took a deep breath. "I wish I could say I was having luck running down leads in finding that building they took you to, but I'm not. We may have located the Brooklyn cabdriver who picked you up the night they let you go, but he's in the hospital after a rear-end collision he had with a stalled dump truck on the highway yesterday. He has a serious head injury and his speech is incoherent, so we haven't been able to get any answers out of him. When he comes around, if he remembers you, we should be able to narrow down the location of their hideout. Up till now, we haven't had any success finding a mission in the area, not one with a sign out front hanging vertically over the walk, as you described, with the word mission in neon lights."

"I distinctly remember seeing that sign," Linda insisted. "It hung vertically over the sidewalk in neon lettering as I'd described. That's one detail I do remember clearly. It was no illusion, I'm positive of it."

"OK. I've got a man looking specifically for this mission and I'll keep him on it."

Matheson paused while pondering his next words. "I want to take a few minutes to confer with you about your family background. I'm particularly interested in hearing what you can tell me about your mother and father to learn something about your past."

"My father died near the time of my birth, and my mother raised me by herself. She was the sweetest, kindest person I've ever known."

"She died not long after you were married, didn't she?"

"Yes, she'd been ill for some time before passing away, but I'm grateful she was there for the wedding."

Matheson straightened up. "I'd like to tell you the true story of an American GI who met and fell in love with a young woman when stationed in Germany. The girl had survived an automobile crash as a child, which resulted in the deaths of her parents and an older brother, and as it was, this couple married and had twins, two girls.

"A couple weeks after the birth of their children, this soldier and his wife left the infants with a sitter and went off to spend the afternoon together. This was the first time the couple had any time alone since coming home from the maternity ward, and on a sunny spring day, they set out to have a picnic. They chose a scenic spot on a hillside next to the burned-out ruins of an old cathedral where an unexpected storm came up with high winds and heavy rains. Surprised by the unsettled weather, they raced to the cathedral seeking shelter, and a wall, badly weakened from a fire which gutted the building some years before, suddenly gave way against the strong wind and collapsed, killing them both. The authorities notified the soldier's family. In the meantime, a foster home temporarily took in the infants, but one received treatment in a hospital when it became critically ill with a lung infection.

"Not long after the GI's parents learned of their son's death, his father had a fatal heart attack, leaving his wife all alone. Months later, knowing her son and daughter-in-law had adorable twins with no surviving family on the mother's side, she went to Germany to locate the twins to arrange to bring them back to America. Upon her arrival, she learned how the twins had come to be separated, but doctors had released from the hospital the one infant undergoing treatment. However, through an unusual set of circumstances, a family had legally adopted the healthy twin and was now refusing to give her up. The grandmother spent over a year in Germany trying to reunite the twins, but facing a drawn-out court battle to do this, she gave up on contesting the adoption. She then went ahead with adopting the unhealthy infant, who was now fine, and returned home to raise the child as her own."

Linda leaned her head back. "I suppose I'm the infant girl who came back with her to America. In a way, I knew all along this Evelyn Werner and I looked far too much alike for it to be just a coincidence, but I never could've anticipated anything like this."

"Our people conducted an extensive investigation before compiling this story, and that detailed analysis of your early life gives insight as to how this mistaken identity came about. Your grandmother was a heartbroken individual who chose to raise you as her own and never mentioned that you had a twin."

Linda reflected on her childhood, saying, "She might have tried telling me, but I was too young to understand at the time.

I have a memory of coming home from school one day when I was in second grade and finding her sitting in the living room by herself, crying. I remember her showing me the picture of a young man she held in her hands whom I'd never seen before, and come to think of it, he may have been in uniform. I recall her commenting that he was my father, and I reacted by going to her bedroom and fetching from the nightstand the picture of the man who I believed was my father." Linda's voice grew faint. "But I now understand the person in the picture from her bedroom had to be my grandfather, and it's a sad realization."

Shaking the thought, she began again, "I presented the picture from the nightstand to her proudly, but her facial expression looked so sorrowful. I knew her feelings were hurt about something, and I burned the incident into my memory, but there was never again a word said about it. I suppose it was too painful for her to try to make me understand, and after so many years of acceptance as her being my mother, she may have thought that the truth might stir resentment. I was all she had in the world and she must've come to terms with the fact that it was easier for the two of us to carry on as mother and daughter. I know I never once questioned it, and now it's strange how such outlandish circumstances have allowed me to find out I have a sister. I don't know whether to be happy or cry over it."

"It's only natural that you need time to put this news into perspective, but I thought learning these facts might take your mind off some of your troubles."

Matheson drove her to within two blocks of her home where she could easily walk the rest of the way, and sorry for having put her through all this, he watched her walking away from his car. There'd been times when Matheson didn't like his job, and this was one of them, but he could do little to change Linda's predicament. He knew better than to form an attachment to people linked to a case, but he admired her for what she'd done tonight. He thought about how bravely she'd acted by going to the cemetery to meet these dangerous people, and nearly getting herself killed. This was a person with courage and fortitude...

CHAPTER 12

A Long Search

After arriving home, Linda placed the disc in a shoebox, and believing it was in a secure place, left it there overnight for safekeeping. She was expecting the kidnappers to phone her by 11 a.m. the next morning, but they didn't. Out of worry she may not hear from them again, she phoned Matheson.

After listening to Linda express concerns that they'd lost contact with those holding her son, Matheson replied, "I expect the death of this man Gensler to make matters worse. These are very vigilant people, but I do expect they'll eventually phone you. They must know by now that an automobile struck and killed their man, and uncertain about whether he fell into an ambush, right now they're assessing the situation. Incidentally, Gensler was a man with a long criminal history, both here and abroad, and he had connections to the man named Kleistner I told you about."

Matheson then asked, "Would it make you feel any better if we contacted your ex-husband and had him flown into New York?"

"The only thing that can make a difference for me is getting my son back home where he belongs."

"There's little we can do for now but wait, Mrs. Moreland. However, I'm committed to doing everything possible to getting your son back, and those aren't just words."

Linda interrupted Matheson, saying, "I know you and your people haven't had any luck finding the building they took me to when I was first abducted, and I've been thinking that I'd like to try finding it. I'm convinced their hideout is in the same vicinity as the Mount Sinai Cemetery and Our Savior Church. They're no more than eight blocks from each other, and that's no coincidence."

"That's a high crime area, and as I've mentioned before, I've got a man looking for that mission. If it's in Brooklyn, he'll find it."

"I'm not going to just sit around waiting for a phone call that may never come, not while my son is in the hands of those people."

"You're going on next to nothing to find their location. So far we've been unable to find a mission with a neon sign hanging out over the walk, and what if they call and you're out?"

Linda's voice raised a few decibels. "If I have to sit here for another hour waiting for that phone to ring I'll go crazy. Louise will be here to take a message, and she can give them my cell phone number if they wish to speak to me directly. All I want to do is find the place where they're keeping him, and I'm not going to be carrying the disc with me so you don't have to worry about them taking it away from me."

"OK, but I think you'll be going on a wild goose chase, and stumbling into these people may prove disastrous."

"Mr. Matheson, it's a chance I've got to take. I'm at the end of my rope."

"Should you come across a worthwhile lead, I'll be available by phone."

By 1 p.m., Linda had taken a cab to Brooklyn to see if she could locate the kidnappers' hideout. She thought Matheson and others of his agency competent people, so there had to be a reasonable explanation for why they couldn't locate the mission she'd seen the night they'd released her. Expecting she may be traveling by foot a long distance, she'd rummaged through her closet and chosen a comfortable pair of soft-soled walking shoes to wear. Studying a map of Brooklyn, she familiarized herself with the city streets around the church and cemetery and made a printed copy to take with her.

Wearing her blazer and a lightweight scarf around her neck to cover the marks left by Gensler's rope, she set out to make a thorough search of that immediate area. Riding in the cab, questions kept surfacing. She was unable to understand why they had gone so far as to try killing her last night when they practically had the disc in their hands. All they had had to do was release her son to her and she would've handed the disc over without resistance, but they apparently didn't see it that way. Fearful of losing the only link she had with the people holding her son, she believed they must now suspect that the authorities ambushed Gensler at the cemetery, prompting them to cut off communication with her. Immensely concerned at what might happen to Allan if she didn't make contact and sway them from believing she'd gone to the police, she saw it important to bridge a line of communication with them. Whether they believed her or not, she was counting on the disc to bring them back to negotiating with her.

It needled her to think her son was nothing more than a bargaining chip in this game of cat-and-mouse. Nevertheless, she knew the only way she could help Allan was to carry on. The government's primary goal was to get the man behind their intelligence leak, and as long as there was a chance of him surfacing, she played an important role to the Defense Intelligence Agency. Locating the building where they'd originally taken her for questioning would give agents a lead they could concentrate on, for they could place it under surveillance. At the same time, she'd proven herself useful to the kidnappers by having obtained the disc they valued. The disc made for an influencing factor in her son's survival.

She'd set out to concentrate on an area within the radius of Mount Sinai Cemetery Park and Our Savior Church west of Prospect Park in Brooklyn to find their hideout. Since Brooklyn was where these people arranged their meeting places, and these locations were geographically less than ten blocks from each other, this was the area where she had to start looking.

The day of her abduction, minutes following the moment they released her in a dazed state, she remembered seeing a mission—she had this clear mental picture of a sign in neon letters vertically making the word MISSION. The electric sign showed the establishment was still in operation, and having described this landmark to Matheson, nothing irritated her more than that they hadn't located it. There had to be an explanation.

Making two quick visits to places of refuge for the poor, she found neither building had the neon sign she'd remembered seeing. Before leaving the last location, she had a word with a nun who told her of one more mission in the area, but it was out of the way in correspondence to the church and cemetery. She concluded she was doing nothing more than covering the same ground Matheson and others in his agency had already covered. She kept thinking there had to be a logical reason for why no one could find this mission, and in her mind, locating it was the key to discovering where their hideaway was and getting her son back.

The cabby waited for further instructions, asking, "Is there any place else I can take you to, miss? I know Brooklyn like the back of my hand."

Linda had a thought and replied, "Take me to Our Savior Church. Do you know where it is?"

"Sure, I grew up in that neighborhood."

Bothered by whatever reason the kidnappers had for choosing Our Savior Church for a meeting place, she had no idea what role that church played in this affair. However, they'd seemingly used that appointed time for their meeting at the church because they knew it was usually empty at that time of day. At least one person in their group must be a Catholic, and this made her think of the woman, Adele. She may have gone to a parochial school when growing up, gaining knowledge about the Catholic religion, before falling in with these criminals. Needing a meeting place where they could exchange information without someone identifying them, confessionals made for an ideal way to confer while hiding one's identity. They saw how the doors to that particular confessional worked to block a person's view and shield them as they exited the church.

As the taxi pulled up in front of the church, Linda realized she'd be losing precious time investigating what was nothing more than a typical Catholic church. Time being critical, she knew the kidnappers still hadn't phoned her home because Louise would've contacted her as soon as that occurred. Choosing to instruct the cabdriver to take her to Mount Sinai Cemetery, after the taxi dropped her off there, she glimpsed the map she carried while walking to the very spot where Gensler met his death the night before. Looking at the path begun by a dead man, she noticed the fire department must've hosed down the pavement to wash away his blood.

It came to her that he had a definite course in mind when choosing to run in this direction, as it may have been the shortest route to their hideout. For now, this was her best lead. It appeared he was aiming for the alley across the street before the chase ended, but the alleyway looked like no place for her to travel. She decided to take to the street running just south of the alley, walking in a northwesterly direction, but parallel with the alley Gensler ran for. She'd thought it a strong possibility that their hideout was between the cemetery and Our Savior Church, but realized, as Gensler was moving in a northwesterly direction, he was moving away from these locations. She passed by a string of deserted row houses facing her from each side of the street. The neighborhood was rough and run down, and coming to a street corner, she nearly decided to turn back. It seemed useless to go on, but she remained steadfast, telling herself over and over again, *Just one more block.*

Linda came upon a black woman carrying a grocery bag from her car, and she approached her. "Excuse me, could you tell me if there's a mission close by?"

The woman's eyes squinted. "A mission?"

"What I mean is a place of refuge for the poor, a home, or shelter for unwed mothers, anything that may be a charitable organization?"

The woman shook her head no. "There's nothing like that in this neighborhood that I know of. Are you sure you know what you're looking for?"

Linda sighed. "Not exactly, I just know I'm looking for a mission and I was led to believe it was located in this area."

"You're not going to find anything like that down this way, and if you journey just a few more blocks you're going to come to the Upper New York Bay area where there's nothing but commercial plants."

Linda gave a nod, and said, "Well, thanks."

Linda had been walking northwesterly on a street south of the alley that Gensler looked to be going for just before the car struck him. She now deliberated on whether to walk to the next street on the opposite side of the alleyway before starting back. The idea was to make a turn at the next intersection and then walk to the following corner before reversing direction for starting back to the cemetery. That way she'd be walking parallel with the next row of houses backing up to the same alleyway, and by doing so, she'd be able to see more viewing area on her walk back to the main boulevard. Turning right at the next cross street, she passed the alley in question, and then walked on to the next intersecting street to turn right and go back to the boulevard where she'd begun her trip by foot. Trying to grasp the memory of that night when they released her, but recalling few details, she still felt convinced that Gensler had a particular reason for starting for that alleyway. Proceeding to walk parallel with this same alley, but going in the opposite direction to head southeast, she kept imagining in her mind that MISSION sign she'd seen.

What she saw up ahead didn't look promising, but then the wind changed and Linda caught a whiff of a familiar industrial odor that aroused her senses. Remembering that unmistakable chemical odor made her believe she was on the right track. Knowing they were holding her son somewhere nearby, it annoyed her to think she was so close, but with so little to go on, she had no idea of where to go from here. She felt lost without seeing a landmark to give her a fix on which way to go, as catching sight of the neon MISSION sign hanging vertically over the walk was her best chance for finding the kidnappers' hideout.

Not wanting to quit and head back now, but having no idea which direction to turn to, she saw little use in carrying on the search for the kidnappers' hideout. At the next corner, she stopped when her eyes caught sight of the tail-end of a car sticking out from the garage entrance of an auto repair shop halfway down the street. Buildings and residences on the block were basically the same red brick style, but there was no doubt something about that auto repair shop drew her attention. The only commercial building on this street, she then saw how there were few cars parked near this garage for servicing.

Crossing the street to begin moving in the direction of the auto repair shop, she turned her focus to the sign attached to the structure. A sign jutting vertically over the walk read TRANS-MISSION, and studying the design of the letters, she said out loud to herself, "The sign—that's the neon sign!"

Running toward the garage, she scrutinized the lettering in detail, and following their shape, she detected a break in the coiled tubular glass. The break came after the first syllable in the word—TRANS, at a joint that linked it with the remaining letters—MISSION. Expecting this to be why she had seen nothing more than the word MISSION, she then saw a sign in the window which read Transmission Specialists and another that read Transmission and Motor Service.

She passed through the garage entrance beneath an overhead door looking to ask someone to switch on the sign as a way to prove to herself she was right. Crossing a concrete floor blackened with grease and oil stains, there were two cars propped up on hydraulic racks, and in a third stall was a delivery van with the hood open. A pair of legs in dark overalls hung out from beneath the van, as the mechanic was lying on his back on a flat cart, tampering with something underneath the vehicle as he maneuvered a droplight.

Unable to see the mechanic's face, she tried to think of a reason to converse about the sign, saying, "Excuse me, but could I trouble you for a minute?"

He remained beneath the vehicle, saying in a grumpy voice, "If it's an estimate you need, you'll have to wait for Ralph. He just left to go for parts."

"Your sign out front on the building...I believe it's in need of repair, and I know it's an odd request, but could I ask you to turn it on?"

"The sign's been on the fritz for about a week, and Ralph is considering replacing it, but he'll be gone for at least another hour running for parts."

Growing impatient because of the loss of valuable time, Linda was convinced the sign hanging outside was the one she saw that night. Turning to the overhead garage door, she saw an exposed electrical conduit channel from a wall switch running up the wall, and understood how this switch controlled electricity going to that outside sign. She flipped it, then went outside to view the sign. The first five letters from the top down—TRANS—were out, and the remaining letters pulling power had lit up to read MISSION.

Finding accomplishment in this discovery, she went back inside to switch the light off, and closed her eyes to think back and recall her movements from before the time the taxi picked her up. Her memory was foggy, as they'd just released her after the interrogation, and she had trouble getting her bearings for considering which way to go. Moving along to a string of deserted, connecting brownstone row houses with jutting bay windows that looked familiar, at the next corner, she stopped to retrace her steps.

Managing to double back the way she'd gone that night, looking down a dead end street, she saw a ten-foot-high chain-link fence where there were huge stockpiles of coal. Deciding to go in the opposite direction, after walking a short distance, she saw parked in the alleyway a gray four-door Mercedes and approached the automobile. A pair of dark sunglasses hanging from the rearview mirror gave her mixed emotions, sparking remembrances of her abduction from a Manhattan street corner. In her mind, she saw the car's rear door thrown open and a dark-haired man peering over his sunglasses at her from the driver's seat. She knew the Mercedes to be the car used in her abduction, and they'd parked it behind the building where they'd interrogated her. Now taking notice of the building's rear exit and remembering leaving the building that night, she recognized the light fixture over the door that had drawn a swarm of flying insects.

The building's door suddenly opened and out came the one-armed man, John Mehlnick, with a set of keys dangling in his only hand. Surprised and dumbfounded by her presence, he dropped his keys and reached inside his sport coat to grab a concealed revolver, but never revealed it.

Alert and watchful as he stepped back inside the doorway, he asked, "What are you doing here?"

Just now taking notice that he had one arm, she said, "I've come to tell you I'm still willing to make the trade if you people are ready to deal straight with me—the disc for my son."

He looked about for a sign of police, and coming to assume that she came alone, he removed his hand from his coat. "OK, come with me."

Linda wasn't sure if she was doing the right thing by entering the building, but not wanting to fuel these people's suspicions, and hoping to see her son, she stepped inside.

Bracing his foot against the door to allow Linda to enter the building, Mehlnick then bent over to pick up the keys he'd dropped, and then closed and secured the door.

Turning abruptly, he took out his revolver, pressing his forearm against her chest while placing his pistol's barrel against her cheekbone to force her against a wall. "If you've brought the police I'll blow your head off!"

Her eyes gaping at the hand holding the revolver, she insisted, "I came alone."

He used his pistol to point, signaling for her to lead the way, and they started up into the building, taking a staircase to a landing where four doors intersected. Mehlnick rapped the butt of his revolver against the door twice, and Adele opened it to see Linda standing next to him. "You fool," she hissed. "You shouldn't have brought her here."

"I found her in the alley. What do we do with her?"

Adele looked Linda straight in the eye. "What did you hope to achieve by coming here, Mrs. Moreland?"

"I didn't bring the disc, but I'm still willing to make the trade and exchange the disc for my son. Can I see him?"

Adele coldly said, "When we learned the man we sent to the cemetery was killed, we moved your son to a safe place outside the city." The woman then looked to Mehlnick and said, "Keep her here." She passed them by to enter a room at the far end of the landing, closing the door behind her.

The one-armed man kept his gun barrel pointed at Linda, and she asked him, "Can you tell me if my child is in good health?"

Mehlnick replied, "Keep quiet. We'll ask the questions."

Using his one hand, he returned the pistol to the inside of his jacket and brought out an open pack of cigarettes. He shook it to raise a few from the pack, using his lips to pull one out. He returned the pack to his coat and then lit the cigarette with the flick of a lighter, taking a deep drag while shifting to a more relaxed stance.

Linda could hear Adele speaking to someone, and then she opened the door to stand at the threshold. "Bring her in here."

The dark room ahead was unoccupied except for a set of chairs accompanying a desk with a lamp. Linda immediately recognized it to be the room they'd interrogated her in, but it no longer held the bed. Staring at the desk and lamp, Linda felt uncomfortable about being there and it showed.

Mehlnick closed the door and stood guard while Adele spoke with a tone of authority. "Your visit comes as a surprise." She took a chair at the desk, a cell phone lying in plain view on the desktop. "Won't you please sit down, Mrs. Moreland. We don't intend to keep you long."

Linda took a chair to sit opposite Adele, who said, "We want to hear your account of what happened to the man we sent to meet you last night. He was supposed to bring us the disc, but instead he got himself killed, so describe what occurred at the cemetery and tell us how his demise came about."

"He tried killing me. I came expecting to trade the disc for my son, but when I found out he didn't bring my son, I resisted giving him the disc, and then he tried strangling me." Linda removed the scarf from her neck to display the marks left by the rope.

Adele commented, "Before your son is released, we must verify that the disc is authentic. When you wouldn't hand over the disc, he must've become carried away with his orders, but no harm would have come to you if you'd given him the disc."

"You people have given me every reason not to trust you. The understanding was that you were to give me Allan when I first delivered you the file at the cemetery. The same thing happened the other day at the church—you people wouldn't allow me to see my son then either. When am I going to be able to see him?"

"Before continuing our discussion, tell us how this man was killed."

"He lured me to the mausoleum's lower level by lying to me about having brought my son to the cemetery, and then demanded I give him the disc. When I refused, he tried strangling me with a length of rope, but I fought him off, and in the struggle, his eyeglasses were broken. I escaped with him chasing me into traffic on that boulevard, and that's when a car struck and killed him."

Adele scoffed, "I don't believe you. The idea this man was killed in such a way is ridiculous."

"I don't care if you believe me or not, the real trouble is that you're finding it difficult to trust me, and you're making it impossible for me to trust you."

Adele glanced at her one-armed associate, and then reached for the cell phone lying on the desk to talk to someone who'd been listening on speaker. Taking the phone off speaker, she said, "I suppose you picked up her voice well enough to hear what she said?"

She then paused to listen, before replying, "Mrs. Moreland says she's still willing to exchange the disc for her son, and

I will explain everything to her carefully to make certain she understands."

Unsure of what they were going to do, Linda's eyes kept going from Adele to Mehlnick.

Adele placed the cell phone back on the desk. "If you want to be reunited with your son, you'll have to bring us the disc, and it will have to be examined at the time of the trade. We're not going to make an exchange without knowing what we're trading for. There must be verification that you're not handing over to us nothing more than a blank computer disc."

She changed her tone to add, "There's truth in what you've said about us both operating in an atmosphere of mistrust. I know you were disappointed when we asked you to return to Washington for the disc. It was unfortunate that the file didn't contain the information we needed, but we would've completed the trade already if you'd complied by bringing the disc to the church as we'd requested.

"Tomorrow morning at 10 a.m., you'll receive a phone call giving you a new set of instructions, and if they're followed correctly, you'll be allowed to spend time with your child while we confirm the disc's authenticity. I promise you won't be disappointed the next time we meet. Your son will be present, and I assure you that if the disc is genuine, you and your child will be free to go. If the disc is not what we hoped it to be, so long as we have no reason to believe you've deceived us, you and your son will still be given your freedom. It's that simple."

Her face held a serious expression as she added, "I find it necessary to warn you again, Mrs. Moreland, that if you go to the authorities you'll never see your son again. I have given you my word and pledged our cooperation in this matter—we want mother and child reunited. I cannot stress enough the importance of getting past this impasse. We must move ahead in good faith and remove the barrier of mistrust before failure leads to disastrous consequences. I hope I'm making myself clear."

"Can I at least see him?"

"Your son is not here, but if he were, I would say yes."

"You're just going to let her walk?" asked Mehlnick, standing at the door.

Adele leaned back in her chair. "If the authorities were here they would've moved on the building by now, so let her go."

Escorted out of the building by Mehlnick, Linda squinted as her eyes adjusted to the bright sunshine, but she still saw the license number of the Mercedes and memorized it. Her surprise arrival had alarmed them, and starting back toward the cemetery, she knew that even though they were highly suspect of her going to the police, they let her go. It was nice to see them in the hot seat for once, but the woman had given her clear warning that their next meeting must go off without a hitch. She had the distinct impression they were under pressure to show results, as though this ordeal had dragged on too long, and a time-sensitive element was urging them to acquire the disc.

Linda recalled how after her arrival, Adele had made a phone call, and after conferring with someone, her icy composure had returned. What had she learned during that phone call that restored her confidence? Could she have checked with the spy who'd infiltrated American intelligence? Had he given her assurances that all was safe, and had it been him who had conveyed the instruction to permit Linda to leave the premises?

The interrogation room had reawakened remembrances of being under the influence of a powerful drug as they questioned her beneath a lamp. It crossed her mind that the agent Matheson wanted to identify may have been one of those figures in the room. Reliving how the drug had lowered her resistance and imposed a willingness to answer questions, she tried recounting what had transpired in an attempt to see others standing in that dark room, but couldn't. This so-called double agent must stay in contact with his collaborators to monitor their progress in their quest to obtain the disc, using whatever means at his disposal to warn his comrades of any threat of outside intervention. Constantly on her mind was whether her contact with Matheson had leaked out, but it seemed unlikely they'd let her go had they known this. Or were they simply growing desperate in their efforts to acquire the disc?

Linda knew this test of wills had to end soon, as she couldn't hold them off much longer, and the tight spot the government had placed her in had her worried. Her next chilling thought was, *In the event that they learn about Matheson, or if they already know of his involvement, what's going to happen to Allan and me once they get their hands on the disc?*

CHAPTER 13

A Game of Mistrust and Evasion

Linda waited until she'd distanced herself a few blocks from the kidnappers' hideaway before calling Matheson's number, pushing her hair back to bring the cell phone firmly against her right ear.

"Hello?"

Barely hearing Matheson's voice over street sounds when nearing the corner, she covered her left ear with the palm of her left hand. "It's Linda Moreland. I've found their hideout."

"Do you have an address?"

A truck shifting through gears drowned out the sound of his voice. "I can't hear you."

"An address, do you have an address?"

"No, I've only seen the rear of the building from the alleyway, but I can show you where it is."

"Where are you calling from?"

"I'm in Brooklyn, standing at Third Avenue and Ninth Street. I can see a recruiting station across the street, and if you can hang on for a second I can get you an address."

"I'll be there in less than thirty minutes. Wait inside the recruiting station."

A short time later, Matheson pulled up in front of the recruiting station and Linda joined him. Having written down the license number of the Mercedes, she handed it over to him, and then directed him to their hideout while describing what had happened. She explained how she'd mistaken a sign for an auto repair shop for a mission, and what had occurred after she spotted the Mercedes parked behind the building.

Nearing that building's location, she saw a dark thunder-cloud, but immediately realized it was black smoke and ash from a fire rising into the atmosphere. Up ahead, fire and emergency vehicles had the street and alleyway blocked, and a firefighter perched three stories high on a ladder was spraying water into a window where there were flames.

She downheartedly said, "The building in flames is their hideout."

Matheson steered to the curb, turning the car's engine off. "Wait here. I'm going to get a closer look and see what I can find out."

"I want to go with you. Allan could be in there."

"How will it look to the kidnappers if you're seen standing out here? Just stay put and I'll be back in a few minutes."

Linda watched and waited as Matheson disappeared into the crowd down the block. She slumped in the car seat to avoid looks from passersby who may be part of the kidnappers' organization. She thought she'd lost her last chance to get her son back, as this could have been their revenge for her going to the authorities, and she feared for the discovery of Allan's charred remains later in the rubble.

Matheson returned to the car in a matter of minutes, saying, "Firefighters believe the building was vacant at the time it caught fire."

Suddenly, the building's roof collapsed, causing people to scatter as smoke and flames rose into the sky, and the sight of it disturbed Linda.

Matheson drove her back to Staten Island, and during the ride, he phoned his department to learn the license number registration for the Mercedes was the same as the address of the fire. Holding the gut feeling she'd failed her son, Linda saw little chance of ever seeing Allan again.

When Matheson dropped Linda off near her home, she put her hand on the door handle, but hesitated pulling it long enough to say, "It's unlikely I'll hear from those people again. Perhaps the person who infiltrated the CIA learned about the Defense Department's involvement and after telling the others, the building was set on fire to destroy evidence before they pulled out."

Matheson replied, "I know you're worried about your boy, but I doubt they would've released you had they suspected you'd gone to the authorities. Judging by what you've told me, the woman did say she'd phone you in the morning, so there's a high likelihood they're going to make at least one more attempt at an exchange. If they do call, you'll be able to complete the trade, so don't give up hope. However, at the next meeting I expect the individual responsible for the leak in security to come forward to verify the disc's authenticity, and that means this may be my best chance to identify him."

"What if you're somehow able to catch a few of them, but they still have Allan? What's going to happen to him? You people aren't concerned about what happens to my son."

Linda got out of the car, and watching her walk away, Matheson felt lousy about how things were, and as much as he wanted to do more to help her, there was nothing he could do. He was having deep feelings for this woman who had radiant beauty, stamina, and nerve, and she'd won his respect by standing up to these people. Unsure of how much more of this she could take, he thought she must hate him for being a part of this awful predicament she'd fallen into.

That evening, Linda wasn't sure whether she'd hear from the kidnappers again, but the woman calling herself Adele had told her to expect a call at 10 a.m. She sensed urgency from them, and the fact that they'd given her freedom to leave their hideout gave her a glimmer of hope that they'd contact her. In the event a foreign power was willing to pay an enormous amount of money to obtain information on the disc, the potential buyer may have been becoming demanding and impatient.

Before going upstairs to bed that night, she asked Louise, "Is Mr. Koenig still with us?"

"Oh, yes, but I think he's feeling ill. That man drinks too much coffee."

In response to Louise's concern for Koenig, Linda remarked with a touch of contempt, "The poor dear."

Linda did not sleep well, and was dressed and watching the phone long before 10 a.m., when precisely at that time, her home phone rang. Upon answering it, she heard a voice say, "Bring the disc to the Ambassador Auto Leasing Agency in the Plaza Shopping Center in Staten Island, and ask for a man named Robert Kranze."

She phoned for a cab, but then used her cell phone to call Matheson to let him know she'd received instructions to meet a man named Robert Kranze at this leasing agency. Matheson told her he'd catch up to her there and he'd have her under surveillance, but cautioned her that the opposition would also be watching her. He then advised her not to use her cell phone to make calls, but asked her to leave it on in case he needed to reach her.

Wearing the same blazer she'd worn in recent days when out and about, she had the disc, and soon a taxi picked her up to take her to the auto leasing agency. Dropped off at the entrance to a modern commercial building surrounded by late model cars of various makes, she paid the driver and entered the building.

A young woman at an information desk gave her a pleasant smile, saying, "Hello, may I help you?"

"I'm looking for Robert Kranze."

"Mr. Kranze stepped out for a moment, but if you'd care to take a seat, he'll be back in a few minutes." The girl turned her attention to paperwork spread before her.

Linda sat down in a comfortable chair to wait, wondering what sort of elaborate game the kidnappers were playing now. Less than a minute later, she saw a white Ford Taurus swing into a parking space in front of the building, and the driver, a tall, lanky male in a dark blue suit with dark, wavy hair, got out of the car.

Linda thought he might be Robert Kranze, and when he entered the leasing agency, the woman at the information desk motioned for him to take notice of Linda. "Bob, this young lady wishes to speak with you."

He looked at Linda. "Hello. You must be Mrs. Moreland."

"Yes, I am."

"Please come this way to fill out a couple of forms." He ushered her to another counter where he had paperwork laid out.

Confused about the situation, Linda followed, keeping her mouth shut.

"Your neighbor Mrs. Dressler mentioned she felt awful about her son running into your car and how she was trying to avoid involving her insurance company, while at the same time compensating you. She paid three days rental fee on a car, even paying for additional insurance coverage, but since you'll be driving the car, as a matter of procedure, I'll need to see your driver's license and a major credit card."

Linda withheld comment, speculating Mrs. Dressler was Adele, and she'd made prior arrangements with the leasing company. A copy of a receipt showed she'd furnished cash as payment.

After he'd finished taking down information to complete the forms, the salesman photocopied her credit card and license. "There are some definite advantages to leasing, and I'd like to leave this brochure with you so you can acquaint yourself with some of them." He handed her the brochure with a copy of the rental lease, and returned her cards to her with a business card of his own. Linda put them in her purse with her billfold.

"Should you wish to keep the car longer than three days, you'll have to stop by so we can update the paperwork." With that, he picked up the vehicle's keys, saying, "That Ford Taurus I just parked in the space out front is your vehicle."

She followed him outside, where he handed her the car keys, saying, "On the passenger seat is a manila envelope Mrs. Dressler asked me to give you containing insurance information pertaining to the accident her son had with you."

After thanking him, Linda sat behind the wheel and reached for the envelope lying on the seat beside her to find explicit instructions left by the kidnappers. A folding map with a route highlighted in yellow indicated her destination in rural southern New Jersey. From the car rental agency, she was to get on the New Jersey Turnpike and take it to Camden, and from there head south on Highway 55. Getting off at one of the Vineland exits at Highway 56, she would drive west before coming to the Indian Hills Motor Lodge, where she had to locate cabin number 12. The letter made mention of Torre's filling station at the Vineland exit, which allowed her a place to stop and top off her fuel tank if she needed to. The letter emphasized in capital letters: FOLLOW ONLY THE DESIGNATED TRAVEL ROUTE AND TALK TO NO ONE.

Not wanting to delay and draw suspicion, she started up the car's engine and drove onto the boulevard bound for the New Jersey Turnpike. Soon getting on the Staten Island Expressway's entry ramp, she looked in her rearview mirror and recognized Matheson tailing her in his tan Impala at a distance of three car lengths. He temporarily removed his dark sunglasses to show her it was him, and she merged into traffic and climbed to the fifty-five miles per hour speed limit. Matheson gradually dropped back until he was out of sight.

When reaching the New Jersey Turnpike, Linda took a winding ramp to get on I-95. Heading southbound, she saw Matheson in her rearview mirror, but soon lost sight of him again. Nearing Camden, she again spotted Matheson in the mirror following her at a safe distance. She got on the interchange to take Highway 55 southward, and it being essential that Matheson keep his distance, he eased back out of sight.

Occupied with the road, she remained in the center lane, wondering what may be awaiting her at this Indian Hills Lodge, and soon she noticed storm clouds forming. Scattered raindrops on the windshield quickly multiplied, and crackling thunder vibrated the dashboard as she switched on the windshield wipers. The rain soon came down heavily, and while some cars pulled over, Linda kept going, but slowed down to forty miles per hour, switching the wipers to high and doing the best she could to keep the automobile in its lane.

She heard the chime of her cell phone, and answered it. "Hello."

There was static on the line, and then she heard, "It's Jack Matheson. Before I lose you, can you tell me what your destination is?"

"When I reach Highway 56 at one of the Vineland exits, there's a Torre's filling station where they gave me the OK to stop and top off my fuel tank. From there, I'm to go west on Highway 56 for five miles until reaching a place called the Indian Hills Motor Lodge where I'm to locate cabin 12."

"I'd suggest stopping and filling your tank because you may still have more driving ahead of you." The phone went dead as Matheson hung up.

After a short time, the heavy rains halted, the sky began clearing, and seeing a vivid rainbow on the horizon, she pressed the accelerator to retake the speed limit. Occasionally glancing in the mirror, she hadn't seen Matheson for some time, and taking in the view of the scenic rural countryside, she saw rich, fertile farmland neatly sectioned off for corn, vegetables, and wheat.

When seeing signs for the Vineland exits, she slowed down to give Matheson time to catch up, but never saw his car behind her. Veering to the far right-hand lane, she caught sight of a sporty blue BMW she'd seen behind her earlier. The blue sedan kept its distance as it followed her. Taking the Vineland exit at Highway 56, when approaching the bottom of the ramp, she kept watch of the BMW through the rearview mirror, and as she signaled to turn right, the blue sedan signaled to turn left.

Braking for the upcoming red light, she tried to get a look at the driver of the BMW as he momentarily came up beside her, but hardly got a glimpse of him. After completing her right turn, she pulled into Torre's filling station, splashing through a puddle before stopping at one of the pumps. The cool air after the storm felt refreshing, and certain there'd be someone watching her filling her gas tank, she acted as if she didn't notice Matheson as he drove past the station.

After leaving the gas station, Linda traveled west on Highway 56, a recently paved two-lane road, and looking in her rearview mirror, she saw no one following her. Matheson knew Indian Hills Motor Lodge was her destination and that she was to go to cabin 12, and she believed he'd gone on ahead to the lodge to keep watch there.

The storm had scattered freshly broken tree limbs on the road, but the sky appeared to be clearing, and before reaching the motor lodge, she saw a sign for Rainbow Lake. Soon afterwards, she came upon a large tree in the road brought down by a lightning strike, and county workers were making slow progress dismantling it with chainsaws.

Stopped behind one of their trucks, she rolled down her window to speak to a man wearing a yellow cap and a bright orange ski vest, asking, "Will it be long before the road is opened?"

"It may be another twenty minutes, but some folks have avoided the wait by doubling back and heading north to go west on Almond Road, which snakes around."

"Thanks, but I'm unfamiliar with the area, so I think I'll wait the twenty minutes."

The highway worker looked into the sky. "They say more bad weather is expected later this evening."

The next time Linda looked in her rearview mirror, she saw a man in a white trenchcoat standing in front of a blue BMW parked thirty feet behind her on the roadside. Thinking it to be the same BMW seen following her earlier, she didn't recognize the car's driver. Considering he may be one of them, he had a grim expression and dark hair with a touch of gray.

Workers cut a large limb from the tree lying across the road and dragged it out of the way to open up a lane for traffic. Linda went on her way, but the blue BMW wasn't following. The man in the trenchcoat remained standing outside his car, and she suspected she may be seeing more of him later. Losing Matheson disturbed her, and she didn't think there was much chance he'd gone on ahead of her. He would've had to wait for the road to open just like she had.

Linda arrived at the Indian Hills Motor Lodge. This picturesque area was much like being in the mountains, and the main building was a stone structure set in a hillside amid tall fir trees. Remembering the instructions told her to find cabin 12, she followed the drive moving up an incline, and veered off to the right where the road split off in front of the lodge. A decorative stone wall encircled blocks of stone etched with letters that read Indian Hills Motor Lodge.

Linda took the paved road around to the rear of the lodge where there was a parking lot. From there, the road began a wide, sweeping circle around a cluster of mature trees shading the grounds. Patches of sunlight and shadow ran across the hood of the car, and well-spaced A-framed cabins came into view facing the drive, each marked by a white number above their door. There was sufficient parking for two cars in front of each cabin, and a few recreational vehicles occupied these spaces. There were barbecue pits teamed up with picnic tables at each site.

Passing the tenth and eleventh cabins, and noticing a big spread to the twelfth, she saw a station wagon parked at that next cabin where youngsters were tossing around a Frisbee. Looking at the number above the cabin door, she was surprised to see the numeral 13. She stopped to look back and view the last cabin she'd passed.

Passing the cabins, which ran in numerical order, she found it hard to believe she'd passed by cabin 12, but she apparently had. Backing up the car until she could read the number over the door of the last cabin, she saw the numeral 11 and she asked herself, "What happened to 12?"

The spread between cabins 11 and 13 caused her to make a visual search of the open ground between them. All that remained of cabin 12 was a stone fireplace and chimney stack that blended with the surroundings. Cabin 12 had burned down long ago, and remembering the burning building in Brooklyn, she wondered if the remnants of this burned-out cabin were supposed to mean something, but concluded it was merely a meeting place.

Linda parked the car, stepped out to stretch her legs, and began walking about a concrete slab that had once been the floor of cabin 12. While she waited at the site, Matheson was also waiting, as he didn't want to show up too soon at the Indian Hills Motor Lodge out of concern his presence may ratchet up the kidnappers' growing suspicion and mistrust. Should those people spot anyone in the vicinity of the lodge looking anything like a government agent, it could endanger both Linda and her son. He knew outwitting these people wasn't going to be easy, and understood she may not be at this cabin 12 for long, expecting they'd take her to another location. In the event that he lost her, he believed he could still track her by the GPS in her cell phone.

CHAPTER 14

Outsmarting the Opposition

Pacing the open space formerly occupied by cabin 12, Linda waited ten minutes before hearing a car coming, and sunlight reflecting off the windshield flashed in her eyes. The automobile was the blue BMW she'd seen earlier, and not knowing what to expect next, she knew she was going to have to play by the kidnappers' terms to see her son. She posed no threat to them, and hoping they'd cooperate this time and complete the trade, she assured herself that once they had possession of the disc, they would have no reason to detain her and Allan any longer.

The BMW pulled up beside the white Taurus, and she sensed the driver was the replacement for the man who'd strong-armed her at the cemetery and later died after getting hit by a car.

The man stepped out of the blue sedan in his white trench-coat, leaving the car door open as he placed his forearm against the roofline. "If your name is Linda Moreland, I'm supposed to take you to your son – that's if you've brought the disc."

"I've got it. I suppose I'm to follow you?"

He shook his head no. "I'm to take you there myself, and if everything goes as planned, I'll bring you back to your car later."

"I don't like leaving the car here. Why can't I follow you?"

"That's not for me to say, but if you want to see your boy, you'll have to come with me and wear this." Dangling from his left hand was a black blindfold.

"What assurances do I have that my son is still alive?"

"I wasn't sent here to persuade you to come, but I saw your boy earlier today and he's doing just fine. Your car is perfectly safe where it is. Leave all of your personal belongings in the car, and just bring the keys."

This man was a little more polished than some of the others Linda had encountered, but his uncaring attitude didn't fool her. These people were counting on her desire to see her son to lure her into coming along with him, and right now, she'd walk barefoot through a bed of red-hot coals to get him back. Having little choice in the matter, but not wanting to be blamed for losing the disc, she wondered where Matheson was.

"Are you declining the invitation?"

"No, I'm coming."

Placing her purse on the floorboard of the Taurus, she remembered Matheson telling her that her phone had a global positioning transmitter, and she made sure she still carried it in her coat.

"One last thing. Before we go you'll have to show me the disc."

Pulling the case out of the hip pocket of her blazer for him to read the TRIAD inscription, she then returned it to her pocket and locked the car door. She came over to the BMW, and he gently but firmly turned her around to put the blindfold on her, and after securing it, he ran his fingers up and down her body to search for weapons. He felt the disc in the hip pocket of her blazer and in the other hip pocket was some cash he gave little attention to. Discovering her cell phone in the inside breast pocket of her blazer, he allowed her to keep it, but switched it off, and then guided her down into the backseat of the car where he had her lie down.

Linda heard him get in the driver's seat to start the engine, and listened while concentrating on the car's shifting movement as her journey began. The car soon took to the main road, and momentum pulling her to the passenger side gave indication the car was turning left to go in a westerly direction. Later feeling her weight shift again to the right, she now believed the car had turned southward, but numerous dips and curves made it difficult to follow any change of direction.

A jolt came as the car turned onto a gravel road. In less than a minute, the car came to a halt and the engine lost power. She estimated the trip had taken twenty minutes. She listened for the driver's movements as he got out of the car, and then he opened the rear passenger door to help Linda to her feet.

"Careful now. Rise up slowly so you don't bump your head."

Steady on her feet, he guided her twenty paces. "We're starting up some steps, and we'll take them one at a time."

The steps felt solid underfoot, like stone or concrete, and when they came to a porch area she heard a door open. After stepping inside, she heard it close. He removed the blindfold and she saw a spacious entry hall with a high ceiling, dominated by the sweeping curve of a staircase, and an elegant Persian rug in brown, blue, and gold partially covered the hardwood floor. A cherry wood table, with a ceramic vase holding a decorative floral arrangement, was centered in the curve of the staircase. At the end of the hall, beyond a doorway, she saw a long dining table before white curtains, and opposite the base of the stairs, tall sliding doors hid what Linda assumed to be the parlor. She waited patiently, not knowing who may come.

Matheson arrived at the resort twenty minutes behind Linda's departure from the lodge. He wore a look of dismay when he came upon the white Ford Taurus, and saw that no cabin 12 existed. He'd avoided entering the lodge grounds sooner for concern they might recognize his car as one they'd seen on the highway, but now he realized he'd made a mistake, for he worried that he'd lost her. He ran his fingers through his hair before attempting to track her by the GPS transmitter in her phone, but his phone's receiver wasn't picking up a signal. He concluded it may have been because of this remote location or interference from storms in the area. Unsure if she was still carrying her phone, he looked in the car's interior and saw her purse tucked up against the car seat on the floorboard.

Guessing their true destination wasn't far from the resort, he recalled Linda's description of a gray Mercedes she'd given him the license number for. The registration had connected it to the fire-damaged building in Brooklyn under the name of a nonexistent company, but he believed they'd used this vehicle to transport her to their hideout. He reported to Washington.

Losing her nearly resulted in a huge dragnet being thrown over the area to find her and recover the disc, but his supervisors decided it best to hold back and give Matheson more time. Their concerns were that such a move would alarm the kidnappers, putting Linda and her child in danger, but the Defense Intelligence Agency's first priority still remained to snare the man responsible for the leak in classified information. First and foremost, Matheson's assignment was to track down and identify, or dispose of, the party accountable for the leak in top secret material. Eliminating their security leak was of the utmost importance, and they understood that any large scale attempt to locate Linda was sure to alert the individual they were closing in.

Defense Intelligence dispatched a few more agents to scour the area to locate their best lead—the gray Mercedes. A search of the white Ford Taurus left agents believing Linda still had her cell phone with her, and agency technicians had begun using a sophisticated tracking system to pinpoint the signal from Linda's cell phone. They even engaged defense sources especially equipped for accurately chartering the geographic location of military objects to make a computerized link-up with the tracking device in her phone, but that all took precious time.

Consequently, Matheson went on searching for her. He felt relieved at having been granted time to locate Linda, but he also felt pressure, as a favorable outcome depended on him finding her soon. Entangled in Linda's fate, he knew Linda had walked into this situation with faith that he and his department would provide her protection, and he didn't want to fail her. For the time being, she'd be completely on her own and would have to do what she could to survive this latest ordeal.

The next twenty-four hours were critical. If they hadn't located Linda and the disc by then, there would be great danger that the kidnappers would murder her, while fumbling the agency's best chance for discovering the source of their leak. Matheson expected that, before that time, intelligence services would deploy a massive search involving local law enforcement to locate the disc. Such a move could invite media coverage that would expose Linda, endangering mother and child.

Adele came to meet with Linda in the entrance hall of this stylishly decorated home, and the driver of the BMW walked into the dining room, turning left to disappear from sight.

Wearing the intimidating grin Linda had grown to loathe and despise, Adele spoke cordially, saying, "I'm glad you chose to come, Mrs. Moreland. Please follow me."

Linda followed her host as they passed through the dining room. They went to the right to enter the library, where an entire wall housed books. Curtains drawn on two sets of French doors enabled her to see a terrace and a rose garden outside. Between these sets of doors sat a bulky desk and a burgundy leather-upholstered wingback chair. On the wall behind the desk hung an attractive oil painting of a mountain scene, done in fall colors, that gave life to the room, and there were more paintings in various sizes above a velvet maroon sofa. Seeing a tall set of sliding doors similar to those off the entry hall, she imagined these doors gave access to the adjoining parlor as she thought that room backed up to the library.

"Allan is a delightfully well-behaved child, and I don't mind saying I've grown fond of him over these past few days. We've purchased numerous toys to keep him contented, but because we've given him the run of the house, he's difficult to keep track of. May I see the disc?" Adele put her right hand out with her palm up for her to hand over the computer disc.

"The agreement was that I see Allan."

The woman smirked. "I'll be back in a moment with him."

After Adele left the room, Linda paced until she saw on the desk the original file she'd stolen from the defense installation in Washington, D.C., recognizing the bold symbol of an eagle on its cover. The back of the house faced westerly and sunlight reflected off a paperweight into her eyes. Shifting her head's position, she glimpsed outside the French doors to see a rolling downhill slope with few trees. At the bottom of the hill, over fifty meters away, she saw high brush before a raised levee supporting train tracks, and even further beyond were high trees bordering a wide-stretched cornfield.

Growing impatient, she turned when hearing something, but saw no one there. Walking to the far end of the room, she noticed the tall sliding doors were open a few inches. Peeking into the parlor from an angle, she saw fine antique furniture, and although the room appeared unoccupied, there was a small fire flickering in the fireplace. Moving to view another section of the room, she saw Allan on the floor playing with a widespread collection of toys.

A grin grew on her face as she placed her hands between the doors to draw them open, and Allan showed youthful exuberance when running into his mother's arms. "Mommy!"

Tears filled her eyes as they embraced, and kneeling to kiss him, she then gazed at his face—those bright eyes, that smile with those little teeth, and his hair had grown fuller over the past few days.

Suddenly seeing an opportunity, she took hold of her child's arm and led him hurriedly to the French doors to find them locked by a deadbolt requiring a key to unlock. With her heart beating fast, she bit down on her lower lip while squeezing the pocket of her blazer to feel the disc's casing, reassuring herself she still had it.

Thinking Adele and the others were looking for Allan and they'd soon return, she mumbled aloud, "Got to get out of here."

Allan looked up at her with an innocent expression. "What, Mommy?"

She pulled him close to get his full attention, saying in a near whisper, "We're going to leave here and you must be very quiet."

"Quiet like a mouse?"

Linda nodded, placing her index finger to her lips as if to say, "Shhh."

Knowing they'd kill her for leaving and taking the disc, she snatched the defense file from the desk, and beneath it discovered a scribbled message on a notepad. It read, "Wednesday—10 p.m., Auburn Airfield," and had the name Crawford underlined at the bottom of the page.

Allan held her hand tightly, and tucking the file beneath her arm, she escorted him through the dining room to get to a door which she thought led to the kitchen. Remembering the driver of the BMW had gone this way, she hesitated, not knowing who or what lay beyond this door, then decided that her best avenue of escape was to go out the front door.

Intending to get to a car, and hoping to find the keys in it, she stepped into the entry hall, but hearing the sound of voices she stopped. Remaining watchful from the edge of the dining room, she heard faint voices echo down from the staircase to the entrance hall, indicating Adele was conversing with a man at the top of the stairs. Peering at the staircase until she heard their descending footsteps, Linda backed up into the dining room and then to the library. She slipped through the parlor's tall sliding doors where she feverishly sought a way out of the house.

Now trapped in the parlor, she had little time to get out of the house before they found her gone, and she closed the doors quietly behind her. She and her son moved to a nook in a corner where they stood beside a tall glass case displaying colorful ceramic dishes. Standing on end, each bore a picturesque scene from Germany. Finding little space for her and her son to stand in this recessed area, there seemed little chance of anyone seeing them here unless they fully entered the room.

Linda was surprised when the parlor doors opened from the entrance hall. One-armed Mehlnick entered the room, saying, "The last time I saw the boy he was in this room playing on the floor, but he's not here now."

Linda stood stiffly still behind Allan with her hands resting on his shoulders, the glass cabinet shielding them from Mehlnick's view.

She overheard Adele complaining as she stood in the entrance hall. "I'd asked you to keep an eye on him. You don't think he's hiding from us again, or that he's wandered outside?"

"Who knows? He's always disappearing," replied Mehlnick, and after his eyes scanned the room, he closed the sliding doors.

Allan looked up at her and grinned, as though enjoying this game of hide-and-seek, and Linda put her finger to her lips in a serious gesture to let him know he must keep quiet.

Remaining still in the corner of the parlor with her son, Linda now heard activity in the library, and Adele abruptly opened the sliding doors to stand but a short distance away. She stood still, waiting, wide-eyed, for this woman to enter the room and see them.

The woman's voice carried as she announced angrily, "Now the mother's missing. I left her waiting here in the library only a minute ago, and I suspect she's taken the boy and run. I want you and Schmidt to comb the grounds for them immediately."

Adele left the doors linking the library to the parlor open, and their voices dissipated, but Linda then heard activity from the entrance hall, making it evident that they had begun searching the house.

She moved to the fireplace, and after crumpling the file and its pages, she fed it into the fiery hot coals. They quickly smoldered before catching fire. She considered doing the same with the disc, but since Matheson had never given her the OK to destroy this so-called classified information, she decided it may be wise to hang on to something everyone regarded as such a valuable commodity.

Going to one of the room's tall, oblong windows to unlock it to escape the house, but spotting Mehlnick outside viewing the surrounding landscape, she moved from the window without him noticing her. She now went to the tall sliding doors giving access to the entrance hall. She found them left open enough to view that area and see that it appeared unoccupied. She pulled one of the doors open and made a beeline for the front door with her son at her side.

The door to the house was solid oak and larger than most, and opening it ran the risk of meeting up with the kidnappers, but she had little choice. A hard yank pulled it open, and finding nobody on the porch, she went for the gray Mercedes-Benz and BMW parked in a circular driveway, the passenger sides of the cars facing the house.

Hurriedly guiding her son in the direction of the Mercedes in hopes of finding the key in the ignition, a quick glance through the front passenger window allowed her to see the ignition empty. Ducking in a stooped-over manner to approach the driver's side of the BMW, she made it to the driver's door before seeing Mehlnick coming around the house after having circled it. He paused to light up a cigarette while surveying the land.

Adele and the driver of the BMW came out the front door to stand on the porch, and they all appeared mystified about what had happened to Linda and her son. The man in the trenchcoat, who Adele had referred to as Schmidt, wore a serious expression, and she appeared steaming mad as she peered about.

Her voice suddenly rang out. "They couldn't have gone far without transportation, and that woman's a danger to us all, should she get away, so don't stop looking until you've found her."

Holding a crouched position next to the driver's door of the BMW, Linda looked over the rim of the car's body and beyond its interior to observe them through the automobile's glass. Mehlnick flicked his cigarette, and he and Schmidt split up in different directions to continue the search. Adele waited behind on the porch, as though calmly considering Linda's options.

Linda was unable to see if the keys were in the BMW's ignition, and seeing Adele holding the same pose, she opened the door while leaning and scooting forward onto the car seat. Anticipating the buzzer to sound off if the keys were in the ignition, she heard nothing, and yet went on to feel around the steering column to make sure they weren't there. Now thinking her chances of getting away were slim to none, she closed the door ever so gently to get it to catch. Peeking over the rim of the car, she saw that Adele had moved from the porch.

Adele appeared behind her, wearing an ugly scowl. She shouted at the top of her lungs, "I've found them!"

Linda picked up Allan in her arms and made a mad dash in the only direction that seemed to point to freedom—the long downhill slope to the raised levee where railroad tracks ran. This was one way they couldn't pursue her by car, but to have any chance for getting away from them she needed to make the levee before any of the others caught up to her.

"It's useless to run! You'll never get away!" Adele called out, following at a fast walk, confident the others would intercept Linda before she'd gone far.

Unable to make any speed carrying her son in her arms, Linda looked to the bottom of the hill to view the steep levee, imagining it would be difficult climbing the gravel-packed, six-foot-high earthwork. Having doubts whether she'd made the best choice running for the levee, it was too late now to change direction, and she continued pushing herself. The wind against her face, her lungs driving hard to inhale and exhale, halfway down the slope she was barely able to keep up with the rampant pace of her own feet. Realizing that if she kept picking up speed, she'd soon fall flat on her face, she cut back on her stride, and her feet started gliding out from beneath her on the wet, slippery grass. Managing to catch her balance and stay on her feet, she slowed down, but still feared that her feet would slide out from beneath her on the incline of wet grass.

Adele shouted, "Don't let them get away! Shoot her if you must!"

Linda neared the bottom of the slope. Rainwater draining down the hill had left the ground saturated. Hearing the oncoming trot of someone behind her, she never bothered to look back. The one closing in on her was one-armed Mehlnick, and hearing a rumble behind her, she glanced back to see him go down on the slick grass, sliding in a spill that allowed him to gain ground on her. He awkwardly rose to his feet to resume the chase, his clothes and one side of his face smeared with grass and mud. Clumsily advancing, but barely able to stay on his feet, he lost his footing and fell to the ground a second time.

Adele and Schmidt had come halfway down the hill, continuing their descent as they watched Linda arrive at the base of the slope where a wall of thick brush separated her from the levee. Panting from the hard run, she waded through tall grass and waist-high weeds, feeling moisture seeping into her shoes. She sank up to her ankles in soggy, spongy mud. She almost fell trying to pull one foot out of the gooey mud, and leaning forward to recover her balance, she grabbed hold of the stems of weed stalks, their roots holding firm to keep her standing. When trying to pull her right foot out of the mud, her foot came out of her shoe. Then the same happened with the left, and she was able to make steps with soupy mud squishing between her toes. The closer she came to the levee, the more the embankment of packed gravel looked like a big obstacle to climb.

Linda arrived at the mound of gravel and rubble with Mehlnick fast approaching. He'd made it to the weeds trying to catch up to them, but was unable to make better time than her. Stones began to shift and give way as Linda helped Allan up its loosely packed crust, the child crawling on his hands and knees to make it to the top. He stood upon its crest waiting for his mother, but she was out of breath and had trouble getting her footing. Elevating herself partway to lunge for the train rail, her fingers fell short by inches. Falling back, she dug her toes in while pushing off to extend her reach until her fingertips caught hold of the rail.

Mehlnick caught hold of her ankle with a stubborn grip and wouldn't let go, but Linda hung on to the rail. Mehlnick kept tugging on her leg, pulling relentlessly, using his weight to his advantage, and Linda finally released her grip on the rail, sliding on her stomach when slipping back down. She dragged loose stones with her, and when she hit bottom, she slipped in the mud, but Mehlnick braced her up, and now they stood breathless together in the muddy slime. Linda heard something plop in the mud, but whatever it was eluded her, and feeling her blazer to make certain she hadn't lost the disc, she then gave up on whatever it was.

Mehlnick pinned her against the levee. "Don't try anything cute. Just stand still."

"Mommy! Mommy!" Allan screamed as he thought harm was coming to his mother.

Mehlnick reached for the child. "Come here, little boy. Don't be afraid."

Tears flowed down Allan's cheeks, and he cried out, "No!"

Linda felt too exhausted to put up a fight, and standing to the left of the one-armed man with her back resting against the levee, she tried catching her breath. Shifting her weight from one leg to the other, her right hand got a feel for a jagged stone jutting out from the levee, and as it loosened and dislodged from the others, she gripped it.

She swung the stone with force. Mehlnick caught sight of it just before it struck his skull, and he collapsed in the muddy slop with blood running down the side of his face. He watched with a dazed expression as Linda gained a foothold to raise herself up on the levee, and just as she came to face the fading sunset a gunshot rang out. The bullet struck less than six inches from her right leg and she froze in thinking whoever fired missed her deliberately to deter her from going over the levee.

"Now turn around slowly," said Schmidt, speaking to her from the hillside, but she didn't respond.

"I'm going to ask you again to turn around slowly. Don't make me shoot you."

Linda turned around, brushing her hair from her eyes to look at Adele and Schmidt standing on the grassy slope, the sun shining on their faces, and she sat cross-legged, Indian style. Adele was furthest up the hill, but slowly coming this way, and Schmidt stood nearly eye-level with Linda, poised holding a 9-mm pistol aimed for her. Mehlnick had begun pulling himself out of the mud, but he was dizzy and blood was draining from the gash in his head.

Adele made a loudmouthed command. "If she takes one more step, Schmidt, kill her!"

Linda thought the man pointing the pistol at her appeared unstable wearing black imported dress shoes on the wet grass, and when he carefully inched forward, his feet suddenly went out from beneath him.

Acting fast, Linda grabbed Allan's hand and scrambled to the far side of the levee. Schmidt fired a shot, but they'd cleared the levee and were out of sight. Hopeful she'd seen the last of those people, but feared they'd follow. She felt a sense of satisfaction picking up her child to run through a patch of woods bordering a cornfield. Seeking to make it more difficult to detect their position, she plowed into the dense, leafy cornstalks. Allan seemed mystified by the tall vegetation.

An hour later, lost with no sense of direction, Linda thought to use her cell phone, only to realize that the phone was what had plopped in the mud when Mehlnick pulled her down from the levee. She still had the disc and some cash tucked away in the other hip pocket of her blazer, and with Allan leading the way, they moved out of the cornfield to scamper along the edge of a far-reaching bean field. Holding hands, they cut across farmland, daylight turning into a faint glow at the edge of the horizon, darkness beginning to engulf the landscape. Concerned for the unpredictability of her situation, she hoped they'd get through this to find help.

CHAPTER 15

Seeking Shelter

The dark of night fell on the land, and walking barefoot in the soft soil of the bean field with Allan at her side, Linda had grown tired of the sight of this remote area. Grateful to have Allan's company, she was well aware she had a long way to go before her problems were behind her. Another encounter with the kidnappers could prove fatal for her and her son, for she knew these people would be out for blood after she'd destroyed the file in the fireplace. She hadn't completely lost hope in the Defense Intelligence Agency, and wondered where Matheson was now when she needed him most. Her best chance lay with him finding her before the others did.

Eager to find some semblance of civilization, she kept thinking they'd eventually find a farmhouse where the residents would allow her to phone the authorities to get help. As they came to a field of leafy vegetation that Linda thought might be spinach, moonlight broke through a cloudy sky to illuminate the land, and she saw another adjoining corn crop that could provide cover if their enemies appeared. Hearing a nearby disturbance caused Linda to crouch next to her son, her eyes looking about searchingly for whatever it was she'd heard. The quiet stillness was broken by a strange shrill that made her heart jump, and she glimpsed what she thought to be a bird lifting off from one of the plants, fluttering its wings as it took to the night sky.

Allan's eyes enlarged. "What was that?"

"It's just a bird," Linda explained, holding a stooped position as her left knee sank in soft earth, and coming to her feet, she brushed soil free from her knee.

Moonlight enabled her to see how wedge-shaped fields of spinach plants and cornstalks met at fencing bordering the roadside, but she hadn't seen a car's headlights as yet. Dwindling, dwarfed, and sparse cornstalks ran out at the fence, and Linda was curious about what lay beyond in the next connecting field, only to then notice her son standing with his hands tucked between his legs. Realizing he needed to relieve himself, they stopped long enough for him to do so as they listened to the sound of a lone cricket.

Drifting clouds dimmed the moonlight while the wind rustled the stalks before falling still, and she then spotted the headlight beams from an approaching car coming down the road. Unable to identify the make of the car, she was concerned it may be the kidnappers, prompting her to keep out of sight. She watched the vehicle follow a bend in the road. It passed by their location moving slowly, as though its occupants were searching the area.

In no doubt that their pursuers were mad as hornets and on the prowl looking for them, Linda decided to avoid the road, and moved toward the fencing to see what awaited them in the next connecting field. Brushing aside leaves of dwarfed cornstalks, she saw barbed wire fencing supported by awkwardly leaning cedar fence posts that linked up with the fence running parallel to the road. Faint moonlight allowed her to survey a gently sloping wheat field carrying as far as the eye could see, and in the distance she spied an obscure Victorian farmhouse encircled by patches of trees and shrubbery. The house looked to be over a hundred yards away. It had a roofline with a projecting tower or turret up front cresting over three stories, and there was a large barn.

Wanting to find refuge and if possible get to a phone, she saw no lights to indicate that people occupied the dwelling, but she expected farmers usually turned in early. Shifting clouds blocked the moon, and no longer able to see the house with any detail or clarity, she then heard the distant rumble of thunder. Feeling a raindrop on top her head, she knew she had to take a chance on finding shelter at that house, and when placing her hand on one of the cedar fence posts, she found it wobbly. Two of the posts had rotted out at ground level, and she pushed over one of the slumping posts to make it lay flat on the ground, standing on it to allow Allan to cross over to the wheat field.

"Is it going to rain?"

Another drop caught Linda's eyebrow, causing her to blink, and expecting a hard rain to fall any minute, she said, "I'm afraid so."

The wind blustered to rustle the cornstalks, moving the soft blanket of wheat in waves running to the farmhouse, and the next round of thunder grew nearer than the last. As raindrops began falling more frequently, Linda picked Allan up in her arms and broke into a run to cross the sea of wheat and reach the farmhouse. She moved with the wind against her back. A short flash of lightning preceded crackling thunder, and sensing a cloudburst coming, she wondered if she could reach the farmhouse before the sky cut loose with a downpour.

The wind turned cool. The next lightning strike accompanied a rumbling crackle of thunder, but the flash enabled her to see the washed-out farmhouse with more detail, the windows covered with shutters. The front porch, from the side, looked to have ornamental spindles, which gave the impression it must have been a grand home in its day. Where the bed of wheat ended, what appeared to be shrubs from a distance was thick brush strung out over a wide area, and wading through it, she passed a coiled piece of plowing equipment encrusted in rust. Trees swayed with the strong wind and she came to the house in a roundabout way to avoid the thickest patch of high weeds, her steps quickened by the storm's threat.

Seeing a rundown and deserted house, she saw no chance of getting to a phone, but she still had hopes of finding shelter. Linda passed the ragged barn that had a sagging roof. A rope dangling from the barn's loft beat against its weatherworn siding, and her aim was to reach a porch extending from the back of the house. Vines and overgrown plant cover was thickest around the porch area, making it difficult to get to, and the next burst of lightning allowed her to see a door and a bare, broken window. Finding the porch steps rotted out, she lifted Allan over the collapsed steps to the decking and then hopped them herself. Gripping the handrail for balance, she nearly fell backwards, but managed to stay on her feet. When moving across rough and badly warped deck floorboards, her foot penetrated a plank, but she recovered to pull it free and dashed for the backdoor to find it ajar.

Linda took Allan's hand just as the full brunt of the storm unleashed its fury with a gushing downpour, and she pushed the door open to stare into the home's dark and uninviting interior. Deliberating on whether to enter, wind and driving rain drove them from the doorway into the house. A flash from a streak of lightning allowed her to see the outline of a large room and a tattered linoleum floor, but the following roar of thunder caused Allan's grip on her hand to tighten. The child's fear came through in his stiff walk with his shoulders raised, and concern for his health helped Linda to overcome her fear of the unknown.

She removed her blazer and wrapped it around him. The raging storm produced another blast of lightning that unveiled a raised porcelain sink near a window and a sagging, tilted wall cabinet. Rainwater plunging from a dislodged gutter poured down with torrential force outside the door, and she turned around to hold her feet out one at a time to rinse them off. The cool water raining down from above soothed the stinging cuts and scratches she'd acquired walking through brush, and she wished she had a towel to wipe them clean.

On the far side of the room lay a doorway of pitch-black, and wanting to space herself from the kitchen to avoid exposure to the elements, she ventured down a hallway that had a wood floor. Gritty dirt stuck to the bottoms of her feet, and she froze as she felt the spring of creaking floorboards sinking beneath her. Lightning lit up the way ahead once more, accompanied by violent thunder that rattled the house, raising concerns for its stability.

The intense clash of thunder brought Allan to her side shivering, and unable to speak, he used both his hands to clench his mother's arm tightly.

She tried reassuring him that he was safe, saying, "It's OK, Allan. You've heard thunder before."

Suddenly, lightning flashed through shutters at that room's only window, and the outline of the burst of light took an oblong shape on the floor, lasting long enough to reveal a bare, rectangular-shaped room. She saw a door lying on the floor off to one side, its handle leaving it tilted, and noticing two other doorways branching off from this area, a strange uncertainty kept her from exploring further. Deciding to stay in this room, she thought it may be the dining room since it connected with the kitchen. Feeling a single drop of water land on top her head, she touched the spot with her fingertips just as another hit her hand, so she moved to avoid what must have been a leak in the roof.

The clamor of thunder shook the house as Linda left Allan to feel along the wall to go back to the kitchen to close the door, pressing her shoulder against it to force it shut against a relentless wind.

Missing his mother, Allan called out, "Mommy!"

She returned quickly. "I'm right here. I just closed the door to keep the wind and rain out, and now we need to try and get some sleep to make a fresh start in the morning."

Finding a comfortable position to lie down on the floor made for a challenge, and she pulled the blazer snug around Allan before cuddling up close to him. Lying on the floor facing each other for some time, even though circumstances weren't the best, she was glad to have him with her. While unable to sleep, Linda rubbed her feet against her pant legs to thoroughly dry them off, and as the thunder grew distant, her ears kept touch with the steady rhythm of rainfall. That constant drip inside the room continued at an uneven pace to help keep her awake, and another drip began somewhere over by the window.

"This house is scary." The tone of Allan's voice came across showing fear.

Realizing her son was still awake, Linda tried to take his mind from this eerie environment by saying, "Did you hear that echo?"

Allan lifted his head as he perked up. "What?"

"Lie down," she told him, and his head settled back. "You know what an echo is. That's when a mountain climber yodels and his voice comes back over and over again."

The thought inspired him to test the room's acoustics, and he playfully sounded off, "Boo!"

"OK, I think that's enough now. Let's go to sleep."

Lying nearly face-to-face, her eyes had adjusted to the dark, and she leaned over to kiss his soft cheek. Hearing the rain letting up signaled how the storm was moving on, and her mind kept working to try and think of a way out of this mess. Between her wondering and fears, she had time to ponder Matheson, for he was undoubtedly looking for her, but would he find her before these criminals caught up to her? Entering a deadly phase of this game, it wasn't likely Adele and the others were going to give up their quest for the disc, and she held concerns for what they'd do if they captured her. Prompted to ponder what the new day would bring, to have any chance at survival she'd have to find transportation or get to a phone to contact the authorities for help.

She turned her head to stare at a narrow section of wall, barely picking up the outline of where decaying plaster left wood lath exposed near an open doorway. She assumed the door lying on the floor in the foreground to be the door that previously hung there, as it had apparently pulled loose from its hinges to fall sometime in the past. Inside that nearby door opening she saw a wall, barely visible, with a bar running crossways for hanging clothes, indicating it was a closet. Hiding the disc crossed her mind, but the article was too valuable to be misplaced or lost. Over time, the rain slowed, the drips in the room ceased, and she fell asleep.

Meanwhile, Matheson was going out of his mind with worry for Linda and her son. He couldn't understand why, with all the technology and sophisticated equipment the Defense Intelligence Agency had available, they still couldn't zero in on the signal from Linda's cell phone. He believed it may be the interference of storms blanketing the area, or perhaps the kidnappers had confiscated her phone and removed its batteries to stop it from transmitting a signal. In a fit, knowing the types of people she was dealing with, there was little he could do but keep looking for the gray Mercedes-Benz that he and others in his agency were searching for.

CHAPTER 16

Avoiding Her Pursuers

L inda couldn't shake the cold chill that woke her in the early morning hours of the following day. Her feet were freezing as she reached for her son, who slept next to her coiled up in a ball. Dim sunlight came through the shutter's louvers, and gazing about the room, she again noticed a decaying section of wall by the closet where there was a small hole. Crumbling plaster left bare wood lath visible above a baseboard, and she thought again about hiding the case inside the house, but decided not to.

Rubbing her feet to produce heat, Linda thought the importance of the disc should bring the opposition out early looking for her, and she bundled Allan up in her blazer to carry him. Feeling the pocket of the blazer to make certain she hadn't lost the disc, she then saw how water had dripped throughout most of the night to stain the room's wood floor in two places. One spot was by the window, and the other was a wide area she couldn't avoid. She walked across damp floorboards to get to the kitchen.

When she stepped out on the porch, the sun was coming up over the horizon, and she saw a mist hanging over the wheat field they'd crossed on their way to the house. Her breath steamed in the cool morning air, and she took a short leap off one side of the decking into a patch of high weeds where the plant growth was damp from either the night's rain or the morning dew. Coming around to the front of this dreary house, she walked in one of a pair of ruts that were a gravel drive leading from the road to the barn.

155

A clear blue sky had but a few powder puff clouds, and hearing the chirping of a bird, Linda looked down at Allan, feeling happy about having this new start. Her child's hair had thickened over the time they were apart, and his complexion had good color, indications his health was improving. However, Allan quickly grew heavy in her arms so she stopped to get him to stand on his own, and before coming around, he leaned one way, then the other.

His eyes opened drowsily, and wearing a pouting expression, he grumbled, "I'm cold."

"I know, but once you start walking you'll warm up."

She put the loose-fitting blazer on him, and the coat and its long sleeves dragged along the ground to make him look a bit comical. After running her fingers through his short hair, they began walking together. It wasn't long before his crankiness wore off, and when they reached the paved road, he asked his mother to remove the blazer. Linda took the coat off him and shook it to remove debris it had collected before putting it on, once again making sure the disc was intact in the hip pocket.

Watchful for cars as they walked along the roadside, before long they came upon a two-story frame building on the other side of the road. It had the looks of a small-town grocery store with a short, slanted roof over the building's front deck where a bench swing hung. A sign on the building read in bold print **TURNER'S FEED AND SUPPLIES**. There was a large storage barn connected to the store where a high-step stake truck had backed up to a loading dock, and two men were stacking canvas sacks in staggered fashion up front by the truck's cab. One of the men wore a dark blue cap with an emblem of grain stalks on the front, and his dark hair hung out in a flip from the back.

A sign by the door read "Bait and Fishing Tackle," and Linda and Allan crossed the blacktop road to enter a store that had a curious odor of chemical additives or insecticides. Assorted bags of seed and fertilizer were in stacks, and shovels and other long-handled implements hung from the walls, most covered by a crust of dust.

The merchant standing behind the counter wore a T-shirt under faded blue jean overalls covering a well-rounded belly. His gray hair worn in a crew cut, and his cheek bulged with a wad of tobacco. Photos on a wall showed him wearing similar overalls in the company of young people paired with a collection of various farm animals, and in a few photos, they proudly displayed blue ribbons. Another cluster of photos showed fishermen holding up their catches, and some of the fish were whoppers, nearly forty inches long.

The man in the blue cap came to the front of the store to converse with the shopkeeper, and the two went over a checklist as Linda and Allan browsed the store. Walking barefoot on the worn plank floor that had a sandy feel, she waited for a break in their conversation to approach the man wearing the cap who she assumed was the truck's owner.

As soon as the heavyset man in overalls finished talking to the truck driver, he turned his attention to Linda, and asked very plainly, "What can I do for you, miss?"

"Do you have a telephone?"

He put his thumbs inside his shoulder straps. "Sure do, but the storm put it out, and there's no electricity too." He slid a box wrapped in plain brown paper across on the counter, calling out to the truck driver, "Hey, Joe, don't forget to drop this package off at the parcel service in Camden."

Linda had a thought, and turning to the truck driver, she asked, "Excuse me, but could I impose on you for a lift to town?"

The driver flashed his eyes at Linda, then he looked to the man in overalls, and there was silence.

Linda turned to address the merchant, and asked, "Is the truck yours? I guess what I mean to say is if your phone worked, I wouldn't have to trouble you, I could call someone, but I'm in a terrible jam and only need a ride as far as the nearest town."

Feeling awkward about her situation, Linda pulled two ten dollar bills from the pocket of her blazer, separating them. "I'd be willing to pay for the transportation."

Seeing how Linda was barefoot and sensing she was in trouble, the merchant gave a friendly smile. "You're not from around here, are you, ma'am?"

"No, I'm not, but I am in a tough fix."

"Put your money away," said the tobacco-chewing merchant, who turned and spit in a wastebasket. "Joe will take you to town if you need a ride."

"Oh, thank you."

Then, seeing the driver pick up the package from the counter, she became inquisitive. "If you don't mind my asking, is this a parcel delivery service you often use?"

"Occasionally," answered the merchant between chews.

"I'm carrying something valuable and I'm not sure if I want to go on carrying it or if I should let your delivery service ship it."

Removing the stainless steel casing from the pocket of her blazer, she placed it on the counter. "It's urgent that I get this to New York, and I think it may be safer to let them handle it."

The merchant picked it up while curiously examining it, and read the printing. "Triad—what is it, something for a computer?"

"Yes, it's a computer disc, and what's usually the procedure? How much does it cost to send a package of this size to New York?"

"It can be sent COD, provided the receiving party's willing to pay the shipping charge, and the cost shouldn't be much for something that small, but it can't be sent like that." The man paused to spit in the wastebasket before continuing. "We'll have to put it in a bubble mailer envelope, and I can provide one for a small charge."

Allan tugged at his mother's arm to say, "That man spit, Mommy."

"I know. Just be still for a minute, Allan."

The merchant put the disc casing inside an envelope and produced a black felt marker. "You'll have to print the address you want it sent to with a return address, and the parcel service will do the rest."

Concerned the gray Mercedes or blue BMW might show up at any minute, Linda quickly wrote her home address for both, and then handed the package to the driver, who went outside and started the truck's engine.

Linda had now lost track of Allan, and finding him climbing on bags of fertilizer, she took him by the hand to start toward the door, saying, "I appreciate all your help."

"Can I trouble you for one dollar to cover the cost of that envelope?"

Returning to the counter, she had nothing smaller than a ten dollar bill, and placed one on the counter, saying, "Thanks."

Rushing out of the store to the stake truck, Allan slipped over into the middle of the seat, taking interest in how the driver threw the floor shift in gear. After Linda climbed in the vehicle, the truck driver engaged the clutch and they started rolling, only to stop when the merchant flagged them down to hand Linda her change. Finally, the truck began moving, and confident they were on the road to freedom, Linda looked to her young son and ran her hand across his bristled hair. She figured on turning the disc over to the first police officer she saw in the next town, and if she didn't see a policeman, she'd let the parcel delivery service ship it.

After going a few miles, Linda saw a filling station coming up on the right. The truck's engine bogged down, and she turned to the driver. "Why are we stopping?"

He hit the blinker, pressing in the clutch as he braked and downshifted. "Gotta get fuel."

Seeing the gas gauge nearly on empty, she looked ahead and saw the station was older than most with a connecting garage where a late model Ford truck was elevated on jack stands to get its brake shoes changed. She also noticed a new red and white tow truck and a Chevrolet station wagon parked on the side of the building.

The driver got out and inserted the pump nozzle in the truck's tank to fill it with diesel. Linda realized that if they had electricity for the pumps to operate, then the station phone may work. Seeing the envelope containing the disc lying in the sun on the dashboard, she placed it on the floorboard, and after removing her blazer, she laid it on top of the envelope.

Getting out of the truck, she helped her son down, and said to the truck driver, "I'm going to see if the station phone is working. I'll be right back."

Inside the station, she met a dirty-faced mechanic coming in from the garage. His shirt had cut-off sleeves, and he wiped his hands off with a rag when giving her his attention.

"Hello. Do you have a phone?"

The mechanic replied, "It's right behind you there."

She lifted the receiver on the pay phone to see if she could hear a signal and the line sounded dead. "I don't think your phone is working. We just came from that Turner's supply store down the road, and the storm knocked out their electricity and phone service."

The mechanic wiped his hands again with the same rag, and stuffed it in his back pocket to try the telephone located behind the counter. He held the receiver to his ear before commenting, "I guess the storm put the phone service out. I'd wondered why there hadn't been any calls, and it's usually just the opposite following a big storm. They have electricity and phone service and ours is out."

Linda squinted while making a pleading gesture. "You wouldn't happen to have a cell phone I could use, would you?"

"Sorry, I don't have one. I get enough interruptions from the shop phone."

Acting in a shy way, but tugging on his mother's arm, Allan said, "I've got to go potty." Then his eyes spotted a snack machine. "Can I have a candy bar?"

Removing the key from the wall marked MEN'S, the mechanic handed it to her. "You'll have to use the men's because the ladies' restroom is out of order. You'll find it on the side of the building."

Linda began escorting Allan out of the station as the truck driver came in to pay his bill. Seeing the restroom key in her hand, he stepped aside to give Linda and Allan passage.

"We'll try not to keep you long," she said apologetically.

Linda located the restroom on the side of the building next to where the tow truck sat parked, and after a few minutes, they finished using the facilities. When coming out to return to the truck she saw a gray Mercedes-Benz turning into the station lot, and acting on impulse, she stepped back inside the restroom. Contemplating a run for the woods behind the station, she considered it may simply be a car resembling the kidnappers' that she'd seen, as she hadn't been able to get a look at who was in the Mercedes.

Sticking her head out to take another look, she observed the Mercedes parked in plain view, and Mehlnick stepped out from the driver's side wearing a white patch over his left eye. A tall man in his mid-thirties with an athletic build and wavy blond hair got out on the passenger side to stand like a soldierly subordinate.

Mehlnick walked from the car, saying, "Wait here, Kepler. I'll ask if anyone's seen them."

Allan looked up at his mother with a curious expression. "What's wrong?"

"Nothing. We'll go in a second."

Believing she had little time before Mehlnick learned they were here, Linda wanted to run to the woods before he came back, but she couldn't risk leaving the restroom without drawing this other man's attention.

She then heard Mehlnick shout, "This way, Kepler! They're back here!"

Kepler's eyes widened as they shifted to the door where Linda stood, and as Mehlnick hurriedly came around the building, Linda pulled the door closed and locked it.

Pulling her son close to her, she saw the door handle jiggle from Mehlnick's hand as he tried turning it, and stepping aside, he gave Kepler an order. "Kick it in!"

The tall blond man charged and rammed the door, but it was metal and it didn't budge. Linda began screaming, "Help! Somebody, please help us!"

Mehlnick spoke anxiously. "As soon as you get in, grab the boy, and I'll take care of the mother."

Kepler again drove his shoulder against the door with a pounding force that jarred the door handle, but the lock held.

Fear turned to desperation, and seeing a wall vent, she stepped on the toilet seat to scream at the top of her lungs, "Help us! Please help!"

Hoping someone heard her calls, she grabbed her child and embraced him. "When that door opens, you run for help."

The next jolt impacting the door drove it open. Kepler reached for Allan, but Linda attacked him, throwing blows that enabled the Allan to slip by and run outside. The blond man chased after him. Allan took to a zigzagging pattern to elude him. Mehlnick came angrily through the door to block the way.

"Help!" she screamed once more, backing up as he came toward her, and he clamped his hand over her mouth, shoving her against a wall to shut her up.

Linda cowered in the corner, and he said, "If we leave without you, your boy dies. Do you understand?"

Mehlnick moved to the door to watch his partner carry the child under one arm to the Mercedes, the boy's legs kicking as he shrieked. While Kepler stuffed the child in the car, the mechanic came marching around the building's corner with a large wrench in his hand. He had an angry look on his face when coming toward Mehlnick.

Holding the door open with his foot, Mehlnick stepped back inside the restroom to reach inside his coat for his revolver. He slipped the weapon inside the hip pocket of his suit coat, keeping a firm hold on the gun's grip and his finger on the trigger. He then turned to Linda. "You've got two seconds to put on your happy face, or you're going to see people shot to death before your eyes."

Linda heard the mechanic's approach. "Do you wanna tell me what the hell's goin' on here, mister?"

The station attendant saw the damaged lock, and the driver of the stake truck joined him to find out what the commotion was all about.

The mechanic spoke demandingly, "I heard that woman screaming as though you're killing her—just who do you people think you are?"

Mehlnick kept a firm grip on the pistol in his pocket as he exited the restroom, looking down at the wrench bobbing in the attendant's hand as he said, "She needed assistance. The door jammed."

"Don't give me that. You kicked that door in deliberately to get to her."

Linda came to the doorway looking battered, and the driver of the truck asked, "Did this man strike you, miss?"

She thought Mehlnick would end it by shooting these men in cold blood, and unable to hold back escalating fear and emotions, she broke down in tears.

The truck driver stepped forward to confront Mehlnick. "You've got a lot of nerve."

"No!" Linda's eyes froze on Mehlnick's hand where he kept his pistol concealed. Unable to let these men die without knowing what they were up against, she added, "Nothing happened—really."

The mechanic's eyes glared at Mehlnick as though he was thinking about clobbering him, the big wrench held firmly in his hand. "What about the damage to my door?"

Stepping back, Mehlnick attempted to defuse the situation by saying, "I'm willing to pay for the damage, whatever it takes to square everything."

The mechanic and truck driver stood by watching as Mehlnick drew from his pants pocket a big wad of cash, using his teeth to separate three one hundred dollar bills from the others. Linda kept silent while looking to the Mercedes-Benz where the other man held her child. Allan was raising a fit.

Mehlnick stuffed the cash back in his pocket, and handed over the $300 to the mechanic. "Here. Sorry about the door, but this should take care of the damage."

"Before we say everything's square," began the truck driver, "what's this other fella in the car doin' with this woman's child?"

The one-armed man kept calm, returning his hand to the company of his revolver. "If you gentlemen haven't already guessed, you're getting involved in a domestic squabble." He turned to the mechanic. "If you're satisfied, then we'll be on our way before we cause either of you any further inconvenience." Distancing himself from the others by stepping around them to go to the car, Mehlnick then turned and addressed Linda. "Are you coming?"

Believing the lives of these two men and the fate of her child depended on what she said and did next, she began walking to the Mercedes.

"Are you sure everything's alright, miss?" inquired the truck driver.

Turning to respond to him dejectedly, she said, "Everything's fine, and I'm sorry about the trouble we've caused you."

Linda shuddered at the thought of leaving with these men, but believing Mehlnick would commit murder if need be to force her to come along with him, she had little choice.

Making no attempt to retrieve the envelope containing the disc from the stake truck, she got in the Mercedes-Benz. She expected the truck driver to turn the disc over to the parcel delivery service to have it delivered to her home, and wondered what was going to happen when these people learned she no longer had the disc. Thinking they wouldn't kill her, at least not until they had their hands on the disc, she hoped this may buy the Defense Intelligence Agency time. She even thought that having the disc delivered to her home might place her in a better bargaining position because they may need her to gain possession of the disc.

The truck driver and mechanic stood together watching the Mercedes leave the station lot, and the driver turned to the mechanic, saying, "Did you see the way that guy held his hand in his suit coat pocket?" He motioned his hand to his side to pose the way the one-armed man stood. "I think he had a gun."

"Yeah, I know, and I was thinking that too, but how does a woman that looks like her get mixed up with a guy like that in the first place?" Then he examined the damaged door.

Returning to the truck, the driver saw Linda had left her blazer on the floorboard, and then learned she'd also left the envelope lying on the floor of the truck. His first thought was to catch up to the Mercedes-Benz, but the automobile was long since out of sight so he went on his way.

The Mercedes sped down the road passing a tan Chevrolet Impala traveling in the opposite direction. Linda recognized Matheson driving, who in turn spotted the Mercedes he'd been looking for. Matheson turned around and accelerated to pursue the Mercedes, and once he had it in sight, he stayed back more than 500 feet to trail it on a snaking road. When seeing it turn off the main road, he drove on a good distance further before pulling over on the road's shoulder.

He got out of his car to double back on foot, and crossing a drainage ditch off the road's shoulder, he soon saw a large house set back in some woods where the Mercedes sat parked in a circular driveway. To get a closer look he approached a mature oak tree at the edge of a clearing where meticulously well-kept grounds surrounded this impressive home. Ivory curtains tied back in the windows tempted him to move even closer yet, but he decided he needed backup. It was now time to contact his agency and get the help he needed to capture these criminals.

CHAPTER 17

Meeting the Mastermind

Mehlnick and Kepler ushered Linda to the library where, after being searched, she explained that the truck driver back at the station had the envelope containing the disc. She'd seen Matheson on the road, but wasn't sure if he'd seen her, and her spirit was down after watching Allan throwing a tantrum and Adele whisking him away to another part of the house. She sat on a maroon sofa for a short time before a short, astute-looking man with a prominent pointed nose and black-rimmed eyeglasses entered the room to stare coldly at her. Of German descent, having a thin and mousy build, he wore a well-tailored blue suit with a charcoal tie, and his salt and pepper hair gave him a look of a man in his fifties. He held a long, skinny cigar close to his lips. Linda thought this to be the man named Emeric Kleistner, who Matheson had shown her a photograph of, and she closely studied his movements.

"Where's the disc?" When no one gave an answer, he again snapped, "Where's the disc?"

Linda never saw him before, yet clearly recognized his voice as the badgering voice that had questioned her during the interrogation, and there was also something familiar about the glint in his eye.

Mehlnick responded by saying, "She just told me she gave the disc to a truck driver who's supposed to turn it over to a parcel delivery service that's to send it to her house."

"Is that so, Mrs. Moreland?" asked the little man, examining her reaction with a distastefully snooty expression.

"It's true. I gave it to a truck driver in an envelope that has my address."

Kleistner looked at Mehlnick. "Did you search her?"

Mehlnick nodded, "Yes, and it wasn't on her."

Then Kleistner looked at Linda, taking a drag from his cigar. "We found what was left of the file in the fireplace. Would you mind telling me where you slept last night?"

"Some old deserted farmhouse a few miles from here."

"Probably the Morgan farm," Mehlnick blurted out.

Looking over her soiled clothing, Kleistner said, "Take her to the unused bedroom upstairs to let her clean up, and Adele will see to it that she gets fresh clothes."

"I want to be with my child. Can't you keep us together?"

Finishing another drag from his cigar, a puff of smoke swirled from its end, and his lips made a bitter frown before his voice amplified. "From now on you'll keep your mouth shut and do as you're told. You've caused me a great deal of aggravation, Mrs. Moreland, and you're certain to soon learn how people who inconvenience me tend to shorten their life expectancy."

Kleistner turned away, then swung back. "Up till last night I had expected our trade to be a success. We had every intention of keeping our word." The demanding tone in his voice increased. "Until we have the disc in our possession, you'll not see your child. That way there'll be little chance of your trying to escape."

Kepler escorted Linda from the library to a second story bedroom with an adjoining bath, and then took a chair in the hall outside her door.

Matheson had thoroughly surveyed the house from the outside and started back to his vehicle, but when reaching the edge of the woods, on the roadside he saw a BMW parked behind his car. Hesitant about emerging from the cover of trees to get to his car, his eyes searched the surrounding area, and a hard, blunt object suddenly pressed against his back.

He heard Schmidt's voice from behind him. "Don't move, and I won't put a hole in you."

Schmidt kept the pistol pressed firmly against his back, using his other hand to reach for the .45 caliber automatic holstered under Matheson's suit coat. Removing the weapon from its concealed position, he placed it in the pocket of his trenchcoat, and then did the same with Matheson's wallet.

Matheson held still. "What's this all about?"

"Let's save the conversation until we get inside where it's nice and cozy. Clasp your hands behind your head and turn around slowly, and if there's any funny stuff, my finger twitches and you die."

Schmidt stepped away, using his 9mm pistol to point the way to the house before turning it back on Matheson. "Let's go."

Matheson glanced down at the barrel of the handgun aimed at him. "What if I refuse?"

Schmidt grinned. "You don't look that stupid to me. You want to end it right here and now, or would you rather go inside where we can play question and answer games?" He aimed his pistol directly at Matheson's heart. "I'm going to have to insist you either begin marching, or say a short prayer, because time's up."

Reading in his eyes that he meant to go through with killing him if he didn't comply, Matheson reluctantly decided to do as he asked, clasping his hands behind his head as he started toward the house.

After entering the interior of the home, Schmidt escorted him to the library at gunpoint. Matheson recognized Kleistner sitting comfortably at his desk, and Schmidt placed his pistol and wallet on the desktop.

Kleistner picked up the wallet and sat back in his wingback chair while fingering through Matheson's wallet to find identification for a man named Thompson.

Schmidt coldly commented, "He was outside snooping around, but he doesn't even have to speak a word. He has the stench of trouble fuming from him."

Kleistner adjusted his eyeglasses. "You look uncomfortable standing in that manner. Why don't you put your hands to your sides, Mr. Thompson? We've had a rash of break-ins and burglaries in the area, so we're naturally suspicious of strangers prowling around our home. Why don't you tell us about yourself so we can get this matter cleared up as quickly as possible?"

Matheson was worried about spending any lengthy amount of time in the house. Hidden inside the pocket of his suit coat was a compact billfold that held his true identification, which would expose him as a government agent. "As you can see from my card, I'm an independent insurance adjuster based in Jersey City, and I was having trouble finding the address of a client living in the area who recently filed a claim."

"Tell me, Mr. Thompson, how long have you been an insurance adjuster?"

"Eleven years," answered Matheson, turning his eyes to the door where one-armed Mehlnick and Kepler had made their entrance to stand on either side of him. Schmidt put his weapon inside his coat.

"Eleven years," began Kleistner, lowering his eyeglasses on the bridge of his nose to study Matheson's expression. "And what exactly did you expect to gain by approaching this house?"

Matheson's face expressed disgust. "Like I told you, I was looking for an address on your house to get a fix on locating my client whose name, by the way, is Johnson. I didn't want to turn down your drive and cause a big commotion just to get an address, as it looks like I've done, but I wasn't snooping, just looking for an address."

"The number is on the mailbox out on the road, but I don't suppose you thought of that."

"Well, I'd already passed it by before glimpsing your house, and I didn't know how far I'd have to drive before seeing the next mailbox because I'd seen so few. So that's mainly why I pulled over. I didn't realize your home was so far back from the road when I started my walk back to view an address number."

"You say you're looking for a client named Johnson, and I've lived here a good many years without knowing a family living nearby with that name. Perhaps if you can provide us with an address, we can do the neighborly thing and assist you in finding the house you're searching for."

"I've got that information on a clipboard in my car, but you act as though you've never heard the name Johnson before. It's about as common as Smith or Jones."

While pondering, the mousy man adjusted his eyeglasses to examine Matheson's driver's license and two credit cards from his wallet.

"You carry a gun, Mr. Thompson. Why is that?"

"About a year ago I was beaten and robbed by two men, and I've carried a gun for protection ever since. Now that I've explained my business and my purpose for being on your property, I need to be on my way, so if you'll allow me to have my personal belongings, I won't be troubling you any longer."

The room was silent, and although Matheson thought he played his hand convincingly, he worried about gaining his freedom.

"Like good citizens, we're cautious of unexpected visitors, Mr. Thompson. If Thompson is your real name."

"What's that supposed to mean?"

Kleistner calmly gripped Matheson's pistol and pointed it at him. "It means I have my suspicions about whether you're an insurance adjuster."

Matheson felt himself perspiring. "Well, if you think me a thief, why don't you phone the police and have me arrested for trespassing?"

"This is not a police matter, for we have our own way of dealing with thieves and trespassers."

Kepler and Mehlnick each latched onto an arm to restrain Matheson and pull him against a wall. He fought to get free. "You have no right to hold me!"

Schmidt came to face him, and Matheson used their arm strength and hold as support for raising his right leg to kick Schmidt in the chest, then he kneed Mehlnick in the groin. Mehlnick doubled over, but held his grip on Matheson's right wrist while using his hip and body to shove him into the wall. Kepler strong-armed him at the same time.

Trapped in a crowded corner with Mehlnick and Kepler aggressively pulling and tugging at his arms to hold him, Matheson struggled to get free, but saw little chance of that now.

Schmidt had regained his composure and reached inside his coat to grip his pistol. He raised it and smacked Matheson across his head with its butt, knocking him unconscious. Matheson fell to the floor.

Kleistner rose from his chair. "He's obviously American intelligence. Search him thoroughly, then get him tied up so he can't cause us more trouble. I'm entrusting you with keeping an eye on him, Schmidt. Mehlnick and Kepler will take his car with any personal belongings he has into town to throw off others who may be in the area, and when they get back, they'll go to work getting answers out of him. Use whatever techniques you wish to make him talk, but don't kill him, and let me know the minute our Peeping Tom starts speaking the truth."

Linda had showered and then dressed in clothing Adele left her on the bed. She now wore a pale yellow blouse, denim jeans, and comfortable shoes. Thinking of Allan prompted her to work on a way to improve her position with the kidnappers, and to save her own neck she needed to prove to Kleistner that she was more valuable alive than dead. This meant convincing these people she'd be willing to retrieve the disc from her home and deliver it to them in exchange for her and Allan's freedom, but she didn't know if they'd agree. Viewing time and fate as elements closing in on her, she feared they'd surely kill her if they didn't get their hands on the disc, for she'd lost hope of help coming. She'd counted on Matheson and Defense Intelligence to come through for her, but not understanding why help hadn't come, she now believed she only had herself to rely on.

CHAPTER 18

Hoping for Help to Arrive

After nightfall, Adele had brought a dish of food to Linda. After finishing the meal, she now sat in one of the bedroom's broad windowsills on the second floor, giving thought to her situation. She'd used the older style keyholes on the doors to observe goings-on outside the room she occupied, and saw Mehlnick replace Kepler on watch in the hall. It appeared they were preparing to take a trip in the near future, as she'd seen the others making trips back and forth carrying boxes and suitcases.

All was quiet now, and Linda turned her attention to the keyhole to the adjoining room where earlier she'd seen a telephone on a nightstand next to a bed. She couldn't attempt an escape so long as they had Allan, but that telephone looked to be her only line of contact with the outside world. Determined to get to that phone, while uncertain if this rural area had 911 emergency service, she intended to have the operator connect her with the state police. It even crossed her mind to phone Matheson's associate Walter Koenig, who must be still monitoring calls coming to her home, and if she could hold the line long enough, the authorities could trace the call. However, for any of these things to happen she had to first get to that telephone, and she felt eager about doing so because she didn't know how much time she had before they'd come for her.

When viewing this connecting room by keyhole, she found it difficult to penetrate the darkness, but she hadn't detected any activity in the room. Keeping the light off in the room she occupied helped her eyes adjust to the dark, and moonlight illuminating from a window on the far side of that room allowed her to see the telephone on the nightstand. To get the door open she needed to improvise a workable key, and looking about, she took interest in the window curtains, removing a large curtain hook from the drapes. Sticking the sharp tip of the curtain hook snug in the door's lower hinge, she crimped and bent its point at an angle to give her the leverage needed to pick the lock's internal parts.

Inserting the crimped end of the hook into the keyhole, she quietly began working on the lock, angling the hook while turning and twitching it up and down, to the left and to the right. The curtain hook caught something and she thought she had a hold, but she lost it. Persistently repeating the same move, she continued to work and rework the hook in the same fashion. She kept this up until, holding the hook at an awkward angle and using the rim of the keyhole for leverage, she heard a click when she turned it.

When opening the door, the hinges began to creak, but she'd opened it wide enough to squeeze through. Her eyes focused on the telephone and nightstand. She unconsciously snagged a loose wire with her foot that went to a tall hurricane lamp resting on a round table, and by the time she felt the tug of the wire there came the faint jingle of glass. She turned to the tipping lamp that held two decorative glass globes and caught hold of the larger one resting on the top, but as it dislodged, the rest of the lamp fell to the floor with the smaller, oval-shaped globe shattering.

Wearing a look of failure, she closed her eyes while placing the globe she held in her hands on top of the round table, and the door to the room she'd occupied opened. Light streamed in, and she heard the footsteps of a shadowy figure approaching. Mehlnick came to stand beside her, surprised she'd succeeded in getting the door open.

Noticing broken glass from the lamp on the floor, he asked, "What are you doing in this room?"

"I want to see my child. Where is he?"

His eyes scanned the room until he saw the phone on the nightstand. His hand latched onto her arm. "You'd better come with me."

She resisted, but was no match for his pulling strength. "Alright, you don't have to paw and manhandle me."

"Go then," he sharply replied, and he followed her.

Linda went down the stairs to the first floor, and soon stood before Kleistner in the library. He was sitting at his desk in the company of a large man of Indian-Pakistani descent whose appearance alarmed her. The man sitting in the armchair across from Kleistner wore a dark suit, and she found his presence somewhat perplexing, as he had thinning black hair, a wavy black beard, and thick black eyebrows. She was most conscious of his penetrating eyes, eyes that made her feel uncomfortably vulnerable, and it bothered her to be in the same room as him.

For Linda, this man's quiet gaze was more of a hypnotic stare. Darkened circles around his eyes were a helpful reminder that his were the ones she'd seen when under the influence of the truth serum. His haunting eyes were the ones she'd seen in her dreams.

Kleistner gave his attention to Mehlnick. "Dr. Rishankar and I have important business to discuss, so I hope there's good reason for this interruption."

"She picked the lock to the connecting room, and she may have used the telephone."

Linda insisted, "I did not make a call from that phone."

Adele entered the room and Kleistner slid a stack of papers toward her. "Burn these papers with the others and tell Schmidt to watch the road. He should notify us the second he sees suspicious activity, and inform us which direction the authorities are coming from so we can elude capture."

After Adele left the room, Kleistner looked to Mehlnick. "You'll be replacing Schmidt watching the road soon. Let me know if you see anything out of the ordinary." He then scowled as he looked to Linda. "We monitor the police radio, so we'll soon know whether you've used the phone, Mrs. Moreland, and if you did, you'll regret having done so."

Rising from his chair, he came around the desk to snap at her, "I wasn't sure about what to do with you, but you've made a nuisance of yourself for the last time."

"I didn't touch that telephone."

Kleistner momentarily paused to introduce her to the man with dark features, whose presence disturbed her so. "I didn't mean to be rude, Dr. Rishankar, this is Linda Moreland... Mrs. Moreland, Dr. Rishankar."

The doctor nodded with a grin. "I believe we've already met."

Linda avoided eye contact with him, turning away without saying anything.

Kleistner and Mehlnick escorted Linda to another room at a far corner of the house where Linda saw Kepler sitting in a padded armchair, flipping through a magazine by the light from a table lamp. He had the window shade pulled down, and on the table next to his chair was a pack of cigarettes, an ashtray full of short butts, a pair of black leather gloves, and a 9mm pistol.

Linda's eyes turned to a man tied to a chair in the middle of the room who sat slumped with his head hung low, his mussed hair hiding his facial features. She recognized Matheson, but said nothing.

Amused by her expression, Kleistner said, "I want you to take a good look at this man and tell me if you know him."

She knelt before Matheson, placing her hands gently around his face to carefully lift his head to see he was barely conscious and his left eye was swollen. He'd taken a terrible beating and was a pitiful sight—blood ran from his lower lip, nose, and a cut above his left eye.

"Did you have to do this to him?"

"I take it then that you know him?"

Looking closely at his battered face, she said, "I know him."

"You ignored the warning of what would happen if you went to the authorities, leaving me no alternative but for you to share in this man's fate."

"I can get the disc for you."

Kleistner gave a short and abrupt reply. "Of course you can, and if you'd delivered it to us, we wouldn't be having this conversation now."

"I can get it for you," she spoke pleadingly, "and I won't fail you this time. Just once I give it to you, please let the three of us go. That's all I ask."

"If it weren't for this man's arrival, we could afford to take one last chance with you, but now that we know the authorities are involved, experience tells me you're an unreliable expenditure. As it stands now, you can't be trusted. You know too much, and you're too smart for your own good."

Going to the door, Kleistner looked to Mehlnick and Kepler. "Keep them tied up together until it's time to get rid of them."

Still on her knees in front of Matheson, Linda had a lump in her throat when turning to Kleistner. "What about my son?"

Kleistner's hand hung on the door handle. "Adele has expressed an attachment to your boy. She's unable to have children of her own, and while considering what other fate awaits the child, I think you'd agree that he's better off remaining in her care."

Unable to find words to convince Kleistner to change his mind, Linda looked at the floor, and after Kleistner left the room, she gazed caringly at Matheson.

His swollen left eye began blinking. "You should've told them you never saw me before."

Her eyes held a sympathetic look as she leaned over to place her head against his leg. "They wouldn't have believed me, Jack, but what's going to happen to us?"

When he didn't answer, she pushed back Matheson's hair to examine his eye, and her fingertips scarcely had to touch the swollen area above the cut eye to make him flinch.

"If you want to do something, see if you can persuade one of those goons to loosen these ropes." He squirmed to make an adjustment, but the ropes held tight.

She turned to watch Mehlnick bringing in another chair from the dining room, and he placed the second chair back-to-back with the one Matheson sat in.

Linda said, "Can you loosen these ropes? They're cutting off his circulation."

"Sit down here," was Mehlnick's stern reply. He pulled his pistol out from the inside of his coat, and then he looked at Kepler. "I'll hold my weapon pointed at them while you tie them up."

Kepler put the magazine down and came over to tie Linda in the chair that backed up to the one Matheson sat in. He finished by tying Linda's legs together before returning to his seat by the window, grabbing a handful of magazines from the shelf beneath the table to sift through. Mehlnick left the room.

Linda used a soft voice to disclose to Matheson how she'd burned the file and let him know she'd had the disc delivered to her house. She then asked, "Is there any chance help will come?"

"There are agents looking for us, but there's not much chance of them finding us at this house. We were reading the GPS signal your cell phone was transmitting until we lost you in this remote area during the time the storm passed through. I had everyone looking for that gray Mercedes, and when seeing you in it on the road, I followed it to this location, but then clumsily stumbled into the driver of the BMW. His name is Schmidt, but he also goes by the name Fischer. I only recently saw a file on him. He has a deadly reputation."

Linda whispered to him, "Could any of these men be the person behind the Defense Department's leak?"

"I haven't seen anybody so far who fills the bill, but the little guy is the mastermind I'd told you about—Emeric Kleistner."

Her voice changed to a higher pitch. "I'm afraid they're going to kill us, and I don't want to die."

Kepler turned his head their way. "Enough talking. Keep quiet."

Except for Linda's soft whimpering, the room became quiet, and a few hours later Schmidt came to relieve Kepler's watch. Kepler stood to leave the room, stretching and stuffing his weapon inside his belt before making his exit.

Schmidt lifted the window shade, which allowed them to see it was daybreak, and then he cracked the window open before taking a seat in the armchair.

In the late morning, Adele set up a table beside them, arranging it to support a tray of sandwiches, and Schmidt came to his feet to point his pistol at Matheson as Adele undid the ropes.

Matheson stood and rubbed his arms to get his blood circulating, and Linda stretched while Adele arranged their seats against a wall to allow them to sit side by side.

"Did you get any sleep?" she asked.

"A little," replied Matheson, twisting his head from side to side, arching his back and shoulders while stretching his arms.

Taking their seats, Linda passed Matheson a sandwich, and looking at him, saw his cheek bulge as he ran his tongue across a tender area inside his mouth. His eye looked a little better.

"How are you feeling?" she inquired, lifting the top layer of bread on her sandwich to see the white meat of chicken breast before sinking her teeth into it.

His left eye twitched as he commented, "A couple of aspirin wouldn't hurt."

A minute later, Adele delivered three drinks clutched in her hands, giving the first to the gunman, and then she came their way with glasses extended in each hand.

Linda took a glass, asking, "When can I see Allan?"

"Seeing you would only upset the child," she replied in her usual cold manner, and she turned her back on Linda to leave the room, hearing but ignoring Linda's final words.

"How can seeing his mother upset him?"

Soon afterwards, Mehlnick replaced Schmidt, who left the room, and Matheson calculated his next move while examining the one-armed man sitting comfortably in the armchair. Seeing the revolver holstered inside Mehlnick's unbuttoned jacket, he studied the floor space separating them, looking for an opportunity to disarm him and take him out. However, Kepler soon returned, appearing fresh and well-rested. Lighting up a cigarette, he looked down at Mehlnick, muttering something in German.

Mehlnick turned his head to Linda and Matheson, and with a dumbfounded expression, said, "Are you sure about that?"

Kepler nodded, exhaling a puff of smoke.

An overwhelming sense of doom swept over Linda, as she sensed they were talking about doing away with her and Matheson.

Stepping forward with the cigarette hanging from his mouth, Kepler used a commanding tone when giving an order. "Get up." Opening his suit jacket, he withdrew his pistol from a well-concealed shoulder holster, then removed a silencer from the hip pocket of his jacket and screwed it to the pistol's barrel. "Face the wall, and kneel at your chairs."

Mehlnick moved the table and tray of dishes out of the way, a look of surprised anxiety on his face, and drawing his weapon, he kept his distance while watching what was about to happen.

Linda stood facing the wall, now terrifyingly convinced they were going to be murdered execution-style. She looked at Matheson, who did as they'd ordered him to do, kneeling at his chair, and leaning forward on the seat as if praying. Linda's knees locked as she held a stiff, upright position, and Kepler said demandingly, "Kneel!"

He placed his hand on her shoulder, applying downward pressure to get her to comply, and her knees buckled as she sank to take the same position held by Matheson. Breathing short puffs of air, she leaned forward while bowing her head. Tears streamed down her face to land on the chair seat. Raising her hands clenched together to her mouth, she bit hard in the fat of the index finger of her left hand, and closing her eyes, she heard the room's door open.

"Kepler," Schmidt's soft-spoken voice traveled across the room. "I hope you're not thinking about doing it here. We can't leave a couple of bodies behind in the house." Giving a slight chuckle as he saw humor in the situation, he added, "Can you imagine the mess? The cleaning lady would be shocked."

Mehlnick looked relieved as Kepler returned his silencer and pistol to their previously concealed places, and when Schmidt crossed the room there was a jingling, clinking metallic sound, perhaps like keys, but audibly different.

"I've got something much more dignified in mind for these two. Get up, both of you, and stand where you are."

Linda had broken out in a cold sweat, and she sucked in a deep breath of air when standing up, but her knees were weak so Schmidt lent her assistance. He held a pair of metal cuffs connected by a heavy chain thirty inches long, and he connected one of the wide bracelet-shaped cuffs around Linda's left wrist.

Schmidt commented, "Some years ago, a previous owner of this house was the warden at a prison farm for this county. Delegating chain gangs for roadwork, he supposedly brought trusted inmates home to maintain the grounds, and these were the chains commonly used to transfer those convicts. I think it rather convenient that he'd leave this chain and bracelets, as they ought to work fine for the purpose I have in mind."

Schmidt smiled when turning to Matheson, and holding the other cuff open for him to place his right wrist in, he remarked, "Kepler has a way of approaching his job with such enthusiasm."

Matheson's fist swung suddenly to knock Schmidt to the floor.

Kepler took a long stride, planting himself in Matheson's way, and they locked in hand-to-hand combat, trading blows until Matheson's hurled fist clipped Kepler's jaw, driving him back.

Mehlnick came forward to deliver a chopping blow to Matheson's neck, but Matheson caught his wrist, elbowed him in the midsection, and when doubling over he fell into a flip that landed him flat on the floor.

Linda came forward to help Matheson, but Schmidt grabbed her by the arm and flung her to the floor.

Whirling an outstretched leg, Matheson tried delivering a kick to Schmidt's left temple. Schmidt blocked it with his forearm, and then lunged forward propelling his fist, but Matheson ducked to dodge it.

Kepler tackled Matheson at the waist, taking him down, and while the two wrestled on the floor with Matheson struggling to break free, Mehlnick stood over them and drove his foot into his ribcage.

Linda rushed to give aid to Matheson, but Schmidt spun her around, pulling her through the door. Seeing Kepler and Mehlnick working him over, she screamed, "Stop it, you're killing him!"

Schmidt began dragging her out of the room, and she hung on to the doorframe until he pried her hand free, resorting to pulling her by the chain connected to her wrist. He took her through the entry hall to the outside, and they waited beside the Mercedes-Benz and BMW for the others. Kepler and Mehlnick came out of the house dragging Matheson. Each one had a grip on one of his arms, pulling his limp body down the porch steps, and they placed him in the backseat of the Mercedes.

Schmidt had Linda sit in the backseat on the passenger side next to Matheson, attaching the loose cuff to Matheson's right wrist. He then moved to open the trunk lid on the BMW to reveal three one gallon containers of gasoline, saying to Mehlnick, "Place these in your trunk."

While Mehlnick placed the gallon-sized containers in the trunk of the Mercedes, Schmidt turned to Kepler. "I have to go back inside the house for something. Don't take your eyes off those two."

Kepler held his pistol pointed in the direction of their captives while Linda heard activity behind her in the trunk, and she caught sight of Mehlnick loading the containers of gas in the Mercedes-Benz's trunk.

Worried about the outcome of this trip, she wondered, *Why the gas?*

Schmidt came out of the house wearing his trenchcoat and carrying a large, black leather duffel bag in his left hand, holding in his right hand a 9mm pistol. Entering the front passenger side of the Mercedes, he let the bag rest on his lap as he turned to the passengers in the backseat and saw Matheson slumped lethargically against the backseat driver's side door.

Kepler came around to get in the backseat on the same side as Matheson, being careful when opening the door so that he wouldn't fall out of the car when doing so. After joining the hostages in the backseat, he stuck his weapon's barrel firmly in Matheson's belly, holding it there with his finger on the trigger.

Mehlnick closed the trunk lids on both cars before taking the driver's seat to start the Mercedes, and he turned the wheel sharply while accelerating to complete the circle drive. Stopping at the two-lane blacktop road, he looked both ways. "Where to?"

"Turn right. We're going to the Morgan farm," answered Schmidt, turning his head to look at Linda and letting the barrel of his 9mm rest on the back of the seat. "At the next fork in the road, turn right again, and we'll cross over some railroad tracks."

It took fifteen minutes for them to reach the old house where Linda and her son had taken shelter from the rainstorm, and when it first came into view, she recognized the roofline of the old house. Feeling a strange fluttering and churning in her stomach, she realized time was running out for help to arrive, and it was as though the imminent threat of death was causing her to shrink from within...

CHAPTER 19

Turning Up the Heat

Arriving at the farmhouse, Mehlnick drove around back, parking the car a good distance away from the house, and left the Mercedes facing the wheat field. He and Schmidt acted diligently to remove the gas cans from the trunk, while Kepler opened the car door and stepped out, his weapon pointed at Matheson. "Out."

Linda and Matheson slid across the seat to exit on the driver's side of the car. As they stood handcuffed together, Linda noticed Matheson holding his right side with his left hand.

Schmidt placed his 9mm inside his trenchcoat to enable him to carry the black bag in one hand and one of the gallon-sized containers of gasoline in the other. Mehlnick and Kepler carried the remaining two cans. Kepler used his gun hand to close the trunk lid, then gestured with his weapon for Linda and Matheson to begin moving to the house, giving the order, "Move it."

Walking beside Matheson, Linda spoke under her breath, saying, "What are we gonna do?"

Kepler placed the barrel of his pistol to her back. "Keep your head straight and your mouth shut."

Directed to the front of the old house, Linda was gripped by a nervous tension, as whatever cruel fate these people had in mind for them left her stifled. They came around to the front porch where the foliage of a mature tree shaded the rotted and splitting front steps, and the deck's weathered floorboards had cupped.

Gathering on the porch, Linda felt her world closing in around her. The moment seemed surreal until Kepler took aim at the door lock. The gun blast that followed made her jump.

Schmidt used his foot to push the door open and stale air belched from the building's dark interior. "OK, let's go in."

Filing into the house, they saw the shape of a large room. A tilting handrail post had dislodged from the base of the staircase some time ago, and a lone armchair sat in the room's corner. They placed the gas cans together inside the front door, and Schmidt placed the black bag on the floor to take a look around, moving into another room where sunlight shone dimly through a far doorway.

"Bring them in here," Schmidt called out.

Kepler stuck the barrel of his pistol in Matheson's back, warning him, "Don't try anything—you won't get far chained together."

When joining Schmidt in the next room, Linda recognized the impoverished room as the one she and Allan had slept in the night before last. The shutter's louvers blocked out most of the sunlight, but at the room's far end, sunlight streamed in from the kitchen's back door. The closet door lay on the floor the same way she had seen it last, and Schmidt turned his attention to the decayed plaster wall near the opening to the closet where there was exposed wood lath and a small hole.

"This will do," Schmidt said, placing his foot against the edge of the door resting on the floor and shoving it to give him space to examine the deteriorated section of a wall where wood lath was visible. The wall drawing his attention divided this room from the living room they'd just entered the house from, and going down on one knee, he began prying away pieces of lath.

Watching Schmidt tear free these slats to enlarge the hole in the wall, Linda had no idea what he was up to, but Kepler held his gun pointed at her and Matheson as the work continued.

Schmidt tore out enough wood lath slats to expose one of the studs, and the aging plaster he disturbed kept crumbling to the floor. He'd created an opening above an existing baseboard six or eight inches in height and about twenty-four inches wide, and the missing plaster and lath allowed one to view a portion of the wall's hollow interior. Pausing to gaze about the room for something his mind had a purpose for, and not seeing what he wanted readily at hand, he got up and went into the kitchen.

They heard him prying loose a three-quarter-inch piece of corroded galvanized pipe from beneath the sink, and he returned to slide his foot across the floor as a way to clear the floor space of fallen plaster. He then stooped to resume work on the cavity, using the pipe to probe while driving and ramming it to penetrate clear through the wall to make two fist-size holes on both sides of the stud support. He then leaned over to make certain he'd created space to see clear through to the living room on both sides of the stud, seeing light coming in from the front door entrance.

Having accomplished what he'd set out to do, he tossed the pipe to a far corner and then brushed his hands together to free them of dust. Reaching inside his shirt pocket to produce a key, he handed it to Mehlnick, saying, "Take the cuff off the woman."

Kepler held the barrel of his weapon to Matheson's ribs while Mehlnick unlocked the cuff on Linda's wrist.

Schmidt remained stooped on one knee as he looked up at Matheson. "Sit down on the floor here with your back against the wall."

Matheson was slow moving, so Kepler jammed the barrel of his pistol into his gut where he knew it would hurt, and he doubled over, grunting in pain. He held his side to ease the pressure on his ribcage as he bent his knees and sank to the floor. Kepler now held the gun to his head while Schmidt took hold of his arm.

"Easy does it."

Everything Matheson saw pointed to his and Linda's demise, and powerless to do anything about it, he knew it wouldn't be long before they achieved their goal. Taking a sitting position on the floor with his back to the wall, Matheson looked beat when saying, "Maybe we can make a deal."

"That's funny," mentioned Schmidt. "If the situation was reversed and I was in your position, I'd be saying the exact same thing."

"You want the disc, don't you?"

"We trust you less than we do her," said Schmidt, and he fished the loose cuff and length of chain links through the hole and around the stud to bring them back inside the room.

Schmidt now reached for Linda's hand, her eyes watering, and having grown apprehensive, she froze, but he took hold of her shaking hand to pull her down to the floor. Situating her on Matheson's right, where she was closest to the closet doorway, he clasped the cuff around her wrist. He then made certain both cuffs were secure before standing up.

He looked down at Matheson. "I don't ordinarily take my job on a personal basis, but I'm going to take pleasure in snuffing you out."

"That's fine if you feel what you're doing is justified," said Matheson, "but why don't you let the girl go? She's done nothing to deserve this, and she knows nothing that can hurt any of you."

"She can identify us," remarked Mehlnick, "and she knew the risks when she contacted the authorities."

Schmidt went to get the black handbag, and crouching down on one knee to open it in the middle of the room Matheson and Linda occupied, he then began adjusting its contents.

Kepler tucked his pistol inside its holster and went to unscrew the lids on the gasoline cans, calling out, "Are you about ready?"

Schmidt came to his feet. "Ready now. We haven't much time."

Kepler followed Schmidt into the kitchen, carrying one of the cans of gasoline, and listened as Schmidt said, "Douse the kitchen floor, and move outside leaving a trail around the perimeter of the house. When you hear the explosion, light it."

Kepler started splashing the kitchen floor with gasoline as he backed up to the rear door, and smelling highly-combustible fumes, Linda and Matheson sensed the volatility of the situation.

Mehlnick remained in the living room. Picking up one of the gas cans, his voice carried with an echoed effect. "This place is going to go up fast."

Schmidt shouted to Kepler, "Hurry up in there," and he lastly turned to Linda and Matheson, saying simply, "*Auf wiedersehen.*"

Schmidt picked up the third container of gasoline, leaving a trail of the liquid fuel as he and Mehlnick made their exit from the front of the house, and the fumes grew stronger than ever.

Immobilized by the cuffs, Linda and Matheson stared grimly at the black bag lying on the floor, and she said, "It's a bomb, isn't it? And if the explosion doesn't kill us, we'll die in a house fire."

Still holding his side, Matheson commented, "I doubt if we have five minutes."

Linda had watched how Schmidt fed the chain with one cuff through the hole, around the stud, and back inside the room, and knowing they had little time, she drew slack out of the chain. To gain their freedom, she'd have to create openings on each side of the stud big enough for her to pass through to enter the next room and then to return to the room they now occupied. Twisting and turning to lie down on her back, she started pounding the wall with her heel. With each kick the wood lath would absorb the shock, but chunks of plaster rained down in a cloud of dust. Matheson turned his face from falling debris and floating dust, and Linda stopped the slamming motion of her feet to franticly pry away pieces of lath from the wall, with some easily pulling free.

"There isn't time. That bomb's going to go off any second now," Matheson asserted, stretching his leg out in an effort to reach the black bag with his foot. He groaned, "Maybe I can reach the bag."

"You're injured. Let me try."

"I'm closer." Matheson grimaced, extending himself, but couldn't get close enough to reach the black bag with his shoe.

"You almost have it," she said with urgency in her voice, giving him what slack she could. She placed her wrist inside the cavity to give him more chain length with which to stretch further across the floor.

Lying with his body extended, he saw the toe of his shoe falling short of the bag. "It's useless, and even if we prevent its detonation, they'll return to finish us."

Rolling onto his good side, Matheson saw the closet door resting nearby, and determining it was reachable, he brought his leg over swiftly to hook the top of his shoe on the door's handle. Pulling the door to him, he could barely maneuver it with his only free arm. He used his foot to aid him in the struggle to uplift the door, and he placed its top end against the black bag. Straining as he put pressure on his ribs, he then carefully pushed the door, and in doing so slid the bag as far away as he could. Not knowing if he'd accomplished anything by moving the bag closer to the room's window, it now rested on floorboards warped from the leaky roof.

Before pushing the door too far out of reach and losing his grip on it, he stopped to pull it back, dragging it toward him. As he gathered himself to the wall and pulled the door with him, Linda helped him stand the door on its side, positioning it quarter-turned sideways to rest horizontally on its hinges. Linda was first to slither around the vertical doorjamb to move inside the closet, and he followed to take a crouched position behind the door, as they squirmed into a narrow, boxed-in, cramped space. Her left arm was extended awkwardly. The cuff and chain held her bound to Matheson with the chain running around the stud, and she felt squeezed, having given him what space she could.

There was hardly enough room inside the closet for the two of them, and expecting an explosion to come at any second, Matheson couldn't get his body completely contained inside. He'd arranged the door in such a way that it spanned lengthwise across the floor to cover the lower portion of the door opening. Ducking while squatting uncomfortably between the door and Linda, he felt off balance clinging to the door handle. The strung-out chain restricted him from finding a better way to brace himself with any stability. He used his knee to nudge the low end of the door out to make it slightly angled, and their only hope was that the door would serve to shield them from the blast's impact.

A tremendous, deafening blast suddenly erupted to shake the house! The door kicked back, sandwiching them. The cuffs held fast, yanking hard while cutting into their wrists. The door pushed Matheson inward to smash Linda against the closet's back wall. Her eyes bugged as the wind was squashed out of her. Time stopped—she thought she'd die.

Blackened gray smoke engulfed the room while plaster settled from the gutted ceiling. The door tipped over with Matheson falling over on it, and Linda fell against him. Dazed but quickly recovering, Matheson saw through the cloud of dust a bright glow from across the room as the window's shutters had blown free from the house. With a *WH-OOO-SH* sound, roaring flames rose from the kitchen, then from the other doorway, and bound by the cuff connected to his right wrist, he felt for the chain to locate the stud inset in the wall.

Breathing through his left sleeve to filter out dust and smoke, he lay on his side kicking against the lath with his left foot to open up the wall, his leg motion irritating the pain felt in his ribcage. More plaster fell from the wall, and holding his left arm against his side, he coughed before shouting, "Linda, you've got to help!"

Stirring and beginning to cough, she heard his words over the ringing in her ears. She rose to resituate herself before stomping her heel against the weakened plaster and wood lath. Ignoring falling plaster, she came to her knees, desperately prying wood lath free to expose more of the wall's interior. When flames from the exits spread to the ceiling with the heat intensifying, her fear escalated to sheer madness, and she kept clawing and yanking pieces of lath free with greater speed to further open the wall up.

Their freedom depended on her rounding the stud the chain ran around and reentering the room to join Matheson. Coughing while gasping for air, she saw her obstacles breaking down. In a frenzied effort, she rose to kick through the hollow gap in the wall, her foot punching clear through to the other side. Another swift kick delivered to the area on the other side of the stud raised the height of the opening while expanding the space for her to pass through. She saw the next room in flames.

Just then, the ceiling in the living room caved in, and collapsing clumps of plaster and debris smothered the flames, but the fire quickly reignited to consume that room. The smoke aggravating her nagging cough until she could hardly breathe, the heat fast becoming unbearable, she drove her shoulder between two upright studs to enter that fiery room as more plaster and dust rained down. Hardly able to see anything, she came around the stud to thrust the upper part of her body between wall studs again, forcing her shoulder and body through to succeed in crossing over to rejoin Matheson.

Soaked in perspiration from the heat's intensity, she dropped to her knees to view fire covering all exits. Fire crackled and spit, and she slapped at small patches of fire on her clothing to put them out. The whole house coming down around them, Linda coughed when pointing to the window where smoke was escaping. They scurried across the floor on their hands and knees. Dodging flaming pieces falling from above, Matheson made it to the window first, but the very second sunlight hit his face, a bullet caught the window frame.

Ducking back, the blaze overtaking the room, Matheson felt the cuff pull at his wrist, and he saw Linda's face at a hole in the floor made by the bomb's blast. Taking a deep breath from the sharp updraft, he joined her to discover a crawl space beneath the house. They worked desperately, ripping up splintered planks of wood from the floor to create an escape route.

Fire had encircled the house, and outside the window, Mehlnick stood with his pistol drawn. Having heard the gunshot, Schmidt dashed toward him. "What are you shooting at?"

"I thought I saw a face at the window." Looking at the window, neither one of them could see beyond smoke billowing from the window.

"There's no way. Your eyes are playing tricks on you." After giving it some thought, Schmidt moved closer to the window, saying, "Stay here and keep an eye on the window. I'm going to walk around the building."

Having made a hole in the floor big enough for them to fit through, Linda entered the crawl space first, slithering between two floor joists. The chain and cuffs connecting them made movement difficult, and her pants leg caught on a nail, but Matheson freed it before following her, squirming through while keeping pressure off his ribs. Far across the dark and narrow space, they saw a small opening where stark sunlight shone forth, and with hardly enough room to go on all fours, they began crawling to get to it. Linda stuck her chin out as she stretched out her right arm to pull herself forward, but the chain connected to her left wrist restricted her movement. She kept her left arm to her side, pulling at the cuff while moving as fast as she could with her belly skimming along the dirt, never bothering to look back.

Matheson followed with his right hand extended, feeling the cuff tugging, and ignoring the pain in his side, he did all he could to keep up with her. Using his left forearm and elbow to propel himself, he was having a terrible time staying on the move. Up ahead, an eight-by-eight timber stretched horizontally to support long-running floor joists merging at the center of the house, but there was one sunken spot that gave them an avenue to continue on.

Linda hurriedly slid beneath the suspended beam, ignoring the black dust and cobwebs covering it, and she saw smoke seeping between the floorboards overhead. Out of breath, Matheson bumped his head while passing beneath the beam and saw cobwebs loosely pulsating from currents of air. A large brown recluse spider scurried to get out of his way. Something heavy crashed against the floor above and they quickened their pace. Reaching the opening where they met daylight, they both laid low.

Quieting their uncontrollable coughs as they tried catching their breath, they pushed aside slow-burning weeds and high brush obstructing their view to gain sight of the outside world. Linda saw how, after ten yards, the scrub brush and weeds blended into wheat, and another thirty yards beyond the wheat field was a tree line where freedom awaited them. Wanting to avoid Schmidt and the others, they had a long way to go to get there without being discovered.

Wanting to give Matheson a minute to recover before moving on, Linda looked at him and said, "If we can make those trees, we have half a chance of escaping those killers."

Concerned he may have suffered serious internal injuries as a result of the beatings he'd taken, Matheson nodded, but he wasn't sure if he could make it.

CHAPTER 20

To Run For Your Life

Linda and Matheson were apprehensive about leaving the crawl space, but they had no choice as the house was fast becoming an inferno. They got to their feet and started for the woods. At first bogged down in the overgrowth of high weeds, when coming to the wheat field they were able to make longer strides. Nearing the woods, they felt optimistic about making it. Looking back as they heard the roof and a section of the second floor collapse, they sighted Schmidt moving toward the rear of the house, but his eyes were on flames engulfing the house. The fiery blaze was sending a column of black smoke and ash into the sky, and Schmidt still hadn't caught sight of them as they aimed to find salvation in the woods.

With the house ablaze, Schmidt was confident that if the bomb hadn't finished the two of them off, they'd surely died in the inferno, but then he saw the opening to the crawl space where the fire had died out. Kepler joined Schmidt, and after they checked the opening, their eyes scanned the outlying area. They spotted Linda and Matheson just as they disappeared into the woods.

After firing two shots, he and Kepler chased after them.

Drenched in sweat and running for their lives with their hearts racing in panic, Linda and Matheson kept an even pace to move into a heavily wooded area where a canopy of tall trees provided shade.

"They're coming for us," Linda said breathlessly, her heart-beat surging, her lungs constantly swelling as her feet pushed rampant through dry leaves.

Matheson clutched his side. "Just keep running."

Both tiring, their legs moved rapidly as they passed between two trees, and when their shoulders bounced together, Linda went down. Matheson grimaced while pulling her up by the arm, and they were soon on the run again, but the expression on Matheson's face showed the intense pain he felt. Coming up on a cluster of small trees, they were able to dodge all but one, and getting the chain caught on it nearly caused them to collide. Linda quickly rounded the tree to get moving again. As the earth turned into a downward slope, keeping afoot on this rugged terrain was becoming challenging, so they slowed down. Flashes of sunlight blinked between the thick foliage above them as the steep incline turned into a deep ravine. Linda's heart pumped hard while she blocked the branches of small trees to protect her face. Another gunshot rang out, the bullet striking a nearby tree, and nearly losing their footing on their descent of steep bluffs, they didn't have much more to go before reaching bottom. They made their way through brush and thick woods to come to level ground where they saw railroad tracks, and across the tracks began another steep rise into more woodland.

Panting hard and out of breath, Matheson stopped to bend over, and doing all he could to stay on his feet, he took a slouched posture to rest his hands on his knees. "There's no way I can make that hill."

Linda took deep breaths as well, her eyes searching to locate their pursuers descending the hillside, but she couldn't see them. To their left, the tracks ran down a dark tunnel, and to their right the tracks cut between the hills and around a bend. When Linda motioned toward the arched stone entrance to the tunnel, they went for it.

Entering the darkness of the tunnel, they focused on the bright opening at the far end, but they weren't halfway through before the pain in Matheson's ribs caused him to stop.

"I've got at least two cracked ribs, and I can't go on," he said, shaking his head as he held his side. Then he leaned his back against the tunnel's stone wall.

Distant, muffled voices echoed from the entrance of the tunnel, and Linda spoke in a whisper, "Jack, if we lie down, maybe they won't see us, and they might not come down the tunnel."

Matheson nodded. They stretched out on the packed gravel alongside the tracks, and Linda watched the end of the tunnel to see Schmidt appear at the opening.

"Down here," he shouted, his amplified voice carrying down the tunnel.

Mehlnick and Kepler soon joined him and their conversation could be distinctly heard as Schmidt said, "I saw them last when I was coming down the hill and they were standing by the tracks. They weren't far enough ahead of me to reach the end of this tunnel without me catching sight of them, so they must have gone up into these woods."

"Can't we afford to let them go now?" asked Mehlnick. "Kleistner's cleared out of the house and there's no reason to return to it except to get your car."

Schmidt looked at his wristwatch and seeing it was 6:30, he said, "We have until ten to look for them. After that, our job's been accomplished and it can't be said that we've bungled orders."

"What if we do catch up to them?" asked Kepler.

"Make it quick and drop them where they stand," replied Schmidt. He then turned to Mehlnick. "We can keep in touch using our cell phones, but for now, go back and move the car, then keep circling the area. You can pick us up later on the road."

Their voices faded as they moved from the mouth of the tunnel, and she last saw Schmidt and Kepler with their guns drawn climbing the hill opposite the one they'd just come down.

Looking to avoid the men attempting to arrange their deaths, but unable to run anymore, Matheson said, "My side is killing me."

Linda responded by repositioning herself to face Matheson. "You'll be OK after you've rested awhile."

Matheson examined the cuts and scratches on Linda's face, and one on her forehead near the scalp line looked deeper than the others. He tore a piece of cloth from his shirtsleeve and wet it with his saliva to clean the cut. There were black patches around her nose and mouth from the inhalation of smoke and dust, and he wiped them off as well. His face looked no better than hers, so she did the same for him. They continued facing each other for a time, keeping eye contact in the dark confines of the tunnel—a look that turned into a romantic gaze, drawing them to each other.

He pushed her hair back, then caressed her smudged cheek— a touch that brought her near to him, and her eyelids fell shut before their lips pressed tenderly together. She felt his whiskers when brushing cheek-to-cheek, and after exhaling, she placed her head against his shoulder as they closely nestled.

Combing his fingers through her hair, he spoke softly, saying, "There was a moment back there when I thought we were done for, and I only wished then that I had time to tell you I love you."

She raised her head to look in his eyes, and they kissed gently and for a long time, but when she opened her eyes, his expression told her that his attention was elsewhere.

"What is it?"

"Shhh, listen." Matheson sat up. "Do you hear it?"

"No. What?"

Going to the train rail to put his ear to it, Matheson was now sure of what he heard, and he said, "A train is coming."

Remaining together and placing his and her wrists close to a railroad tie, Matheson then situated part of the chain linking the cuffs together across the train rail, and said, "Just sit tight."

The train was soon close enough for Linda to hear its approach and seconds later, she lifted her head to see the engine rounding the bend at high speed. Focused on its fast approach, she felt apprehensive about keeping her wrist so close to the rail, and wanting to pull her hand away, she said, "I don't think I like this."

Matheson held her arm and wrist firm, speaking reassuringly. "We're lying below the rail, so we'll be alright. Just trust me and keep still."

The oncoming engine's thunderous noise and the sound of metal riding against metal amplified in the tunnel—the train's sudden quaking rumble and roar was deafening. Feeling urgency to move away from the tracks, her eyes went from the oncoming train to Matheson, then to the rail where the links of chain rested.

He pulled her close to him to kiss her in the most sensuous way. Her eyelids closed, shutting out her fear, and their kiss lasted through the duration of the train's passing. They stayed together until the last car had passed, and then Matheson moved to check the handcuffs' chain and saw that the links lying on the rail had squashed thin under the weight of the train's wheels. He twisted the smashed links back and forth until they weakened and came apart, and they were now free of themselves.

"I don't know what's best to do from here on, but maybe we should split up because Kleistner is planning on leaving the country soon, if he hasn't already. You've got to think of your son now, and you'll be able to make better time on your own to reach the authorities."

It was obvious that Matheson was going to slow her down, and lagging behind may make him easy prey, but Linda didn't want to separate, and insisted, "No, we stick together."

They came to their feet to continue their walk to the end of the tunnel. Linda expressed thoughts. "The day before yesterday, I uncovered a note on the desk in the library of the house where they were keeping us. The note read 'Wednesday, 10 p.m., Auburn Airfield,' and it had the name 'Crawford' underlined." She then added, "Today's Wednesday, and we just heard Schmidt stress the time of ten o'clock, so could it mean that Crawford is the pilot of a plane and they're leaving from Auburn Airfield at ten tonight?"

Matheson replied, "Schmidt said he wanted to continue the chase until ten o'clock, so that may be, but their plans could've changed, and may still change again. I studied a statewide map, and I don't remember seeing an Auburn Airport, but the map designers may not have designated small airfields."

"Would they leave without the disc?"

"By now, who's to say they don't have it? A lot depends on what your Louise Hagen does with the disc when it's delivered to your home, which I imagine might happen sometime today."

Reaching the mouth of the tunnel and the sunlit area that lay beyond, Matheson said, "You know, we were damn lucky back there, and I still think it would be a good idea to split up."

"Jack, if you're thinking of my wellbeing, I could just as easily be the one they catch up to, so splitting up isn't going to accomplish anything."

He looked into the trees once more. "So what do we do?"

"I think we'd be pushing our luck to go back to that house. A blaze like that should've drawn spectators and maybe the authorities, but we may not survive another confrontation with these people. I suggest we go up into these trees, keeping parallel with the tracks and see where it takes us."

Walking arm in arm, they started up into the woods keeping parallel with the railroad tracks until they came upon a rocky stream of cool, clear water. Matheson plunged his upper body into the water, remaining immersed for a few seconds, and Linda cupped her hands together to splash her face before drinking the water to soothe her parched throat. After refreshing herself, Linda cleaned some of the cuts and scratches she'd acquired when tearing a hole through that wall. She no longer had long fingernails, having chipped and broken them all off, and she'd scraped her arms up squeezing between those studs, acquiring numerous splinters embedded in her hands. Glad to be alive, having cheated death, they started moving through a densely forested area remaining watchful for Kleistner's henchmen, while fearing what might happen if they should meet up with them again.

CHAPTER 21

Eluding the Killers

After surviving a brush with death, they remained fearful of being found by the men hunting them and journeyed till sundown to trudge out of the woods in to a clearing where they heard loud country music. They came to the outskirts of a gravel lot where they saw many cars parked near a one-story building that looked like an assembly hall. Matheson didn't appear at all well, and in the last hundred yards of their walk he'd become dependent on Linda to keep him going. She shouldered his weight to get him inside a dimly-lit but crowded establishment where they heard the music with more clarity, and they got looks from some of the patrons. Most people's attention was on the live band playing onstage. A male vocalist wearing a black cowboy hat and vest was singing a popular Garth Brooks song.

Linda and Matheson went down a wide aisle running between the bar and a short wall partitioning a widespread area for round tables surrounding a crowded dance floor. Feeling light-headed, Matheson went for a barstool at the partition, bumping into a man who just vacated the seat.

The patron noticed the dirty smudge Matheson left on his shirt and brushing it off, he remarked, "How'd the coal miners get in here?"

Somebody chuckled, and Linda gave him a hard stare.

Now seated, Matheson leaned on the partition's counter, his forearm knocking over a drink.

"I'm sorry, he's feeling ill," Linda said to the woman whose drink he spilled.

The woman and her companion walked away, with one turning to the other and commenting, "They're filthy."

Drawing a deep breath, Matheson looked at Linda and said, "I'll be alright here, but you need get to a phone and call the state police. Have them contact Richard Bante with the Defense Intelligence Agency in Washington. Give them my name and don't forget to mention that Kleistner and some of his followers may be taking off from that Auburn Airfield at 10 p.m., and hurry."

Linda cut across the aisle to the bar to confront the bartender, whose hands busily exchanged drinks for cash. The clock above the back of the bar read a few minutes after nine o'clock. "Excuse me," she said with her voice raised, "I need to make an emergency phone call."

His eyes never left the glass he filled or the bottle he poured from. "The phone is back by the restrooms."

Linda looked about, her eyes tracing the boundaries of the partition bordering the perimeter of the dance floor. Sets of stairs rose on each side of the stage to reach a balcony that ran the building's length, serving as a backdrop for the stage, but she had no idea where the phone or restrooms were located.

With urgency in her voice, she asked the bartender, "Where are the restrooms?"

"In the rear, next to the pinball machines," he replied, squeezing lemon peel into a glass while pointing with his other hand.

He'd pointed to a corridor where she saw a sign that said RESTROOMS with an arrow, and there were pinball machines with lights flashing off their backboards in the same area. She fought the crowd to reach a pay phone at the far end of the corridor. Waiting for a man in a T-shirt to finish making a call, she realized she wasn't carrying any change, but did have some cash. Traffic steadily coming in and out of the restrooms, she moved out of the corridor to catch the attention of a waitress and exchanged cash for coins.

Seeing the person on the phone hadn't finished making his call, she tapped him on the shoulder and said, "I need to make an emergency phone call."

The individual rudely replied, "One emergency at a time."

Worried their pursuers may show up, Linda discovered Matheson had moved from the place she'd last seen him and was concerned about what had happened to him. She scanned the area trying to locate him. Seeing the phone no longer in use, she dialed 911, relaying information to the state police as Matheson had instructed, and urged the authorities to contact Richard Bante at the Defense Department. Explaining there were armed killers searching for them, she also made it clear that a plane taking off from Auburn Airfield at 10 p.m. could be kidnappers who had her son. After mentioning the plane's pilot may be someone named Crawford, she hung up the phone and then nearly stumbled into Matheson. He looked somewhat rejuvenated after leaving the restroom with his face washed and his hair combed, but still looked pale.

Linda said, "Help is on the way."

The musicians had taken a break, and now hearing Patsy Cline singing the song "Crazy" over the speaker system, she remarked, "They're playing our song."

Matheson smiled. "I think I'm going to have a cold beer to quench my thirst. May I get you something to drink?"

"Make mine a rum and Coke, and as soon as I've freshened up, I'll meet you back at the partition."

In the restroom, Linda worried whether the authorities would get to the airport in time to stop the plane from taking off with her son. Thinking about it made her want to cry. Remembering how close they'd come to dying in that house fire and doing all she could to just survive, it was now up to the police to capture these people. Standing at the sink with the water running, she noticed her ravaged appearance in the mirror and the image shocked her, as she saw a rash of minor cuts and scratches on her face.

Matheson stood by the partition counter where a collection of tall-neck beer bottles had clustered, smoke from a smoldering cigarette going straight to his head. To avoid the irritation the smoke caused him, he moved down along the partition, and when a person came to stand beside him, he turned to see Schmidt standing there.

"We meet again," said Schmidt, wearing a wide smirk.

Matheson looked across the dance floor and beyond the building's glass front to the parking lot. He saw Kepler standing beside the blue BMW's back door with his back to the building. It appeared Kepler was having trouble with the fit of the trench-coat he wore, which may have been Schmidt's since he wasn't wearing his, and he closed and straightened the coat before coming to enter the nightspot.

"Let me congratulate you on your escape," remarked Schmidt. "I never would've guessed you'd be able to get out of that one."

"Haven't you people caused us enough trouble? We don't have the disc. What is it you want?"

"Simply following orders. You know how it is."

"The state police will be here any minute."

Schmidt lifted the few chain links dangling from the cuff connected to Matheson's right wrist. "Where's your female companion?"

"We split up," Matheson replied, watching Kepler standing guard at the entrance.

"I doubt that."

Matheson thought about how grim the predicament looked with their arrival. Linda came around from the corridor, her mouth dropping open when her eyes locked with Schmidt's, and then she saw Kepler standing at the entrance.

Matheson gripped a beer bottle, shattering it over Schmidt's head, and before his body had hit the floor, Kepler threw open his coat, withdrew an Uzi machine gun, and fired a burst at Matheson.

Ducking and running, Matheson covered his head to protect himself from flying glass coming off the partition, diving out of sight just as the music stopped. The weapon had devastating firepower with the capability of shooting 800 rounds per minute, and everyone dropped to the floor in fear as Kepler sprayed bullets indiscriminately.

Kepler started across the dance floor with people scattering to get out of his way, but one man sprang heroically to grab hold of him, only to have Kepler cut him down with a short spurt. He then fired at the bar, taking out the mirror and bottles and drinking glasses. Shattered glass flew until the gunfire stopped, and he shouted, "Stay down, and you won't get hurt!"

Matheson kept out of sight, and no longer seeing Linda, he heard whimpering and crying from people who may be injured. Seeing Schmidt recovering to draw his pistol from inside his sport coat, he moved away to distance himself and started up the balcony stairs crawling on his belly. A short wall shielded him from Kepler's view, but he knew he couldn't dodge them for long because there were no outside exits off the balcony to provide him a line of escape.

"Come out with your hands in the air," demanded Kepler, as though to bluff Matheson into thinking he knew where he was, keeping his finger on the trigger.

Schmidt was rubbing his head when he caught a glimpse of Matheson creeping on all fours on the balcony level to slip behind the backdrop for the stage. He took aim and fired with his pistol, but missed, and losing sight of him behind the partition, he pointed to indicate to Kepler where to take aim. "He's on the balcony!"

Kepler sent a hail of bullets that pierced the backdrop partition to follow the length of the balcony, missing Matheson but hitting others.

Sinking to the floor, Matheson paused to view a fiercely trembling leg belonging to a man whose open eyes were still, and then he continued crawling for the far end of the balcony at the building's front. Searching for a way out, he sensed they were closing in. The quiet was unnerving, and wishing for the sound of sirens to save him, he knew it was too late for miracles.

Finding himself trapped at a corner where steps led back down to the dance floor, he focused on a nearby window's lean wood construction supporting six-by-nine sections of glass panes.

Schmidt had come up to view the balcony level, and taking aim to fire, he shouted, "At the far end!"

Kepler fired just as Matheson dove through the window, landing outside on the walk and rolling before recovering to regain his footing.

Bullets flew as the machine gun rapidly chattered, and Matheson went into a stumbling run for the woods to get away. The stinging pain in his ribs became greater than ever. Putting his hand where he felt a burning pain below his ribcage, he glimpsed his blood-soaked fingers. Realizing a bullet had gone through him, and ignoring the enormous pain within, his heart-beat surged.

Reaching the woods, he fell forward on his palms and chest, sliding on grass and dried leaves before stopping. "God," he said aloud, a single tear running down his face, and he crawled beneath the low sweeping branches of a tall evergreen tree to collapse in a bed of dry needles.

Kepler went outside chasing after him, but Schmidt remained behind, keeping his finger on the trigger of his handgun, hunting down Linda.

Quiet tension gripped the establishment as Schmidt looked about to target Linda, and seeing people everywhere, he realized it may be difficult to distinguish her from so many. Moving to the edge of the corridor where he'd seen her last, he singled out a blonde woman crouched on the floor who resembled her, and when he took aim, her eyes widened in terror as she cowered. Concluding it wasn't her, he moved down the corridor and kicked open the door to the women's restroom, where two women were clutching each other in a corner while squirming in fear.

Linda had ducked inside the men's restroom when the shooting broke out, and she stood behind the door alongside a young man, their backsides flat against the wall.

Listening for a sign the shooting had ended, the guy standing next to her asked in a soft whisper, "Do you think it's over?"

Linda closed her eyes and shook her head no.

Before moving from the corridor to return to the main area, Schmidt stopped at the men's restroom door, and opening it slowly, he froze as he heard the sound of sirens in the distance.

Linda stood straight and rigid with perspiration flooding from her body, staring wide-eyed at the door, thinking this was the end.

Knowing the police were closing in, Schmidt abandoned his search, exited by a clear path left for him, and ran to his BMW to start its engine. Shifting the transmission into gear, he put his foot to the floor to accelerate, and steering the car to where Kepler stood, he threw the door open to him, shouting, "C'mon and get in."

"I lost him in these woods," said Kepler, "but I don't see how I could have missed him."

Schmidt now yelled to Kepler, "Forget him and get in!"

Kepler took the front passenger seat and the BMW sped off into the night.

CHAPTER 22

The Clock is Running

Linda didn't leave the restroom until she heard sirens directly outside the building, and she was a nervous wreck when stepping into the corridor. Awed by the onrush of New Jersey state troopers and county sheriffs storming the building with their weapons drawn, aid was given to the wounded and those in shock. A captain for the state police arrived on the scene wearing a mountie-style hat, and assessing conditions, he instructed his sergeant to allow paramedics inside to give medical attention to those needing it most.

Coming to this police captain with her lower lip quivering, she broke down in tears. "I am Linda Moreland."

He escorted her to a chair. "I'm Captain Ferris and I received notification about your distress call by radio. Can you tell me what happened to Matheson? Was he killed?"

"I don't know. There was so much shooting."

People began showing life, and paramedics tended to a man stretched out on the dance floor whose chest area was drenched in blood, but they immediately pronounced him dead.

"No!" cried out a woman who knew the deceased, and she watched as they covered his body with a sheet.

The sergeant returned to address Ferris. "From what I've gathered from witnesses, two gunmen went on a shooting rampage targeting a man who dove through the building's front glass." He pointed to the window Matheson crashed through, adding, "We've found droplets of blood indicating he was hit, but have not discovered a body thus far."

"You've got to find him—he may be bleeding to death!" blurted out Linda, trying to get up, but the captain restrained her, and she stared at the blood-stained sheet covering the body on the dance floor.

He turned to his sergeant. "Get some cars' headlights pointing into the nearby woods, and initiate a sweeping search following the blood trail."

The sergeant went outside to join other officers, and minutes later, he stuck his head in the door, shouting, "We've found him, Captain!"

Linda ran outside into the woods where emergency vehicles had their lights directed, and a state trooper guided an ambulance driver to back his vehicle up to the edge of the lot where officers huddled.

It began raining and she came to see flashlights beaming down on Matheson's body lying on a gurney, his eyes closed.

While paramedics strapped him in, an officer commented, "Had I not nearly stumbled over him we may not have found him until it was too late, but he's still alive. I saw his eyes open."

Police assisted in hoisting up the stretcher to carry him out of the woods and they loaded him into the ambulance. Linda asked a paramedic, "Is he going to be alright?"

"He has a pulse, but he's lost a lot of blood and the next hour or two will be critical for him, but on the way to the hospital, we'll do all we can to stabilize his vital signs."

"Mrs. Moreland," the captain called out, standing in the form of a silhouette. "I've been informed that two officials from the Defense Department are on their way here, and they should be arriving within the hour."

"We can't wait. I explained when I phoned for assistance that there are kidnappers who have my five-year-old son, and they're supposed to take off in a plane from Auburn Airfield at ten o'clock."

"It's after ten now, but I can't recall where Auburn Airfield is located." The captain looked at his sergeant in the hope he knew where it was.

The sergeant responded with, "Auburn Airfield is roughly thirty miles southeast of here."

Ferris nodded, "OK, I recall hearing over the radio about dispatching cars to an airfield, but what about those officials due to arrive here from the Defense Department?"

Linda replied, "They'll have to catch up to us there."

As light rain came down steadily, Linda followed the captain to his car and sat in the front passenger seat, hoping the plane hadn't taken off.

Ferris spoke into his radio. "Dispatcher, this is Captain Ferris. I have Linda Moreland with me. Please advise Defense Department officials that we are headed for Auburn Airfield. Can you tell me how conditions stand right now at that airfield?"

A voice came back, saying, "We have contact with Auburn Airfield, and police on the scene have stopped all aircraft scheduled for takeoff."

The captain's car became third in a string of patrol cars with their emergency lights on. The lead car was driven by the sergeant. The dispatcher stayed in radio contact with state and local police at Auburn Airfield. Minutes later, the dispatcher reported hearing gunfire when police approached a plane scheduled for departure, and officers returned fire.

"Are police aware that my child is a hostage on that plane?"

"Dispatch, law enforcement at Auburn should be advised that Mrs. Moreland's five-year-old boy is on the plane in question, and they should act accordingly with this child's safety in mind."

"Can't we go any faster?" asked Linda, while the windshield wipers kept time.

"We're pushing it now. These blacktops are slippery when it begins raining, but there's nothing we can do that isn't already being done to gain your son's freedom."

A radio message from the dispatcher came back, reporting, "Gunfire has ceased, but state police have the airstrip blocked with their cars while cornering a Hawker Beechcraft twin turboprop airplane."

In the following radio message, the dispatcher reported that they were arranging for the police to intercept signals transmitted and received through the airfield's tower. Officials had done this to aid police on the scene who wanted to monitor communications and have the option to speak directly with those on the plane. This took a short while, and as the signal came through, Linda heard a voice from the control tower contacting the plane's pilot by radio. The garbled transmission was at first difficult to understand, but she grasped that police were signaling for the pilot of the plane, Darren Crawford, to acknowledge their demand for people to evacuate the plane.

There was a pause as those in the plane discussed their predicament, and the pilot's answer came back, "Negative."

"I repeat," announced the air traffic controller, "your plane must be evacuated. You will not be allowed to take off."

Crawford replied, "Occupants of the plane aren't giving up."

"Looks like we're in for a standoff that could make for a long evening," mentioned Ferris, turning the defroster on low to clear the fogged up windshield.

There was quiet in the car for a time, and then the radio broke silence. "Captain Ferris?"

He spoke into his mike, "Ferris here."

"I have a man from the Defense Department here at the airport who would like to have a word with you—a Walter Koenig."

"Koenig?" said Linda. "What's he doing there?"

"Put him on," said Ferris, glancing at Linda as he took his thumb off the mike. "Who is Koenig?"

"He's a man the Defense Department placed in my home to monitor the phone."

"Captain Ferris." Koenig's voice came over the radio speaker.

Ferris pressed the mike button. "Yes."

"Is there a Jack Matheson or Linda Moreland there with you?"

"Matheson's been wounded and was rushed to the hospital, but Mrs. Moreland is here."

"Can Mrs. Moreland hear me?"

Ferris handed her the microphone, pointing out how to use it. She pressed the button to speak to him. "Yes, I hear you fine."

"Where's the disc?"

"It should've been delivered to my house sometime today by a delivery service. Why aren't you there now?"

"As soon as my office notified me of the search grid they'd set up to locate you and Matheson, I told them I was renting a plane on my own accord to see if I could help. While I was in flight they directed me to this airfield to assist law enforcement officials in securing your son's release."

The captain put his hand out for the microphone, and taking it, he asked, "How does the situation look there?"

"These people are hardened criminals and they're not giving up without a fight. I don't know if you've heard, but we already have one state trooper critically wounded."

"We should be there in no more than fifteen minutes," said Ferris. "Do you have any suggestions on how to defuse this standoff without more people getting injured?"

"I don't know, but I'm thinking of the boy, and I'm afraid if more gunfire is exchanged, a stray bullet may hit the fuel tank on that plane. As much as I hate to mention it, I think I can persuade these people to release the child, but I'll have to guarantee them a clear runway for takeoff. My department's main concern is with the loss of life, just as yours is. There's a classified computer disc we thought to be in their possession, but that doesn't appear to be the case now."

The captain drew a breath. "I just left six dead and nine wounded at another location that those people on the plane are apparently responsible for. Do you know how that sounds to me?"

"You don't have to tell me, but if we're going to salvage anything out of this, we have to think of the boy. The State Department held concerns for the disc, but it's unlikely these people have it."

There was a pause, during which time Ferris held the microphone in his hand. Then he replied, "You're the authority, but to let those people go is a crime."

"Spoken very nobly, Captain, but do you have a better idea?"

"I guess not."

There was a pause, then Koenig came back with, "I was just informed that their destination is supposed to be in Canada, and there's a chance Canadian officials can apprehend them on their end. This situation may make for a change in their plans, but if air traffic controllers can track their flight path without losing them, they may still face justice after all."

"That's a thought," replied Ferris.

"Well, I'll call Mrs. Hagen first and find out if any packages have been delivered to your home, Mrs. Moreland, and if she has received a package, I'll see if I can arrange the child's release."

After Koenig signed off, the radio fell silent and Linda felt some relief in the hope that Koenig may be able to convince these people to let her son go.

Soon, Linda saw a sign on the side of the road for Auburn Airfield, and within minutes, the airstrip came into view with an array of red flashing lights from the roofs of state and local police cars. Ferris turned into the airport's entrance and steered his cruiser for the three-story tower at the end of the runway where the action appeared to be.

Linda watched as a humming twin turboprop Hawker Beechcraft streaked down the runway to take to the night sky, and presumed it was Kleistner and his cohorts taking off for Canada. With traffic jammed near the tower, they could get no closer than within thirty yards of it. When the car stopped, Linda got out and ran as fast as she could for the building. Her legs moved rapidly on the damp pavement to cut across a shallow puddle, and behind the tower's broad glass front, she saw people lined up to view the airstrip from its well-lit interior. She came through the entrance doors with her heart pounding, her eyes scanning the open area in search of her son, and finally turning to see him rushing toward her, she dropped to her knees.

"Mommy!" Allan called out to her excitedly. "I knew you were coming, I just knew it."

Catching him in her arms while beaming with joy, she held him snug against her breast, then looked at him and smiled at how he came through this unharmed and unchanged. Her eyes closed, feeling grateful for the moment, and she thought how this whole terrible incident was at last behind her.

Seeing a man with silver-streaked hair and black-rimmed eyeglasses approaching, she recognized Koenig. Wearing a solemn grin, he said, "I just talked to Mrs. Hagen a few minutes ago, and she said she received a package this afternoon."

Stroking the top of Allan's head with his fingertips, Koenig added, "I told her we'd be heading back to New York immediately and instructed her to lock up the house and not open the door until we arrive. Because Matheson's injured, I'm left with responsibility for the disc, and I'll have to see that it's returned to Washington tonight."

Ferris entered the building and saw Linda embracing her child.

Koenig reached out to shake his hand. "You must be Captain Ferris. I'm Walter Koenig. Pleased to meet you."

Shaking Koenig's hand, Ferris replied, "Seeing mother and child reunited brings some consolation for what my job's brought me tonight."

Looking at the nicks and cuts on his mother's fingers and hands, Allan asked, "Mommy, what did you do to your hands?"

Seeing reporters descending on the building, Koenig looked at Ferris. "Look, if you can stall that mob we'll try to find another door out of here. My plane's right outside."

"I'll try," said Ferris, "but I ought to tell you there are a couple of Defense Department officials on their way here."

Distancing himself from the door with Linda and Allan, Koenig said, "They'll know how to reach me, but I'd consider it a great favor if you'd withhold the release of this lady's name from the media until morning."

Koenig then came to the counter and presented his credentials to the head of airport security. "There's got to be another exit we can take to get out of here."

"There's a service entrance you can use." He tipped back a section of counter to give them access to the area behind him.

212

Following the official, Koenig saw the press coming through the door and Ferris raised his hands for them to halt, using his authority to hold them while promising a story.

They hurried along to Koenig's rented airplane, a single engine Cessna. Within minutes they were racing down the runway, the plane's nose lifted, and they were in flight. Allan, though overwhelmed by his first plane ride, soon turned drowsy from the panorama in the twilight sky, and curled up in his mother's arms to drift off to sleep. Buzzing along in the starlit sky with her son held close to her breast, Linda was completely exhausted, and unable to keep her head up, her eyelids drooped before falling shut.

CHAPTER 23

The Joker in the Deck

Linda, Koenig, and Allan arrived home by taxi in the early hours of the following day to a dark house. After paying the cabdriver, Koenig lifted Allan in his arms. "I've got the boy. Are you going to be alright?"

Feeling relieved to be at home, Linda appeared worn out as she said in a soft drawl, "I'm coming," and stepping out of the taxi beneath a street lamp, the automobile pulled away. She followed Koenig down the walk. He entered the residence ahead of her, and at the door's threshold, pitch-black awaited her.

She heard Koenig's voice carry from the living room where he was placing Allan on the sofa. "I couldn't find the light switch, but be careful, I nearly tripped on something."

Linda switched on the entry hall light, and was shocked to discover Louise lying at the base of the stairs, her legs twisted and tangled as she lay on her side wearing her kitchen apron. She came to kneel beside her and saw her head turned to the living room doorway, her eyes staring into space, and it was plain to see she was deceased.

"I left him on the couch," said Koenig, returning to the hallway, and he knelt beside Linda to take Louise's pulse, but then shook his head before closing the woman's eyes. Coming to his feet to shut the front door and lock it, he then returned to the living room where, when flipping on the light switch, a table lamp lying on the floor came on. Whoever had been here had emptied the antique secretary's desk of its contents and left those articles strewn about on the floor. The room was in disarray, and he found the dining room in much the same condition.

214

Koenig picked up the lamp to set it on the end table, and finding the phone and receiver near the desk, he brought them together to get a dial tone, but the line was dead. Returning to the entry hall, Linda hadn't moved from kneeling beside Louise, but had placed her hand on Louise's shirtsleeve as though showing devotion to a woman she knew well.

He withdrew from his coat his cell phone, commenting, "They've cut the phone line, and the battery in my cell phone is dead."

Wearing a dazed look, it didn't matter to Linda how or why Louise died, only that she was gone, and all she could do was wonder, *Why did this have to happen?*

When Linda gave no response about the phone situation, Koenig gripped her arms firmly to bring her to her feet to stand her against the wall, the eyes behind the eyeglasses holding a grave look. He spoke with urgency in his voice. "We'll have to act on the assumption that they didn't find the disc, which means they may still be outside watching the house. Now we haven't much time to find that disc, so where do you think Mrs. Hagen would've placed a package delivered to the house?"

"On the desk," she answered.

"They emptied out the desk. Where else?" His eyebrows rose as he tried to remain calm, but he was obviously nervous with the pressing threat of these people returning. "After she and I spoke, she knew the package she'd received contained something of importance, and if she found the phone dead and believed the house was under surveillance she would've hidden it, so where would she have put it?"

Standing face-to-face, she felt the wave of his breath, and numbed by Louise's death, she replied, "I don't know."

The depth of the eyes behind the eyeglasses, his nose, and every detail down to the creases and lines in Koenig's face induced thought, as something about this man's features tapped into her memory. Whatever this faint inkling suggested eluded her. The puzzling conclusion that she recognized Koenig from some other occasion kept eating at her, but her mind kept drawing a blank.

He withdrew from his shoulder holster a .38 caliber revolver, and flipping the cylinder out sideways, he made sure the chambers were full before returning the weapon to its holster.

"We may not have much time, Mrs. Moreland. Please think."

Drained mentally, physically, and emotionally, she said, "If it's here, the only way we're going to find it is by looking for it."

"So where do we start?"

Linda drew a deep breath. "The kitchen, I suppose."

Koenig moved to the far end of the entryway pulling Linda by her wrist, and switched on the kitchen light to find the kitchen in shambles. They stood gazing at the mess: the cabinets and pantry were open and emptied out, their contents thrown on the floor, the refrigerator tipped over on its side, and the stove pulled out from the wall.

"They were certainly thorough," mentioned Koenig, stooping over to pick up a large stainless steel canister from the floor. Tipping it upside down, a few egg noodles scattered, and then he tossed it in the pile.

Linda spotted the bubble envelope packaging used to send the disc to her home, recognizing her handwriting on the address, and she picked it up. "Wait, this is the envelope the disc was mailed in."

Koenig's eyes gazed over those items scattered before him. "Then the disc could very well be here in this heap of debris." Catching sight of a computer disc in a plain plastic case, he displayed it to her, asking, "Could this be it?"

Linda remembered the disc as the one Matheson first gave to her, but he had later exchanged it for the true Triad disc which he had placed in the stainless steel case. "No, that's just a blank disc—what we're looking for will be in a stainless steel case stamped with the word Triad. You're sure to know it when you see it."

Watching Koenig holding a crouched position as he fingered through a few items, the idea she'd seen him before he came to the house with Matheson kept getting in the way of her thoughts. Dead tired and unable to unlock suppressed thoughts, Linda rubbed her temples to give her relief from a headache that had developed.

Koenig abruptly turned his head to look directly at her. "It's got to be here someplace," and then he came to stand beside her, as if staring her down to force her to give a response.

Suddenly under enormous pressure, she closely scrutinized his features and said, "We have a computer in a room upstairs, so she may have taken it there."

"I'll have a look upstairs."

Linda replied, "At the top of the stairs, turn left, and the room closest to the front of the house has the computer."

"You're sure you'll be OK for a few minutes down here while I search upstairs?"

Linda nodded without saying a word.

"If you hear anything, just call out and I'll be down in a second."

Hearing him climb the stairs to the second floor, Linda went back to the foyer to kneel beside Louise, but her mind kept trying to go back to another time when she'd seen Koenig. Unable to put her mind at ease, while pondering where her thoughts were leading her, the question she kept asking herself was, *If I've met Koenig before, when could it have been, and where?*

No matter how hard she tried, she couldn't arrive at what her subconscious was pushing to the surface and it needled her, like probing for an evasive word on the tip of one's tongue. She fought this annoyance diligently until composing a mental picture of Koenig's face linked her to an elusive image in the back of her mind, but it faded. Stymied, her eyes fixed on Louise, and placing her hand on her wrist, she found her body cold to the touch and her limbs stiff and rigid as though rigor mortis had long since set in. She'd learned about this condition when she'd found her mother dead: a paramedic estimating her time of death mentioned that rigor mortis usually takes hold after three or more hours.

The revelation that Louise had perished hours before aroused doubt and suspicion as to whether Koenig had spoken to her near the time they'd left Auburn Airfield to start their plane ride back to New York. Linda closed her eyes as her mind became resolute, again imposing a repetition of the thought process to concentrate on the features of Koenig's face. She pictured his eyes peering out of the eyeglasses, staring deep into her own, and this fixation finally revived a memory to play in her mind. Absorbed by the vision of Koenig's face retracting as he backed away from her, a blinding light from a lamp caused her to shut her eyes as she lay on her back while undergoing interrogation…

The memory came to life as she glimpsed Koenig speaking to Kleistner and Rishankar, saying, "The likeness is amazing. We have a unique opportunity here for using her to obtain the file, but time is of the essence."

"Adele has given her a shot to counteract the serum," remarked Kleistner, coming close to examine her eyes, "and in a short while she'll be fully conscious."

Koenig moved around Kleistner to gaze down at her. "Are you certain she won't remember me? If I get the opportunity to come into this, I don't want to have to worry about her recognizing me."

Rishankar then responded, "In her state of mind, she'll remember little of this experience, except possibly the overhead lamp shining in her eyes…"

Linda's mind came back to the present, and she moved quickly into the living room, scooping Allan up in her arms, supporting him with her left arm beneath him as he rested against her shoulder. Returning to the vestibule, she saw no sign of Koenig on the stairs, and approaching the front door to leave, she quietly twisted the turn piece for freeing the lock's latch, then turned the doorknob to open the door.

"Stop," commanded Koenig, fast descending the stairs. "What are you doing?"

Linda continued pulling the door handle to open the door wider so she could step outside. "I've decided to go to a neighbor to ask for help."

Koenig blocked Linda from going out by placing his hand firmly against the door to force it closed. "And what if they're out there, then what?"

Squinting with fear, she looked him in the eye, blinking uncontrollably as she said insistently, "I want to try."

Koenig secured the latch. "Put the child back on the couch." Linda stood defiant, refusing to move, but then he spoke sternly, raising his voice. "I said, put him back on the couch."

Fearing what was coming next, she reluctantly returned to the living room to place Allan on the couch, and for a brief moment, he began to stir. Worried he'd awaken, but hoping he would not, she flipped the light switch to put out the living room lamp and left the room.

Linda returned to face Koenig in the hallway. A man of size, he stood in the way of the entry door wearing a sanctimonious expression. With a tilt of the head, he said, "I think it's time we stopped kidding ourselves, Mrs. Moreland. You've remembered, and you and I both know it."

"What do you mean?" she asked, playing dumb, knowing Koenig would for certain kill her, as he couldn't afford for American intelligence to learn he was working as a double agent.

"I haven't time for games. You're not going to deny you've remembered our first meeting, and if you don't hand over the disc, I'll be forced to do something I don't want to do."

"If I don't have the disc, and I don't know where it is, what do you want me to say?"

Koenig brought his pistol out casually, gazing at it as his jaw shifted to one side. "The fact that you've remembered tells me that you could know where it is, and you're holding out on me."

Staring at the weapon, and fast reaching the point of desperation, Linda pleaded, "But I don't. How can I know where it is when I wasn't here when it was delivered? Louise could've put it anyplace. If I knew where Louise put it I'd hand it over to you."

"I received a phone call telling me to expect the disc would be delivered here today, and growing impatient, when Mrs. Hagen went grocery shopping, I got the idea it might have already come. While she was gone, I had a look around, and after a brief search down here, I went upstairs to rummage through a couple of rooms."

Listening, Linda looked at the front door, wondering how she could reach help.

"A short time later, the doorbell rang, and that's when I realized Mrs. Hagen had returned sooner than expected, as she must've entered from the back door just minutes before. I looked out the window to see a panel truck making a delivery and heard her open the door to receive the package. Then I tried to put things back the way I'd found them. Not a minute later, I was surprised to discover Mrs. Hagen standing at the top of the stairs watching me, and I approached her to explain what I was doing, but she refused to listen to me. She turned away to avoid me, and in doing so, lost her balance and fell down the stairs— the fall killing her."

Koenig took one step toward Linda. "I told you this so you'd know I'm not a cold-blooded murderer, but since you know who I am, you should also know I can't let you live without getting the disc. However, if I'm able to obtain the disc, I'll tie the two of you up and you'll both be found safely in a few hours, long after I've gone."

Holding the gun at his side, his fingers tightened around its grip. "Now I no longer have the time or patience for discussion."

Linda felt fearful for her life, and in a pleading manner said, "I really don't know where the disc is, but Louise must've opened the envelope in the kitchen so it must be down here someplace."

He swung the pistol suddenly, striking her on the left side of her face with the butt of the gun, and she dropped to the floor, lying dazed with blood oozing from a gash in her temple. She sat propped up by her left arm, her knees bent with her legs twisted to one side, and tears streamed down her cheeks while blood ran down the side of her face to drip on the floor.

Koenig leaned over her. "If I don't get the disc, I'll have to kill you!"

The room spinning, Louise's body lying nearby told her the cold truth. Unless help came or she found and gave him the disc, she would be finished.

A high-pitched hum rang in her head, and tears flowed as she spoke beseechingly. "If I knew where it was I'd give it to you, but I don't know where it is. Please don't hurt me."

"I'm giving you one last chance. Now where is it?" he demanded, cocking the hammer on his pistol.

She put her hand to her head, smearing the blood running down the side of her face, and glimpsed her bloodied fingers. "Alright, there's just one other place she could've put it."

Koenig, believing her to be in worse shape than she actually was, helped her up and she chose the moment to strike the hand holding the gun, knocking the weapon to the floor and shoving him back.

Regaining his balance to catch himself, he then backhanded her, the blow causing her to fall to the hallway floor.

She worked her hands and legs in a backward motion as she scooted on her bottom in the direction of the kitchen, screaming, "Help me, somebody please help me!"

Koenig switched off the light, but the streetlight's glow through the door's window allowed her to see a black silhouette coming at her, and she scrambled to her feet just as he overpowered her. His hands clenched her throat to strangle her, squeezing to quiet her screams, and she aggressively clawed at him before pounding her fists against his arms, but his grip only tightened. When this failed, she grabbed hold of his wrists and tried to pry them free from her neck. Her eyes had adjusted to the dark to see him lean forward, grimacing with determination.

Fast succumbing to oxygen deprivation, the strength in her arms dwindling as life drained from her body, and losing consciousness, her cries failed to bring help...

A gunshot rang out! Koenig's eyes enlarged with his pupils rolling to one side as his expression turned to disbelief, then he gave up his chokehold and collapsed on her.

Coughing breathlessly, she pushed him off and sat up. Someone had heard her cries for help. Then she saw the figure of a small boy standing in the shadows, and when lowering his arms the gun dropped to the floor.

"Allan." Her voice sounded gruff and out of tune, and she put her hand to her neck when swallowing to clear her throat before calling out to him again. "Allan."

Startled and stunned by the event, the boy stood speechless, and she crawled on her hands and knees to embrace him, holding him tightly as she rocked him in her arms.

"He was hurting you," the child explained in a shaken voice, realizing what he'd done to defend his mother, and added, "I heard you scream and saw the gun on the floor."

"Shhh, it's alright." They both began crying.

A neighbor who'd heard the gunshot phoned police and they were on the scene within minutes to scour the house and make a determination of what had happened. As soon as Linda was able to speak coherently, she gave her story to police officers huddled in the living room while sitting on the couch with Allan at her side. Her son looked astounded by the number of police in blue coats circulating the interior of the house.

A black policewoman brought in a first aid kit to clean her wound, then covered and secured cotton over the cut with white adhesive tape. "You're going to need stitches," she said bluntly, then applied additional fingertip pressure to the white adhesive tape to help make it stick to her skin.

The house became still as paramedics removed the bodies from the hallway, and Linda's thoughts turned to Louise, thinking of the kind person she was. While this was happening, another officer came from the hallway to approach Linda, and he leaned over to hand her Louise's apron. "This belonged to the lady."

In changing hands, the apron unfurled to give up the stainless steel Triad case contained in one of the pockets and it dropped to the floor.

Linda said excitedly, "It's the disc!" Reaching to pick up the stainless steel casing, she felt more at ease seeing the computer disc inside, as it had been in the pocket of Louise's apron the entire time.

Thinking of the trouble it caused her, and those who'd died from circumstances surrounding it, she said, "I don't know who's in charge here, but I wish someone would take this thing off my hands once and for all."

"I'll take that," said a man in his mid-fifties coming forward from the hallway to produce a photo ID card identifying him as a special agent with Defense Intelligence.

"My name is Richard Bante and I represent the Defense Department. We've been trying to catch up to you all night, Mrs. Moreland." He returned the card to the inside pocket of his coat. Taking possession of the casing, Bante then examined the disc to recognize an identification mark he'd made. He closed the case and handed it over to another plainclothesman that whisked it away. Then, gazing about, Bante added, "Until you're straightened out here we'll arrange for you to get a room at a hotel."

Packing clean clothes in a suitcase, Linda then saw her house vacated and secured, and following a short visit to a hospital where she received stitches, she and Allan took a room at a hotel at the government's expense. After tucking Allan in, she showered, and the spray of hot water helped wash away the residue of the harrowing experiences she'd lived through.

Linda later pondered Matheson's fate, and knowing he was in critical condition from wounds he'd received, she wondered if he was going to pull through. She also had time to contemplate her own future and wonder what price she'd have to pay for stealing that first file from Washington, D.C., to turn it over to her son's kidnappers. These concerns kept her mind occupied for days, but she had a strong desire to see Matheson again to make certain he survived the shooting. No longer able to reach him at the phone number he'd given her, and people from his agency closely guarding any information about him, she had no way of learning whether he survived their ordeal. Wanting very much to see him and thank him for all he'd done to help her and her son, she wondered if she'd ever see him again.

Epilogue

In the following days, Linda made numerous phone calls trying to learn Matheson's condition, but was unsuccessful at finding out what hospital he was in. She tried reaching Richard Bante through the Department of Defense, but nearly always found him to be out of town and unavailable. Days ran into weeks without her hearing from Matheson, leaving her to think he might have died from bullet wounds, and this saddened her, but she never gave up hope she'd one day see him again. Periodically reflecting on the time they spent together, she came to terms with the situation by thinking that what they'd shared had merely been his way of passing time, and for all she knew he could've been married.

Allan seemed to show no bad effects from having shot and killed a man, as though for him it was just a bad dream, and he never spoke of it so Linda left it alone. With all he'd been through and deprived of his mother's company, seeing her that night in a threatening predicament had compelled him to pick up the revolver from the floor to stop a man who was choking her to death. She had no idea if this incident would harm him psychologically, but only knew that given time and all the love a mother could give, he might heal and forget the turmoil he'd experienced. As his health went on to improve, life got better all the way around for him, and by all accounts, he was growing up as any normal child his age. Linda returned to her job in fashion, and just when her life began to get back on track, a story surfaced in the news covering the theft of classified material from Aeronautical Defense Headquarters in Washington, D.C. The federal government indicted her for the theft of high-level classified material, and soon afterwards, her ex-husband's attorney notified her that he was seeking custody of Allan. Knowing she may have to serve time for her crime, and under the growing pressure of an uncertain future, she granted her husband temporary custody of their child. She did this to give her son time to adapt to the change of life she expected might come, but dreaded the idea of relinquishing him.

On the day of her arraignment in Washington, D.C., she walked the main corridor on the second floor of the Federal Courthouse looking for the courtroom where she was to meet with her defense attorney. Arriving early for her case trial, she waited in the hall before entering, hoping to confer with her lawyer. Then she saw Matheson coming out of the courtroom wearing a well-tailored suit.

She quickly turned away, looking out a window to avoid him. He approached to stand beside her and said, "Linda, if you have a minute, I'd like to speak with you."

"Alright," she replied, making eye contact with him, and then staring out the window again as though showing little interest in what he had to say.

"How have you been?"

"OK. I'd wondered how you were, but I had no way of reaching you—the phone number you gave me no longer works and the Department of Defense cared little about helping me to contact you."

"As you can see, I've recovered fine, and it was quite a surprise to learn about Koenig. I'm sorry about what he put you through and for the death of Louise Hagen."

"I take it then that he was the man you were after from the beginning."

"Well, yes, from what we've pieced together, the Russians leaked enough information to lead us to believe a mole had infiltrated the CIA to keep suspicion off Koenig. By accounting for our leak in the CIA, we had little cause to look elsewhere, giving him almost free reign to work as a double agent in defense intelligence."

Matheson paused before saying, "I know about your troubles, and I want you to know that I've gone way out on a limb to stop the Justice Department from issuing charges against you.

Richard Bante is supportive, and he and I have stressed the risks you've taken to help the agency, and how the theft you made wasn't for personal gain. Anyway, because of your cooperation and the fact that you left yourself exposed to danger, as part of a plea bargain, they've agreed to exercise the utmost leniency in your case. The court hasn't disclosed all of the terms of the agreement, and they're in there now working out the final details with your lawyer, but it looks like you'll have to do some time.

"I've used what influence I have to try to meet with the President, but have yet to receive a reply from him. What seems to have the most bearing on circumstances surrounding your case is that this is an era of theft and sale of government documents. There are senators using your situation as a forum to curb this trend, insisting that if you're let off without a prison term it'll send the wrong message to others who may be considering such a crime."

Linda stared out the window, making no comment.

"Evelyn Werner's heard about what you've been through. She's quite concerned, and from what I understand she's hoping to meet you in person soon."

"My heart wouldn't be into meeting her, at least not until I can get these problems behind me." Suddenly overcome with emotion, tears spouted from her eyes. She turned to rush to the end of the corridor where she came to a dead-end, veering to a corner while drawing a handkerchief from her purse.

Matheson followed, coming to her side with a look of concern.

"When this is over with, I will have lost everything—I won't even have Allan, and I suppose I knew what I was doing was wrong, but I couldn't help myself."

Linda finally broke down in tears. Matheson put his arms around her. "I want you to know that since we've been apart not a minute has gone by that I haven't thought of you."

She looked at him. "Then why haven't you contacted me?"

"Before my release from the hospital, I received orders to report to NATO Headquarters in Brussels, Belgium, to give commanders and the security staff an account of this case.

226

Kleistner and his gang of cutthroats eluded capture and are still out there on the run. I tried phoning you several times before leaving for Europe, but I couldn't catch you at home. I would've phoned from Europe, but my superiors warned me that any contact with you before your trial may be detrimental to your defense. I'd promised my help if you needed it, but I didn't want to start phoning you and later have it said that my judgment is biased, which may prove harmful to your case.

"I was confident that you earned amnesty, as you'd done everything humanly possible to rectify the wrong you'd done, and I stated so in my report. When learning the Justice Department moved up the date of your trial, I argued my point insistently, but officials have refused to exonerate you.

"My pledge still stands, and when your attorney confronts you with the offer the courts are making for your acknowledgment, I say to wait and give Richard Bante and myself more time. Bante is right now seeking an appointment to confer with the President on your behalf, and his word carries a lot of clout. If he can get in the Oval Office and explain what lengths you've gone through to come to the aid of your country, I think you'll be granted a pardon, so all hope isn't lost."

He brushed back her hair. "The first time I saw you, I thought you were the most beautiful woman I'd ever seen, and then I came to know a person whom I admired. Looking at you now, those feelings are stronger than ever before. I love you, and I promise to do everything possible to get full custody of Allan for us to start a new life together." They kissed and embraced.

THE END

CPSIA information can be obtained at www.ICGtesting.com
Printed in the USA
LVOW13s2239071013

355762LV00001B/4/P

9 781625 167927